SEAL TEAM SIX: HUNT THE VIPER

ALSO BY DON MANN AND RALPH PEZZULLO

The SEAL Team Six Series

Hunt the Dragon

Hunt the Fox

Hunt the Jackal

Hunt the Falcon

Hunt the Scorpion

Hunt the Wolf

Inside SEAL Team Six:

My Life and Missions with America's Elite Warriors

SEAL
TEAM SIX:
HUNT THE VIPER

DON MANN
AND
RALPH PEZZULLO

MULHOLLAND BOOKS
LITTLE, BROWN AND COMPANY
NEW YORK BOSTON LONDON

Copyright © 2018 by Don Mann and Ralph Pezzullo

Hachette Book Group supports the right to free expression and the value of copyright. The purpose of copyright is to encourage writers and artists to produce the creative works that enrich our culture.

The scanning, uploading, and distribution of this book without permission is a theft of the author's intellectual property. If you would like permission to use material from the book (other than for review purposes), please contact permissions@hbgusa.com. Thank you for your support of the author's rights.

Mulholland Books / Little, Brown and Company
Hachette Book Group
1290 Avenue of the Americas
New York, NY 10019
mulhollandbooks.com

Mulholland Books is an imprint of Little, Brown and Company, a division of Hachette Book Group, Inc. The Little, Brown name and logo are trademarks of Hachette Book Group, Inc.

The publisher is not responsible for websites (or their content) that are not owned by the publisher.

Printed in the United States of America

Originally published in hardcover by Mulholland Books, May 2018
First Mulholland Books mass market edition, April 2019

10 9 8 7 6 5 4 3 2 1

"If a viper lives in your room and you wish to have a peaceful sleep, you must first chase it out."

—Gautama Buddha

Dedicated to the men and women who risk their lives in the global fight against oppression and evil

SEAL TEAM SIX: HUNT THE VIPER

CHAPTER ONE

*Live as if you were to die tomorrow. Learn
as if you were to live forever.*
—Mahatma Gandhi

THE SIX heavily armed U.S. Navy SEALs watched
the battered pickup approach on Highway 47 in Iraqi
Kurdistan as rockets, artillery shells, and mortars exploded in the distance. Team leader Tom Crocker had
a lot on his mind today—the fierce fighting to dis-
lodge ISIS (Islamic State of Iraq and Syria) from
nearby Mosul, the mental welfare of one of his men,
who had just learned that his father had gone missing,
and his own future.

As he stood along the two-lane asphalt road, his
HK416 automatic rifle pressed against his right bicep,
using his left hand to shield his eyes from the dust
that swept up from the gently undulating plain, an
alert came over the radio. A French AS532 Cougar
helicopter had crashed south of the town of Sinjar, approximately fifty klicks (kilometers) from the Syrian
border.

Other concerns quickly vanished from his head.
"Survivors?" he asked into the mike clipped to the top

4 • DON MANN AND RALPH PEZZULLO

of his camos as he waved the pickup to the side of the road.

Davis, the team's comms man, seated in the second Flyer-60 Advanced Light Strike Vehicle, answered, "CC [Coalition Command] is reporting six aboard the Cougar including pilot and co. Several casualties. It came down in contested territory, so medevac can't land until the ground is cleared."

Crocker's eyes never the left the pickup, which slowed to a stop—a sorry-looking bag of bolts if he'd ever seen one, with a front bumper held on with string, a mismatched colored hood, and a right windshield perforated with bullet holes. Another part of his mind remained focused on the downed French helo. "How far?" he asked into his mike.

"How far...what?"

"How far is the Cougar from where we are now?"

"Southwest, maybe twenty klicks," Davis answered. "Take us fifteen...twenty minutes to get there depending on the roads, which are probably shit."

Most of the land in this part of Iraqi Kurdistan was flat, with the exception of the Sinjar Mountains, north. Fresh fields of wheat, cotton, and tobacco interrupted by primitive villages and dirt paths. So off-road travel was an option; so was the presence of mines and IEDs.

"Tell CT to get on the SAW and cover this pickup," Crocker barked into the mike as the vehicle rattled onto the shoulder and stopped.

He was referring to the gas-operated Squad Automatic Weapon (SAW) that sat in the bed of the Flyer-60—a light machine gun with a rapid rate of fire of two hundred rounds per minute and an effective range of eight hundred meters, which had been a mainstay of the U.S. Armed Forces since the 1980s.

The six men—Crocker, Akil, Mancini, Davis, Rip, and CT—were members of Black Cell (a special unit of SEAL Team Six/DEVGRU). African American, six-two, and ripped, CT was a former T-6 Red Squad member and before that an NCAA Division II wrestling champion and martial arts specialist who had grown up in Compton, California. He'd left, he joked, because he got tired of being shot at without combat pay.

He'd recently joined Black Cell and was training to replace Davis as the team's comms chief, as Davis was planning to transfer to an intel job at ST-6's base in Dam Neck Naval Base at the end of the month. Said he wanted to spend more time with his family, and surf. Crocker would miss him. They'd survived all kinds of catastrophes together— helicopter crashes, enemy attacks, captivity, even an avalanche.

Now his right-hand man Mancini (a.k.a. Manny, or by his radio alias, Big Wolf) pointed his MP7A1 submachine gun at the driver and used his left hand to indicate to the occupants of the pickup to get out.

"Refugees," he said sympathetically as a squat woman with a long burgundy scarf tied over her head kicked open the passenger door, and the door slid off its hinges and crashed to the ground.

"Nice ride," Akil commented.

"At least they made it out," Crocker said.

The SEALs had stopped dozens of similar vehicles so far, six weeks into their deployment in Kurdistan. Untold thousands of other Syrian refugees hadn't gotten safely out. Instead, they'd been robbed, raped, and murdered and hung from lampposts and trees by Syrian Armed Forces, gangsters, or one of the myriad armed opposition groups to the regime of Syrian president Bashar Assad.

Around ten million of them had fled that country since the start of the civil war in 2012, creating a human rights disaster of epic proportions. Crocker had seen the teeming, sprawling refugee camps in Jordan and Turkey, and the kids playing in dust-filled alleys between prefabricated Pods that served as temporary shelters. Heartbreaking and hopeful at the same time. Kids in the most difficult situations found ways to amuse themselves.

"Let's get this over quick and go help the Cougar," Crocker growled. He'd grown to loathe Syrian President Assad for committing genocide on his own people, and couldn't fathom why the rest of the world had watched this catastrophe unfold for years without doing anything to stop it.

Out of the cab of the truck stepped a middle-aged woman, two teenage boys, and a five-year-old girl clutching an unclothed plastic doll. They all shared the same thick dark crescent-shaped eyebrows and looked like they'd slept in their clothes. The teenagers stood behind the woman, who Crocker assumed was a relative, with their hands in the pockets of their jeans.

Crocker said to Akil, "Tell the boys we need to see their hands."

The team's operational terp, Zumar, was currently honeymooning with his bride in Beirut, Lebanon, on the Mediterranean Coast, so they were relying on their teammate Akil, an Egyptian American SEAL who spoke Arabic and some Farsi, which were the chief languages in this part of the world, along with various Kurdish dialects.

Akil addressed the boys in Arabic and they

responded by bowing their heads and then holding their hands up for the SEALs to see. They appeared to be brothers. The older of the two had a few wisps of beard and a fresh, jagged scar on his head and trembled from head to toe.

"What happened to him?" Crocker asked.

Akil spoke to the woman and as she answered she waved her arms dramatically and contorted her face, indicating objects falling from the sky, and something landing on their heads. Her voice shook with emotion until it broke and she started weeping and sank to her knees.

Crocker pulled her up. He didn't need to hear the translation from Akil to know the story. He saw the pain in her eyes, and for a second felt the buzz of her desperation reach into his chest.

Akil relayed the details: They were Christians and had been hiding in the suburbs of Aleppo. Her husband had once been a bus driver. They were living in a garage when it was bombed, killing her husband and burying her son. Rescue workers dug the boy out, but he hadn't been the same.

They'd sold practically everything they had to buy the truck. Militiamen and roving gangs had stolen most of what was left. And they hadn't eaten in days.

All this was communicated while CT kept watch with the SAW and Mancini and Rip inspected plastic bags, which were piled in the pickup bed.

"Household stuff and clothing," Mancini reported.

"All right, let's get 'em some MREs and bottles of water and send them on their way. Alert Colonel Rastan's men that they're coming. Hopefully they can find them some cots in the Red Cross camp outside Erbil."

Colonel Rastan was the commander of a ragtag but

hard-fighting company of Peshmerga soldiers who were trying to wrest this part of their native Kurdistan from ISIS control. Erbil was the sleek modern capital of Kurdistan, where oil deals were negotiated by French, British, and U.S. executives luxuriating in brand-new five-star hotels and entertained by Russian and Uzbek hookers.

The refugee mom hugged Crocker and muttered some sort of prayer of thanks as Rip, Mancini, and Akil set armfuls of bottled water and MREs into the back of the pickup.

"Safe travels," he said, as his teammates helped the family back into the truck and lifted the passenger door in place.

The wind picked up, sending a piece of brown paper twisting east toward twin trails of garbage and waste that paralleled the highway to the edge of the horizon.

"Peace!" one of the boys shouted out the pickup window as it passed.

"Peace!" Crocker shouted back, wondering where they'd end up and if they'd ever return home.

Standing with one foot on the lead Flyer runner looking up at the darkening sky, he was already thinking ahead to the fears of another set of victims— the Frenchmen aboard the Cougar—who he imagined were terrified of being captured, tortured, and having their heads cut off by Sunni ISIS militants. The Geneva Conventions of humanitarian treatment of prisoners of war hadn't reached this part of the world.

No small exaggeration. He and his men had witnessed ISIS savagery firsthand in parts of Mosul and other towns and villages in Kurdistan and northern

Syria that had been liberated recently. Mass graves filled with mutilated bodies, human heads lined up on walls, naked bodies hung upside down from street lamps. All of it disgusting and inhuman, and done in the name of Allah, or God.

"Let's go help the Frenchmen!" he shouted as he spit the bitter taste out of his mouth and climbed into the lead Flyer.

Every day of this three-month deployment had been like this. Battles to fight, messes to clean up, militia groups to sort out, and masses of civilians to try to help one way or another. It wasn't a war, per se, it was human tragedy played out on multiple levels with scant resources, and with little concern from the rest of the world. It was the violent destruction of society and the first primitive attempts to put it back together. Realities that people living in New York, London, and Paris could barely fathom.

Where's the outrage? Where are the Hollywood celebrities raising money? Fuck. . . .

CHAPTER TWO

*It isn't the mountains ahead that wear you
down. It's the pebble in your shoe.*
—Muhammad Ali

WIND MOANED through the opening of the passenger window as Davis read the coordinates of the Cougar crash site, and Akil, at the wheel, punched them into the vehicle's GPS.

Dark and brooding behind three days' growth of black beard, Akil muttered, "Pisses me off…"

"What now?" Crocker asked back. Akil wasn't a laid-back, take-things-as-they-come guy.

"The fact that Coalition medevac can't land until the crash site is secured."

"Policy," Davis countered.

"The policy sucks bones," Akil growled.

Crocker shared his teammate's frustration. The coalition opposing ISIS in western Kurdistan was disorganized and changing all the time. At its best, it was an attempt to coordinate military and support units from different regions and countries, including Shiite militia groups from Iraq; military contractors from Colombia, the UK, and the U.S.; pilots from France, the U.S., and the UK; medical teams from Europe and Japan; special operations forces from the U.S., the UK, Poland, and the Netherlands, who came and went according to political contingencies back home; Kurdish Peshmerga fighters; and YPG (People's Protection Units) militiamen from the West—a collection of young anarchists, drifters, idealists, Christian evangelicals, and whack jobs from the States, Europe, and beyond who had come to join the fight.

At its worst, it was a mess of clumsy rules and regulations, and incompetence.

"Whole damn thing gives me a big pain in the ass," Akil barked as he pushed down on the accelerator.

A former Marine sergeant, and Black Cell's navigation specialist, Akil hailed originally from Egypt, loved women and any kind of action, and had been a mainstay of Crocker's team for five years now. Fourteen months ago the two of them had barely escaped from North Korea after a top-secret mission that claimed three other SEALs including an SDS (SEAL Delivery System) pilot and copilot—each one etched in Crocker's memory so strongly that he sometimes imagined they were still alive.

"I mean, somebody's got to be held accountable for this disaster," Akil continued. "Assad, Obama, the Iranians, Putin, other Arab countries. They fuck around and what happens? A half-million dead, ravaged cities, and millions of refugees. Someone's gonna shoulder that karma."

"I didn't know that Muslims believe in karma," Davis commented from the backseat.

"I don't know, either." Akil laughed. "I'm a shitty Muslim. But there's gotta be some kind of greater justice. Right?"

"Right," Crocker agreed.

Two combat jets tore through the orange haze to their right, the flames from the afterburners lighting up the sky. Crocker strained to see if they were American, British, French, Turkish, or Russian.

Mancini's voice came through Crocker's earbuds. "Yo, Deadwood. Big Wolf here. This crash site near anything we're familiar with?" Deadwood was Crocker's radio alias. Mancini, his second-in-command, was seated in the passenger seat of Truck Two.

"It's a few kilometers south of Sinjar," Davis answered.

"Sinjar, no shit…." Mancini said. He was their resident expert on anything ranging from fractals and thrust ratios to ancient history and geography. "That's the town Zumar hails from."

"Zumar, our terp?" asked Crocker.

Zumar's recent wedding in Erbil had been the highlight of the deployment so far. Three days of nonstop partying, feasting, dancing, and celebration, capped off with hours of songs and tributes to the bride and groom. "Epic," Akil had called it.

"Yeah," Mancini answered. "Zumar told us that Sinjar was the ancestral home of the Yazidi religious sect, and he was Yazidi himself. And how the Yazidis were one of the oldest tribes on earth and weren't Muslims, but followed the teachings of Zoroaster."

"Who?"

"Zoroaster, an ancient Persian prophet who saw the human condition as a mental struggle between truth and untruth. He preached good thoughts, good words, good action."

"Like the Franz Ferdinand lyrics," Akil offered.

"Which is why ISIS has branded his followers devil worshippers, rapes their women, and is trying to wipe them out," Crocker added.

"Makes sense, right?"

"It's complicated," commented Mancini.

"What isn't in this part of the world?"

The tribal and religious hatreds rife in the region were a muddle to Crocker. Sunnis loathed Shiites, though they both followed the teachings of Mohammad. Muslims hated Christians and Jews and vice versa. Personally, he believed in God, but all the arguing over how to name him or how he wanted you to worship seemed absurd.

Wasn't it obvious that we were all children of the same creator and meant to treat one another with kindness and respect? What happened to the Golden Rule: treat your neighbor or your brother the way you'd like them to treat you?

Davis interrupted his train of thought. "Boss, I've got Colonel Rastan on the satellite phone."

"Rastaman vibrations, man. Patch him in."

The colonel's deep, British-accented voice resonated in Crocker's ears. Twenty years ago the Peshmerga colonel had spent two years studying at the Royal Military Academy Sandhurst. "Crocker, my brother. Tell me some good news. All I hear are problems, problems, more problems. What's the good word?"

Crocker maintained a minute of silence. Rastan got the joke and chuckled.

"Colonel, two things…" Crocker said, turning serious.

"Yes. Hold on a minute…."

Akil steered the Flyer-60 around a deep crater in

the asphalt road, which appeared to be the result of a recent air strike.

"Crocker?"

He heard heavy ordnance launching in the background. "Still here, Colonel. Where are you?"

"Outside Mosul. Sorry. It was my wife. She's at the hospital waiting for the results of the tests."

Aside from the warfare, people still suffered from regular problems like illness—a troubling mammogram in the case of Rastan's missus.

"How's Lyla doing?" Crocker asked. He remembered a tall, dignified woman with large, dark, soulful eyes.

"Nice of you to ask, but let's talk about that later. What did you want to tell me?"

Crocker switched channels in his head: back to business. "Two things, Colonel. First, we stopped a pickup filled with refugees heading toward the checkpoint at Mosul. A woman, her young daughter, and two sons. They should arrive there soon. See what you can do for them."

"Okay."

"Second, we're on our way now to relieve the downed French helicopter."

"You near?"

"Approximately ten minutes away."

"I hear it came down in the vicinity of Qabusiye."

"What's that?" asked Crocker.

"A farming town. The mayor has reported ISIS activity in the area recently."

"When?" Crocker asked.

"In the last week or so. Criminal acts....Gangs stealing trucks and goats. That's Abu Samir al-Sufi territory."

"Who?"

"The Silent Sheikh, the Viper."

He was referring to an ISIS commander—their leading military strategist—who had once been an officer in Saddam Hussein's Republican Guard. Al-Sufi's men controlled a wide swath of northern Syria and western Kurdistan and swore allegiance to Caliph Ibrahim—a.k.a. Ibrahim Muhammad al-Badri—who was rumored to have been injured as a result of a recent Coalition air strike on Mosul.

The Viper's men were known to be vicious, well trained, and heavily armed.

"I'll send one of my units to support you," Colonel Rastan offered.

"I'd appreciate that, Colonel." Crocker figured he was referring to YPGs, which were groups of Kurdish militiamen and foreign volunteers who roamed the area—a mix of Kurdish nationalists, opportunists, and anarchists and adventure seekers from Canada, the U.S., and Europe—untrained and undisciplined for the most part; Syria's version of Road Warriors, minus the tricked-out vehicles.

"Godspeed, my brother," said Colonel Rastan. "If you and your men are in Erbil this weekend, maybe we can get together at my house. We'll have a party… drink some beers, smoke a hookah, relax."

"Thank you, Colonel. I'd like that." Crocker was trying to remember if this was Super Bowl weekend, or if it had already passed. He wasn't even sure which teams were playing.

The wind picked up, and Akil turned the armored vehicle onto a dirt path heading south through new fields of tobacco. The resulting sandstorm turned the sky from hazy orange to a deep shade of purple.

Today's temp hovered in the low sixties, but Crocker knew it would drop like a stone as soon as the sun went down.

"No way medevac is flying through this," Akil remarked.

"Not likely."

He glanced at his Suunto watch and saw that it was only 1400. Smiling to himself, he remembered his girl-friend, Cyndi, the dimples on her back, and the sweet smell of her hair as she stepped out of the shower.

I wonder what she's doing now.

Her presence was so strong in the moment that he imagined he could reach out and touch her. Then the Flyer-60 hit a deep pothole and jerked right. Despite the seat belt he was wearing, he had to brace himself so as not to slam his head into the side window.

"Dammit, Akil. Watch the fucking road."

"What road?"

"We should be there," Davis announced.

Visibility was shit front, sides, and back. Fifty feet max, before the landscape became completely obscured by churning sand and dust.

"CT. Gunner up," Crocker said through the headset.

CT, in the back of Truck Two, slipped on a pair of goggles, stood in the gusting wind, and readied the SAW.

"What am I looking for?" CT asked.

"A column of smoke, flames, a shattered bird..."

Crocker felt a twinge of foreboding at the bottom of his stomach. Then he thought he heard the crackle of AK-47 fire over the growl of the engine and hiss of sand.

"Stop!" he said into the headset, as he tightened his grip around the HK416, customized with an M320 grenade launcher and Aimpoint sight.

Akil applied the brakes. "What?"

He heard the sound again, this time more distinct.

Even though it was dark, Crocker's NVGs (night-vision goggles) were useless since the cause of the limited visibility was the swirling sand and dirt. Mancini crouched beside him and pointed ahead and to the right.

Squinting through sand goggles, Crocker made out the back of a Toyota pickup and traced the outline of a .50 cal machine gun in its bed, like a crane leaning forward.

He went down on his belly, then whispered into his mike, "One technical…two o'clock." The extended cab Toyota pickup, also known as a "technical," seemed to be the preferred choice of insurgents throughout the Middle East and North Africa. Most of them accommodated some kind of machine gun or antiaircraft weapon. Whoever the dealer was had to be a very rich man.

"Any sign of the Cougar or French survivors?" Davis asked from Truck One, parked 100 meters away.

"Negative."

Crocker took a deep breath, extended his left arm, and led the way to the back of the Toyota. From that vantage, he spotted two more parked at odd angles. Still no sign of the Cougar. Hearing a man's voice ahead, he hugged the ground and became aware of his accelerated heartbeat and the sweat on his chest.

The wind let up for a second and three men came into view. Two of them bearded with black bandanas over their faces. One of them young with long, stringy brown hair. ISIS—an acronym for the full Arabic name of the Islamic State, Dawlat al-Islamiyah f'al-Iraq wa Belaad al-Sham—or Daesh in Arabic.

They were leading a slight man in a tan uniform who appeared to be bleeding from the head. One of the bearded figures pushed the captive from behind, causing him to stumble forward and crash into the side of the Toyota and fall.

Motherfuckers! Cowardice and cruelty never failed to ignite Crocker, and now he had to battle the impulse to shoot at or otherwise engage the sons of bitches. Wanted to see the complete picture first.

"Boss…" Manny whispered through the earbuds.

Maybe fifty feet past the front of the Toyota he caught a fleeting glimpse of the Cougar, lying on its side, and maybe a dozen or more men around it. In an instant, the wind gusted and the image disappeared behind a veil of dust.

"What's the plan?" Manny whispered.

Crocker pointed right, and led the way on his belly, reminding himself that in conditions like these he couldn't depend on his 416. Glad he had a SIG Sauer P226 on his hip. The land dipped slightly, and the air became so thick with crud that it was difficult to breathe.

"Boss…" It was Davis's voice.

"Wait…." Crocker had reached into the pouch on his belt and was tying a scarf over his nose and mouth.

Someone shouted in Arabic and muffled shots rang

out. The wind gusted hard, causing debris to sting his ears and neck, and then it eased, and the dust started to settle and visibility increased.

Ten feet, fifteen, twenty, thirty…He saw that he and Mancini were facing the bottom of the downed Cougar. Its top rotor hung at an odd angle, creaking slowly in the wind. Past its tail sat two more technicals with black flags flapping vigorously. "There is no God but Allah," or whatever the scribble on them meant. The vehicles were bad news, as they multiplied the number of insurgents. He'd never seen an extended cab Toyota pickup without at least six armed men aboard.

Did the math in his head. Five trucks; minimum thirty militants.

"Boss…" It was Davis again.

"Just a sec."

Visibility became decent from the ground up to about four feet. It allowed him to see that they were in an eight-foot-wide gully that swept around the left side of the downed helo. Following the gully back toward the road with his eyes, he spotted a row of four men in olive flight suits, kneeling, and a crowd of militants standing behind them.

A blade flashed through the milling dust and he intuited what was about to happen. Heads would be lopped off, and then the militants would drive away with the other one, two, or maybe three Frenchmen taken hostage.

A high voice pierced through the whine of wind. It was someone reciting an angry vow or prayer in Arabic.

"Manny, you got any M14s on you?" he whispered into the head mike.

"One."

He removed the incendiary grenade from his belt and handed it to his teammate.

"Continue to the right to those two technicals. Take 'em out."

"Copy."

"The rest of you stay in the trucks. Make sure the SAWs are manned and ready. You're gonna hear a blast. See a fire. Soon after that the technicals will be coming your way. Try to disable them, and be aware that they'll be carrying hostages."

"Roger."

"Boss…"

"No time. Go!"

"Boss…"

"Fucking go!"

He heard Manny scurry away, and slithered on his belly toward the downed helo. Closer, closer, and under the rear rotor until he was maybe twenty-five feet from the kneeling Frenchmen. That's when he heard the explosion of the first AN-M14 TH3 grenade. Then another, illuminating the shocked faces in front of him, turning them white, then yellow, then orange.

The light grew brighter again as the chemical mix burned at more than four thousand degrees Fahrenheit, searing through metal and finally igniting the gas tanks, so that the vehicles exploded like twin volcanoes and flew off the ground. Shards of sizzling metal whizzed through the air.

He heard the scream of a militant, then saw the face of another thickly bearded one as he lifted a sword over one of the captured Frenchmen's heads. Crocker quickly aimed his 416 and hit the insurgent in the neck and head, causing him to let go of the sword and fall backward.

Manny, behind Crocker and to his right, opened up with his MP7A1 submachine gun, and total chaos ensued as militants screamed and scattered. Some fired wildly. Most, as he had anticipated, ran back to the other three trucks. The ones who tried to drag the Frenchmen with them, he picked off with carefully placed shots.

That's when he became aware that the wind had let up, increasing visibility, which wasn't good. Engines started, the technicals roared off, and then he heard the thrashing sound of SAWs engaging.

"Bring it the fuck on!" Akil shouted through his earbuds.

The battle grew fierce. SAWs against .50 cals, causing a huge, continuous racket. Even though the four SEALs in the Flyers were severely outnumbered, they had the advantage of being in armored vehicles.

Crocker launched himself forward on a powerful pulse of adrenaline. He was face to face with the four kneeling Frenchmen. He cut through the plastic around their wrists, and helped them to their feet.

"Non! Non!" one of them protested.

"How many are you?" he shouted at their stunned faces, only to realize that they didn't speak English.

"Combien? Combien? You?"

"Américain?"

"Huit," one of them answered.

"Eight, right?"

"Eight."

That's when he heard the rip of a PMK machine gun and a shrill shout of *"Allahu akbar."* He'd assumed the militants had fled together, but was wrong. Pushed the Frenchman down to the ground and went to his knees and returned fire, rounds flying over his head and tearing into the Cougar. Located the young man behind the machine gun and raked him across the chest.

One of the Frenchmen had been hit in the leg. Crocker opened his medical pouch, removed an Israeli trauma bandage and some QuikClot combat gauze, and growled into the headset. "Manny?" His mouth was clogged with mud.

"Boss?"

CHAPTER THREE

*Success is not final, failure is not fatal: it is
the courage to continue that counts.*
—Winston Churchill

MANCINI HAD fought his way back to Truck One and
was now behind the left rear fender using the electric
sight system of his M320 grenade to line up the front of
a technical. He pulled the trigger and the HE round
glanced off the top of the Toyota's hood, sending up a
stream of sparks, slammed into the cab, and exploded.
Blood and body parts created a cloud of red as Manny
slid another round into the side chamber. The second
grenade hit the .50 cal machine gun and tore it out of
its bed.

He was so pumped and focused, he didn't notice
Crocker shouting his name. Imagined he was behind
him at first, and as he turned an AK round ricocheted
off the asphalt and tore into his boot.

"Fuck!"

The disabled technicals burned behind him, casting
eerie shadows and heat as Crocker collected the
Frenchmen. The wounded calf on the one he'd treated
had stopped bleeding. The bullet tore through mostly

muscle and had missed the peroneal and anterior tibial arteries. The other three who had been on their knees awaiting execution appeared to be in various states of shock. One was talking to himself. Another stared at his hands.

The pilot, who he helped from the downed Cougar, had a badly broken leg and possible injuries to his back and pelvis. The copilot had sustained major head trauma and was dead.

Either the firing from the road had stopped, or his eardrums were damaged.

Speaking into his headset, he said, "Davis, report status."

"Daesh has fled north. All good in Truck Two. We're gonna need to replace one of the tires. Will do that now. Minor damage to the windshield and hood."

"CT?"

"Good in Truck One, boss. No significant damage."

"Romeo?"

"Ready for more."

"Rip."

"Can barely hear, but good."

"Big Wolf."

Silence.

"Manny?"

"Nicked in the foot."

"Davis, call medevac. Tell 'em we've got wounded. One seriously."

"Roger."

Crocker's brain spun fast. "Then get on the phone and call Rastan. Tell him to block the jihadists' retreat. I'm gonna need help getting these Frenchmen into the trucks. And we'd better get out of here fast, before Daesh returns with reinforcements."

The battle was over for now, but there was a shit-load more to do.

Colonel Rastan had suggested that they move five klicks south to the town of Qabusiye and wait there for the medevac helo. Which is what they were doing now on the outskirts of town, near a dirt soccer field, as the sun set, turning the clouds ever-deeper shades of red.

The five Frenchmen and the covered body of the copilot waited behind a waist-high concrete wall with a doctor from the town clinic—Housani, he said his name was. Tall, with tight curly black hair. They'd been there for more than an hour, and the air was getting colder. The Frenchmen looked confused and scared.

Crocker cut the energy bars he kept in his pouch in half and handed the halves out to the Frenchmen. Offered one to the doctor.

"No, thanks."

"You speak English."

"I have a cousin who lives in Michigan."

"You spend time there?"

"A few months on vacation. I'm Turkish. From Ankara. A volunteer with Doctors Without Borders."

"God bless you."

The conflict had attracted good-hearted people, too, who came to help ease the massive distress. Doctors, nurses, and humanitarian workers from all over the planet.

Now he jogged around the field to get his blood moving, and stopped beside CT, who scanned the sky through a pair of binos. Glanced at his watch…1805 hours.

"Who's coming? U.S., Dutch, or French?" CT asked.

"The guys in the TOC didn't say." The TOC (or

Tactical Operation Center) located on Erbil Airbase monitored all military air and land traffic throughout the region on huge computer-generated maps.

CT wanted to talk about the upcoming Super Bowl. He was rooting for the Falcons. His wife and mother would be cooking a southern meal—fried chicken, beans, and collards.

"I thought you grew up in SoCal?" Crocker asked, blowing into his hands to keep them warm. He'd given his gloves to the wounded Frenchman.

"Mom is originally from Alabama. My wife's family still lives in South Carolina."

Crocker didn't care about the outcome of the game or the fact that Lady Gaga would be performing. He was more of an Ella Fitzgerald and Sarah Vaughan kind of guy. Dug be-bop and fifties jazz. Currently number one on his listening list was the sublime *Charlie Parker with Strings*. Stirred up memories of his grandparents whenever he heard it.

He was more than happy to discuss the relative talents of the quarterbacks and merits of defensive schemes to pass the time, and distract him for a few minutes from the grim realities of western Kurdistan and the feeling in his gut that ISIS would be back to seek revenge.

Colonel Rastan had told him they wouldn't. That they were concentrating their forces for a counterattack on valuable oil fields east of Mosul. That his units controlled this part of Iraqi Kurdistan. That the ISIS team they'd met at the Cougar crash site had crossed the border from their base in Syria and had likely returned.

Crocker wasn't buying any of that. Angry dogs bit back.

He noticed Davis's blond head near the Frenchmen, and, raising his voice, asked, "What's the latest from the TOC?"

Davis looked at his watch. "ETA, four and a half minutes."

"Then we should be able to see it soon."

CT kept surveying the sky with the Steiner M50rc binoculars. "You ever play ball?" he asked out of the side of his mouth.

"Me? No, I started running and lifting weights in high school. Before that I was a motocross fanatic and gangbanger."

CT shook his head. "You…a gangbanger?"

"Member of the bad-ass Flat Rats. Since reformed."

Davis pointed into the northeast sky and shouted, "There!"

"All right. Let's hump."

He and CT snapped open some Chem lights to mark the field. Slowly the HH-60M Black Hawk came into view, until they could make out the Red Cross symbol on the nose. It maneuvered into position and landed, kicking up clouds of dust.

With the engine idling, the crew chief and flight medic stepped out. The former had his long hair pulled back in a ponytail.

"What have you got?" the flight medic asked in perfect English. He was young and Middle Eastern, maybe Turkish or Lebanese, with a shaved head.

Crocker gave him the medical rundown, and the Frenchmen were quickly loaded aboard.

"That it?" the crew chief shouted.

"No. Wait." He turned to CT and asked, "Where the fuck is Manny?"

Davis answered, "He doesn't want to go."

"He's going! Get him. Get him, now!"

Like he did most nights, ISIS commander Abu Samir al-Sufi, a.k.a. the Viper, was being driven from one town in northeastern Syria to another. The forty-four-year-old with the thick black-and-silver beard traveled lightly—an AK-47 at his feet, an armored vest across his chest, and a backpack stuffed with a change of clothes, a prayer rug, worn copies of the Quran and Sun Tzu's *Art of War,* and the twelve cell phones he used to communicate with his lieutenants.

As he sat upright in the passenger seat of the extended cab Toyota pickup, he spoke to one of them, named Abdul Salam, through the encrypted program Signal.

Salam reported as he did every night on all ISIS activity west of Mosul. "Sheikh," he said in Arabic, "if God is willing we will achieve victory tonight. God is great."

"Yes, Salam," the Silent Sheikh responded. "If God is willing. I felt his spirit today in the children of the town of Tal Afar. They were reciting a favorite verse from the book, Salam."

"Tell me, Sheikh. What verse was that? I wish to know it."

"'Wealth and children are but adornments of worldly life. But the enduring good deeds are better to your Lord for reward and better for one's hope.'"

"Inshallah."

"Inshallah."

"I will recite that tonight before I sleep."

The pickup drove with its headlights off through the dark streets of Raqqa, near the banks of the

Euphrates River. Behind it followed a captured Iraqi Army Humvee with the Islamic State slogan "Repent or Die" sprayed across the sides with black paint.

For the last two years, al-Sufi had waged war against the new Iraqi army, Shiite militia groups, Assad's Syrian army and air force, Hezbollah, special units of the Iranian Revolutionary Guards and Quds Force, and more recently special operations units of the U.S. military. He'd seen the Islamic State give birth in central Iraq and spread through Iraq into Syria. He'd seen their ranks grow from a few hundred to tens of thousands. And he'd celebrated one victory after another.

Recent air strikes by the Russians, British, Americans, and French had reversed that trend. Some Islamic State leaders had been killed and injured. Hundreds of their fighters had died. Hundreds of others had abandoned the cause and slipped into Turkey, Iran, and Jordan.

In the past, the Viper and his men had moved from Mosul all the way west past the city of Aleppo with ease and had attacked towns in between with impunity, ridding them of Shiite, Jewish, and Christian infidels, raping and subjugating their women, and establishing strict Sharia rule.

Air strikes had forced him to alter their strategy and restrict their movements. They had also emboldened Kurdish militia groups like the YPGs and even the YJA-STAR (also known as the Free Women's Units).

Al-Sufi didn't like that. Now he and his men had to hunker down in urban areas under their control, where they were harder to find by Coalition drones and pilots. In cities like Raqqa, their headquarters, they'd built tunnels, trenches, and fortified bunkers. The infidels to his mind were cowards. He defied them to come down from the sky and fight, man to man.

Mayor Araz Sabri, at the head of a long wooden table in a large rectangular room in the Qabusiye town hall, lifted a pewter cup filled with red wine and uttered five words in English: "Friends...welcome... freedom...United States!"

Crocker, seated to his right, smiled and returned the toast. "Thank you, Mayor. We're honored to be your guests."

Translating his remarks was a bookish young man at the mayor's elbow named Dilshad. He claimed to have learned English during the two years he'd spent studying agronomy at the University of Georgia. The language spoken in this part of Kurdistan was Sorani, a dialect of Kurdish and derivative of Farsi.

Mayor Sabri, a robust, red-cheeked man of eighty with a bushy gray mustache and a fringe of gray hair, was a hero of the war against Iraq in the early '70s— a war that eventually caused Saddam Hussein to grant a level of autonomy to Iraqi Kurdistan. Now a federal region within Iraq, the Kurdistan Regional Government boasted its own president, prime minister, and parliament.

It was Colonel Rastan who had suggested that Black Cell remain in Qabusiye for the night because of heavy fighting in the vicinity of Highway 47 at Mosul. Besides the probability that passage to their base in Erbil would be blocked, Crocker and his men were exhausted and hungry. So Crocker decided to accept Mayor Sabri's invitation.

He was happy he did when townswomen brought out trays of grilled lamb and vegetables, couscous and fresh tomatoes and cucumbers, and set them on the table. The smells alone were overwhelming, and the lamb was deliciously spiced and cooked to perfection.

Seated at the table were a dozen of the mayor's friends and aides and the five SEALs. Communication was restricted to nods, smiles, and grunts of approval, except for the discussion between Mayor Sabri and Crocker, translated by Dilshad.

It wasn't a conversation really, more like an oral history of Kurdistan and its people delivered with passion. Crocker, in his state of exhaustion, managed to retain some facts. There were approximately thirty-five million Kurds—"the world's largest ethnic group without a state"—and five to six million of them lived in Iraqi Kurdistan. The majority of the others resided in the Syrian, Turkish, and Iranian parts of Kurdistan.

Kurdistan's predecessor—the ancient Kingdom of Corduene—had been invaded by the Persians and Romans. Subsequently, Kurdistan had been ruled by the Ottomans, British, and French. Though largely Sunni Muslim, the Kurds embraced a wide range of religious beliefs, including some from Shiite Islam, Christianity, Judaism, Zoroastrianism, Yazidism, and Yarsanism. Crocker had never heard of the last one.

He also learned that the Sorani word for "great" is *mezin*.

Abu Samir al-Sufi sat in a tiny, candlelit room in a mosque in Raqqa reciting verses from the Quran. He knew many of them by heart, memorized during his four years spent in the Camp Bucca U.S. military detention center outside of Umm Qasr, Iraq.

"'I will cast terror into the hearts of those who disbelieve.'"

These weren't the words of a prophet, recorded dozens of years after his death by crucifixion and preserved in the Bible. They were the actual words of God revealed to the Messenger Mohammad and recorded in the Quran.

He was interrupted by a knock on the door. "Yes?"

"Sheikh, it is me, Yasir Selah." Selah was his aide-de-camp—a painfully thin man with a perpetually serious face and a bum right leg, caused by a Shiite car bomb attack on a Sunni mosque in Baghdad years ago.

"Come in, my son."

Selah briefed the sheikh about the downed French helicopter, the rescue of the Frenchmen by a small unit of U.S. forces, and the retreat of the U.S. forces into the town of Qabusiye.

"The Americans are still there? In Qabusiye?" al-Sufi asked, stroking the silver tip of his beard.

"Yes, Sheikh. This is so."

Al-Sufi rose and paced the cold concrete floor from side to side. He recalled another passage from the Quran. "If thou comest on them in war, deal with them so as to strike fear in those who are left behind, so they may remember."

Allah had an answer for everything.

Al-Sufi knew that the town was vulnerable and that the infidels' air forces were focused on liberating the oil fields around Mosul. He also knew the infidels were greedy capitalists and generally interested in areas that would yield some sort of economic advantage. Qabusiye was a modest town in the center of an agricultural area. It offered neither oil, minerals, or antiquities.

A learned man who had studied every important military strategist from Alexander the Great to Napoléon Bonaparte, to Hannibal Barca, Erich von Manstein, and North Vietnamese Võ Nguyên Giáp, he considered 2,500-year-old Chinese general Sun Tzu's five essentials for victory.

1. He will win who knows when to fight and when not to fight.
2. He will win who knows how to handle both superior and inferior forces.
3. He will win whose army is animated by the same spirit throughout its ranks.
4. He will win who, prepared himself, waits to take the enemy unprepared.
5. He will win who has the military capacity and is not interfered with by the sovereign.

In every way, it seemed like a perfect time to strike.

CHAPTER FOUR

Many people die with their music still in them.
—Oliver Wendell Holmes

CROCKER DREAMT that he was sitting in the basement of a strange house. A loud party was going on upstairs, but he couldn't join it because he was baby-sitting a two-year-old girl with a chubby round face and shiny black eyes. He couldn't remember who she was. It definitely wasn't his daughter, Jenny. But he had a sense that they were related somehow.

A niece, maybe?

The girl in the blue patterned dress ran and giggled, challenging him to chase her. He did and she squealed as she ducked under furniture and evaded his grasp.

As he stopped to catch his breath, someone spoke through the closed door. "Tom, you can come up to the party now."

He turned to the little girl and suddenly he wasn't in the basement anymore, but in a dark room with a vaulted ceiling. Davis snored from the mattress beside him. He sat up and looked at a triangle of reflected light that fell across the red tile floor. A dog barked in the distance.

Where am I?

Crocker slowly remembered the lamb dinner and Sabri's talk about an independent, unified Kurdistan and the Athenian-style direct democracy they would establish based on voluntary participation. It was a nice idea, he thought, but ideas only worked if put into action. And action in the case of a unified Kurdistan involved an enormous number of variables and contingencies. The first thing they had to do was secure their country's borders and provide security to their citizens.

He heard a whining in the distance like that of a girl crying. It was quickly joined by others to create an eerie chorus. As it grew louder and closer, his body tensed.

Crocker realized what he was hearing and shouted, "Wake up! Wake up! We're under attack!"

A split second later explosions shook the walls and filled the little room with smoke and dust. He reached for his weapon first, then his combat vest. His body moved automatically, rousing his men, pulling on his boots and pants, pulling extra mags from his rucksack and shoving them into his pockets, fitting NVGs onto his head. At the same time, he was acutely aware of the sounds and the directions they were coming from.

So far, all he heard was rockets. No incoming automatic weapon fire. That meant the enemy was still at a distance.

He intuited the rest: Daesh had traced them back to the village. They'd come to exact revenge.

The TOC at Erbil had to be alerted. A defense had to be organized. His team consisted of two gun trucks and five men. It would be impossible for them to defend this town of four or five hundred on their own.

Dilshad burst into the room, coughing from the smoke and wearing black pajama bottoms and a t-shirt. His eyes were red and his wire-rim glasses askew.

"The mayor...Mayor Sabri needs you!" He was gasping for breath and appeared to be in danger of hyperventilating.

"Take a deep breath. I'm going now."

"We're under attack!"

Crocker grabbed him by the shoulders. "Calm down, Dilshad, we'll be okay. You have a Peshmerga detail assigned here or a police force?"

"Only...only the town...militia."

"How many?"

"Thirty...men and boys...with guns."

"Where are they, Dilshad?"

He seemed confused by the question and tried to pull away. Rockets landed nearby and exploded.

"Listen to me, Dilshad. Listen.... Where is the militia? Do they have a headquarters?"

"No!"

"A place where they gather?"

"They have instructions to assemble in the town square, which is close. I'll show you."

"Good. Let's go!"

Davis, Rip, and CT were still gathering their gear. Akil stood at the door, armed and ready. Another series of whines grew closer.

"Incoming!" Akil shouted.

They hit the ground and covered their heads, except for Dilshad, who seemed mesmerized by the sound. Crocker reached up and pulled him to the floor as one of the rockets slammed into the roof and exploded. Plaster and pieces of clay tile rained down on them.

"Go! Go! Go!"

He sprung, powered by a burst of adrenaline, pulling Dilshad with him. Outside, the cold night air was pierced with screams and cries for help. His teammates gathered around him.

He took Dilshad by the shoulders and said, "Show us the way!" He shook him. "Dilshad, take us to the square."

"Yes. Yes! Over here."

They ran in formation, weapons ready. Some with helmets. All wearing Dragon Skin armored vests. Akil beside him, his dark eyes burning with intensity.

"The fire's coming from the northeast," Akil said. "One hundred and fifty meters, I would guess. I'm gonna climb up on one of the roofs to get a better look."

Crocker hadn't seen a building of more than two stories in the entire town. "Okay. You got comms?"

"I got comms."

"We'll be in the plaza."

"Copy."

"Davis, call the TOC in Erbil," Crocker continued, checking to make sure that he had a full mag loaded in his HK416. "You know what to tell 'em. Then see if you can reach Rastan."

Davis's blond hair was matted with plaster dust. "Will do."

He checked his watch. A few minutes after 0400.

They entered the town square, which was surrounded by older buildings with balconies and porticos. A little fountain sat in the middle. Assembled around it were a dozen teenage boys with rifles. More men were arriving via passageways and alleys. Mayor Sabri shouted at them through a megaphone in the local dialect. A man beside him switched on an electric lantern that cast strange shadows against the ground and walls.

Crocker turned to Dilshad and said, "No, no! Tell him to turn that off."

"What?"

He pointed at the lantern. "The light! The fucking light! Off. It gives the enemy a target!"

Dilshad shouted hysterically at the mayor. Sabri threw up his hands and grunted something at a group of townsmen, who helped him down from the lip of the fountain. He got in Crocker's face and snorted in English, "This…is…bad…very bad!"

"Listen."

Crocker pulled Dilshad and the mayor close. Townspeople gathered around them.

"Tell the mayor…"

Akil's urgent voice came through the headset. "Deadwood, I'm looking at six technicals and a shitload of jihadists armed with .50 cals and rockets. I think they're going to hit us east and north. Maybe send a truck or two to probe west."

"Copy. Gather as many men with guns as you can and meet me on the east side of town."

"Roger."

He interrupted Dilshad in heated conversation with Mayor Sabri. "Listen to me.…Listen. Tell the mayor we have to set up a perimeter."

"We need air strikes!" Dilshad exclaimed. "The mayor says we need air strikes!"

"Yes."

"Without air strikes they will kill everyone!"

"Everyone! They kill," Mayor Sabri repeated in broken English.

"Listen, Dilshad, listen....Erbil has been alerted. Airplanes are coming."

"When?"

"I don't know. Listen. My men are going to set a perimeter."

"How?"

Crocker turned to his men on his right. "Rip and CT, you've got south and west. Take Truck Two and set up. Akil, Davis, and I will take Truck One and cover east and north. One man on the SAW, the other organizes and directs the locals."

"Roger."

Looking at Dilshad and Mayor Sabri, he continued, "Mayor, you stay here. Direct your men as they arrive to the different sectors on the perimeter. Northeast and southwest. Does he understand?"

"Yes," Dilshad said, his voice and body trembling.

"Repeat it. Tell him to nod his head if he understands."

The mayor nodded and slammed a forty-five-round mag into his AK-74 Kalashnikov. Crocker hoped he knew how to use it.

"What about me?" Dilshad asked nervously.

"Come with me," Crocker answered. "I need you to translate."

"Why?"

"You have a walkie-talkie? You can communicate with the mayor?" Crocker asked.

Dilshad held up the push-pull model in his hand and nodded.

"Excellent. Everyone's got comms?"

"Check."

"Deploy!"

Rockets exploded in front of them and to their left as they crossed the plaza. Townspeople with guns were shooting in panic, wasting ammunition. Crocker turned to Dilshad and said, "Call the mayor. Tell him to tell his people to stop shooting until they reach the perimeter and coordinate with us."

"How can he do that?"

A woman ran up to them holding a girl who was bleeding from one of her legs. Fear and panic poured from both their faces. Crocker had to fight the impulse to open his medical kit and help her.

"You have a hospital? A clinic?" he shouted at Dilshad.

"We do."

"Where?"

"Down there," he answered, pointing down a dark alley. "Down on the right."

"How far?" The lady was shouting at him in Sorani.

Dilshad held up three fingers. "Three…blocks. Blue sign…"

"Davis, help them. Then hop in Truck One and join me on the northeast."

"Got it!"

Carefully, Davis took the girl, held her in his arms, and ran off with the mother following and shouting.

"This way!" shouted Crocker.

They bumped into Akil as they exited the plaza.

"Let's kick some Daesh ass!" Akil growled.

"You stick with me. Davis will join us. We gotta defend the northeast corner."

"We'd better fucking hurry. Where're the trucks?"

"They're parked back at the town hall. Davis is bringing one. Rip is getting the other."

"Where's CT?"

"He's headed southwest."

The town was small. Only twelve blocks before they reached the northeast corner. They'd gathered eighteen militiamen along the way—mostly young men armed with hunting rifles, shotguns, and AKs.

CT's urgent voice came through Crocker's earbuds. "Deadwood, Daesh is moving toward my perimeter. Three technicals and a swarm of men."

"Copy."

"They're covering their assault with RPG and .50 cal fire. These kids are fucking useless. Some have already cut and run!"

"Organize them the best you can! Rip is on his way with the SAW. We gotta organize them so they know what the fuck they're doing."

"I'll try."

Crocker selected a two-story building on the northeast perimeter. Like the other structures in town, this one featured a flat concrete roof. He waved his arm to indicate to the young men to gather around. Most of them looked scared shitless.

Davis roared up with Truck One.

"Where should we set up?"

Crocker turned to Dilshad and said, "Tell the militiamen to come with me. Davis, you and Akil take the truck and set up a couple blocks away. Give us as many grenades, launchers, and RPG rounds as you can spare."

He selected four of the strongest-looking teenagers to carry the gear from the truck, then led the other dozen or so up a set of exterior stairs to the concrete roof. It was about six hundred square feet with a three-foot-high lip around it.

Soon as they arrived, one of the kids was thrown back by a .50 cal round that ripped a hole in his chest. The kids around him groaned and shouted.

"Down! Down! Tell them to get down on their stomachs and do what I do!" Crocker said to Dilshad.

"The boy…"

"Forget the boy. He's dead. Tell them to get down!"

He turned the kid over and placed a piece of tarp he found in the corner over his body.

Two rockets screamed past and exploded against a building behind them. One of the boys left his rifle and ran toward the stairs.

Dilshad shouted after him.

Crocker heard the SAW start up below. Raising his head above the concrete lip, and peering through the NVGs, he saw jihadists take cover behind their trucks, still one hundred meters away on a flat field of some kind of new crop. The fact that they were being cautious gave him a glimmer of hope.

"Davis, what did they say at the TOC?"

"They're checking on available air support."

"Fuck that."

If they were checking, he figured it might take an hour or more, by which time the town might be overrun.

Communicating through Dilshad, who lay on his stomach beside him, Crocker instructed the young men to stop spraying bullets wildly, and instead do as he did—raising his head every ten seconds or so, locating a target, taking a few carefully placed shots, and then ducking behind the lip for cover.

They were hugely outnumbered and short on

ammunition. A kid to his right already ran through the only mag he had for his AK-47. Crocker handed him a single-shot, break-action M79 grenade launcher and some rounds, showed him how to use it. The kid, who wasn't old enough to grow a mustache, nodded back.

"Deadwood, three more technicals circling south."

"CT, you copy? You see them?"

"Copy, boss. We're taking a shitload of rocket fire right now!"

"You on the SAW? Where's Rip?"

"Copy. Copy on the SAW. He's moving the truck so we're better positioned."

"Rip?"

He heard a loud explosion through his headset, followed by intense incoming. Crocker couldn't deal with that now. AK rounds were tearing into the concrete lip in front of them at an increased rate. He raised his head, saw the jihadists inching forward, growing bolder. Picked out one of them shouldering an RPG and raked him with a blast from his HK416. The boy to his left was struck in the shoulder and started screaming bloody murder.

The other ten kids looked his way with intense fear in their eyes. Crocker sensed he had to do something dramatic to keep them from panicking. More rocket fire ripped into the roof behind him. A woman's scream echoed down the narrow street.

He reached into his medical kit, located an Israeli bandage, and used his right foot to pull an RPG-7 closer.

He handed the bandage to Dilshad. "Wrap this around the kid's wound."

"I...I don't know how."

"Do the best you can."

A bullet ricocheted off the lip, throwing dust and plaster into Crocker's mouth. He spit it out and tasted blood, then loaded an arrow-shaped 93mm PG-7VL round into the RPG and aimed it at one of the technicals.

Pulled the trigger as incoming buzzed toward him. Lowering his head, he heard the explosion and quickly looked up to see flames spreading across the technical's hood.

The kids to his left and right seemed to gain encouragement from that. The enemy responded with a barrage of RPG fire of their own. He lined up another PG-7VL and fired, at the same time calculating in his head how much longer they could hold out. Ten minutes? Fifteen?

A big explosion reverberated from the street below, followed by shrieks and the sound of a wall collapsing. Then cries for help.

"We must surrender," Dilshad moaned.

Before Crocker had a chance to answer, Davis's urgent voice came over comms. "Akil's hit! He and some of the kids with him are buried! They're behind me. Fuck....I can't help him. Can't leave the SAW."

"I'm coming!" Crocker shouted.

Crocker handed his SIG Sauer P226 pistol to Dilshad. "Pull the trigger and shoot! I'll be right back."

"Wait!"

He slammed a fresh mag into his HK416, and rushed down the outside steps, ignoring the bullets that tore into the plaster wall and balustrade.

CT was screaming in his earbuds, which Crocker took as a good sign. He was alive. He could only focus on one thing now—the steps in front of him, the position of Truck One and Akil. He looked north, south, and west.

Spotted a bold jihadist running toward the village with an AK. Dropped him with a short burst of rounds.

Spoke into his body mike. "Davis, direct me!"

"Boss..." The line broke up.

"Davis...what the fuck!"

The sharp buzz of the SAW led him north down the dirt path that ran along the building to the first perpendicular path, where he found the Flyer-60. In the light from a window, he spotted Davis with both hands on the SAW and rivulets of sweat streaking his face. A picture of grit and determination if he'd ever seen one. The air so clogged with smoke and cordite, he could barely breathe.

Crocker shouted to get Davis's attention, but the latter was so intensely focused and the noise reverberated so loudly in the tight space that he couldn't hear. So he climbed up on the back of the truck and slapped Davis on the back.

Davis didn't shift his eyes from the targets in front of him. AK and other small-arms fire was coming at him furiously, and glancing off the armored shield around the SAW.

"Where's Akil?" Crocker shouted over the roar.

"Boss...Boss! Under the pile of bricks at the corner. The whole fucking thing collapsed. I want to...but can't stop."

"Anything new from Erbil?"

"Negative. I keep checking. All air assets are committed to the fighting around Mosul."

There was no point complaining. Not now.

Crocker looked past the Flyer hood and saw that

the insurgents had moved forward and were set up at seventy-five meters. Then he wound around the back of the Flyer to the opposite corner, where the whole side of a building had collapsed and was now a five-foot-high pile of rubble and bricks.

Fuck.

The dust was still settling, and in the dark, an old man and an old woman with a scarf around her head were digging frantically with their hands. He joined them, furiously pulling up bricks and pieces of mortar and throwing them to one side.

Sweating, he thought he heard someone moaning under the rubble. Wasn't sure it wasn't his imagination, or the wailing of the older woman, or maybe his hearing was screwed up.

He hadn't heard from CT, Rip, or Mayor Sabri for a while, and was now able to separate the racket from the southwest from the tremendous firing behind him. Both were getting closer, which wasn't good.

"CT, it's Deadwood," he called into the body mike. "Copy?"

No response.

CHAPTER FIVE

*Talk straight and to the point, without any
ambiguity or deception.*
——The Quran

NINETY MILES away in the Syrian city of Raqqa, Commander Abu Samir al-Sufi slept in a tiny room behind the Al-Firdous Mosque, when his aide Yasir Selah came in to wake him.

"Forgive me, Sheikh," Yasir said. "It is our brother-in-arms Mohammad Balul who is directing the assault on Qabusiye. Our brother seeks your guidance."

It took al-Sufi a few seconds to recall where he was, and picture the face of the young Mohammad Balul, who if he remembered correctly had been born in Qatar and had been fighting with ISIS for more than a year.

"Tell Balul to call me on the encrypted phone. You have the number?"

"Yes, Sheikh."

The heavyset man rose and said a quick prayer to Allah and asked him to look over the wives and children who seemed like echoes from another life. He'd left those still alive behind in his hometown of Tikrit, Iraq—not far from the birthplace of Saddam

Hussein, whose family had been shepherds. Two of his sons had died since the American invasion, and he hadn't seen his favorite and only surviving wife, Fatima, in almost a year.

"What happened with our brother?" the sheikh asked his aide as he reached for the wooden prayer beads at his hip—a gift from Caliph Ibrahim, who claimed to be a direct descendant of Messenger Mohammad.

"Balul is calling soon."

Caliph Ibrahim had given him the nom de guerre—the Viper—because of his quiet manner, skill at camouflage, and lethal bite.

Sheikh al-Sufi had been fighting most of his life. He started at the age of fourteen as a member of Saddam Hussein's Special Youth Corps, sent to man checkpoints in Iraqi Kurdistan. At sixteen, he joined the Iraqi Army, and at nineteen was invited to join Saddam's vaunted Republican Guard. As an officer in the Guard, he had resisted the United States–led coalition twice, once in 1990 in Kuwait and again in 2003.

He'd learned along the way that a military commander has to remain calm under all circumstances. Panic and rash decisions are anathema to victory. As al-Sufi finished washing his face and beard, Mohammad Balul's excited voice came over the encrypted line.

"Commander al-Sufi. Sorry to bother you, wise leader.... May God lead us to victory...."

"*Inshallah.*"

Balul relayed the details of the assault on Qabusiye and the unexpected resistance his fighters had met.

"How many trucks and fighters do you have, Balul?" the sheikh asked.

"Seven pickups and thirty-two men."

"And how have you deployed?"

"We have amassed at the northeast side to maximize our firepower and break through the town's defense."

Sheikh al-Sufi fingered the prayer beads at his waist and sighed. "The problem then, brother Balul, is one of tactics."

"Tactics? What's wrong with our tactics?"

The circumstances of this war had made it difficult to instill discipline and unity of purpose. Many of those jihadists who joined the fight from places like Yemen, Somalia, and Saudi Arabia had lots of motivation, but very little military training. Others, especially those from Syria, were opportunists who had joined the cause to rape and pillage and enrich themselves.

The sheikh put Mohammad Balul in the former category—motivated but lacking experience. Over the cell phone, he said, "In battle it is paramount to always know your enemy. Who is your enemy, Balul?"

"My enemy?"

"The enemy you face now. How would you describe them?"

"Sheikh…We are fighting maybe a dozen U.S. soldiers and the town militia of maybe forty men."

"Are these men untrained and poorly armed?"

"The militia? Yes. Most definitely."

"And they are defending a relatively large perimeter, correct?"

"Yes, Sheikh. Yes."

Al-Sufi could sense frustration in the young Qatari's voice. He asked, "If you look at the situation as it is, what is the best way to attack?"

"From all sides simultaneously?" Mohammad Balul suggested.

"Yes, brother Balul. It's the correct way, it's God's way...."

"God's way. Yes."

"The Prophet Mohammad said, 'Those who believe, and have left their homes and have striven with their wealth and their lives in Allah's way, are of much greater worth in Allah's sight. These are they who are triumphant,'" Sheikh al-Sufi said, quoting from the Quran.

"Thank you for these words of wisdom, Sheikh."

"They are ours to live by. Ours is a just fight, Balul. *Inshallah*."

On his knees and breathing hard, tossing bricks aside and digging through the rubble, his fingertips raw and bleeding, Crocker called "Akil!" over and over.

No answer. One explosion after another pounded his temples and deafened his ears. You didn't leave a teammate behind under any circumstances.

While he continued digging, he looked up to see if the streets in front of him were still clear. They were. No insurgents had breached the perimeter. Not from his perspective. None so far.

The sun had started to rise, and he was making progress on his side of the pile. The woman across from him had stopped out of exhaustion and was sobbing. He felt something smooth, and when he looked down, spotted a Nike swoosh on a sneaker in the dappled light.

The shoe contained a foot, which he traced to a leg and the body of a boy. His head had been crushed on one side.

Seeing the boy's body, the woman pushed Crocker away and flung herself on it with a heart-piercing scream. But not before he established that the boy was dead.

Past her legs he saw something move in the pile. An arm with a tattoo on it?

"Akil!"

Three more rockets squealed overhead and exploded. Debris stung the back of his head and neck. Continuing to dig, he pulled at a rectangular piece of metal with an illustration of a sewing machine on it. Behind it, he found a wide back covered with dirt and pieces of brick. Pushed them off and as he did, felt for signs of life and along his neck and spine for damage.

"Akil, can you hear me?"

Crocker thought he detected something moving inside his big teammate. A pulse, he hoped. Cut the side of his hand on something sharp as he reached around the debris and grasped Akil around the chest and very slowly and carefully pulled him up.

"Yo, buddy.... You hear me?"

Akil wheezed badly. Crocker opened Akil's mouth, reached inside with two fingers, and cleared his mouth and throat. Akil turned his head violently, coughed, and spit out a glob of mud and concrete just as another rocket slammed into the street in front of them, setting off a secondary explosion.

"Mofos," moaned Akil.

Crocker thought of the Flyer. "Davis?" he called into his body mike. "Davis...report!"

"Boss...boss," Akil growled. "I need to wash this shit out of my eyes. I can't see."

"Wait here. I'll be right back."

He scurried back to the Flyer, saw that Davis was still on his feet and firing, flashed a thumbs-up, and grabbed a water bladder and medical kit. By the time he returned to the corner, Akil was sitting up with his back against part of the building that was still intact. The old woman still hadn't let go of the dead boy.

"The kids…got…fucked," Akil groaned.

"Not your fault."

"Brave boys…"

"Lean back."

Two other women had arrived and were talking among themselves and digging. One of them had an old M1 carbine slung across her back.

Crocker lifted the bladder and rinsed Akil's eyes and face. Then handed it to him so he could clean his mouth. The big man had a large gash on his right cheek, and smaller cuts and bruises all over his body.

He winced as Crocker helped him to his feet.

"I cracked a couple ribs."

"Real lucky to be alive."

"Hold up," Akil said. "I need my weapon."

His M4A1 was covered with dirt and debris, and the front window of the EOTech scope had shattered. Neither was functional, but Akil took them anyway as he leaned on Crocker and limped eighty feet back to the Flyer. From the equipment locker in back, Akil grabbed an MK-46 machine gun and several belts of 45mm rounds. Cleared the shit from the pockets of his combat vest, and loaded them with grenades.

"Ready, boss." The gas-operated weapon weighed more than twenty pounds when loaded.

"You crazy fuck, you'd better stay here."

"Not happening. I'm going up to the roof to kill those bastards."

Crocker pointed to the MK-46. "You sure you want to carry that beast?"

He heard CT's urgent voice through his headset.

"Deadwood. Deadwood, it's CT. You copy?"

"Copy." He felt a moment of relief. "What's your status?"

"We're being outflanked west and south. Taking fire from two directions now. Down to four militiamen, me, and Rip."

"Rip okay?"

"Rip's a stud!"

This and yesterday's encounter at the Cougar crash site were Rip's first real combat with Black Cell since coming over from SEAL Team Two.

"Hold fast," Crocker said into the radio. "I'll be there in a minute with reinforcements."

The latter was a fib, because he had none. Still, he'd try to rustle up a boy or two along the way.

Davis saw him leaving and shouted, "Where the hell you going?"

Crocker filled his vest with mags and pointed south. "Same rooftop as before. Then going to help CT. Keep up the good work!"

Davis fed another belt into the SAW and resumed firing. Crocker wondered how many he had left.

The roof was a mess of bodies, blood, spent shells, and smoke, mostly from the building next to them, part of which was on fire. Flames flickered out of the second-story windows. Dilshad was one of six locals still alive, but his eyes were completely frozen, indicating a state of shock.

Crocker lay on his belly beside him, while Akil set up the machine gun and started firing. The racket canceled out everything else.

He cupped his hands over Dilshad's ear and

shouted, "You hear from the mayor? Mayor Sabri. What'd he say? We need more men!…Dilshad!"

When Akil took a break and lowered his head behind the concrete lip, he said, "He's gone, boss. He can't hear you."

"Damn.…"

Crocker came up with his finger on the trigger, saw a jihadist running toward them with a grenade in his hand. Put three rounds in his chest from sixty feet before the black-bearded man launched the grenade. Fell out of his hand backward and exploded.

Akil said, "They're either pulling back or shifting tactics."

"Why do you say that?"

"Some trucks are moving south. Look!"

Crocker poked his head above the lip, fired, and saw the silhouettes of three technicals circling.

"Fuck."

He pulled the walkie-talkie from Dilshad's hand, pushed the activation button, and spoke into it. "Mayor! Mayor Sabri, you hear me? This is Crocker. Copy."

All he heard back was frantic screaming in Sorani. A high voice that didn't match the mayor's.

"Is this Mayor Sabri? Is he there? Get Mayor Sabri. Get him now!"

The line went dead. Crocker tried again. "You okay here?" he shouted to Akil. "I'm gonna help CT and Rip."

Akil nodded without taking his eye from the Trijicon sight.

He ran southeast through the narrow streets and saw the light of dawn illuminating the cloudy sky. Slipping as he turned a corner, he realized for the first time that it had started raining.

He wanted to assume Mayor Sabri had stationed some of the militiamen at the south and west sides of town. But when he stopped in the doorway of a house and tried to reach him via walkie-talkie again, he got no response.

So he pocketed it and moved forward. The distinctive rip of the SAW echoed close and to his right. He slid across a slick concrete slab under the portico of a building on the corner and saw a sudden flash of light and the profile of a Toyota truck. The explosion threw him off his feet and onto his back. Momentarily stunned, he lifted himself out of the mud, and through the flames and smoke saw Rip on the ground, grappling with a jihadist.

The latter seemed to have the advantage.

Fucking hell!

Crocker wanted to shout out the lessons he'd learned from his close quarters defense training. Seeing the flash of a knife in the jihadist's hand, he lifted his HK416 and tore a red ribbon across his chest.

"Rip!"

Rip pushed the big man off him and struggled to his feet.

"Boss? Shit...." Gasping for breath.

"Over here."

The tall man limped over, blood smeared across his face and neck, his eyes wide.

"Where are the militiamen?" Crocker asked.

"All dead."

He pulled Rip close, and craned his head around the concrete column. Saw CT with his back to him on the SAW. Bodies strewn haphazardly around the

Flyer. The technical burning to their right and the sound of more Daesh fighters shouting behind it.

"We're fucked.... They're coming...from all sides...." Rip warned as he tried to catch his breath.

Crocker saw that CT's back was exposed. Soon as the smoke cleared, the jihadists would see the SEALs were trapped.

He pushed Rip toward the Flyer. "Start it up, and get it the fuck out of here!" he barked.

"And go where?"

"Make a loop and flank the fuckers to our right."

"What about the ones coming from the field?" Rip shouted, his eyes bulging out of his head.

Crocker couldn't see them and, therefore, couldn't calculate how close they were. "Do it. Go!"

The situation wasn't good. Rounds were coming hot and heavy from two directions. He made his body small. Clenched behind the column. Heard more shouts of *"Allahu akbar!"* from the jihadists sensing victory.

Past the burning technical, Crocker saw the outlines of six to eight of them surging forward. The Flyer engine growled behind him. It was his job to provide cover. Without the Flyer and its SAW they were certainly fucked.

Someone was shouting through his earbuds. "Boss! Boss! Copy!"

"I can't now..."

"Boss, we're trapped!"

On his belly behind a column of what seemed to be the town's only three-story building, Crocker said a quick prayer to God to look after his friends and family, especially his daughter, Jenny. A colleague whose heart stopped beating for two whole minutes once told him that he felt himself being pulled down a tunnel to a bright white light while seeing scenes from his life.

Crocker readied the 416 and waited. The jihadists seemed to move in slow motion past the burning truck. He held his fire until he was able to take out as many of them as possible with one continuous stream of bullets. He'd get one chance before they turned on him and took him down.

It's been a good life…

Thunder pealed overhead as he pulled the trigger. Jihadists screamed, twisted, and fell to the ground. Two, three, five of them. A split second later, a tremendous explosion rocked the field to his left and lifted him into the air.

His chest hit the concrete under the portico, knocking the wind out of his lungs and snapping his teeth together. Lost consciousness for a moment.

A deafening explosion pulled him out of it. Then another and another.

By the time he could think clearly enough to level the 416, he saw the jihadists had turned and were running toward the technicals, which were backing away. A deafening roar ripped his eardrums, and then a huge metal object screamed overhead.

Looking up he saw a single red star on the wing of a Russian Su-34M jet fighter as it slipped behind some low clouds. The continuous blast of its 30mm cannons rendered him temporarily deaf.

Fucking Russians.…

CHAPTER SIX

The unexamined life is not worth living.
— Socrates

AS PLEASED as Crocker was that the ISIS insurgents had retreated, he was pissed that it was a Russian aircraft that had come to their rescue and not an American one. It might seem like a strange quibble, and maybe he wasn't thinking straight, but that's what stuck in his head. In his half-conscious state, he pictured Russian president Putin leaning back in a red leather chair with a self-satisfied look on his face.

"Son of a bitch," he muttered.

"Who?"

He slowly focused on CT looking down at him.

Crocker saw his big white teeth and the light around him.

"We still alive?"

He closed his eyes for several minutes and woke up in the passenger seat of Truck One. Sunlight reflected off the sides of buildings. He heard people groaning behind him. Turning, he saw the bodies of four wounded townspeople in back.

"Where are we going?" he asked Davis, who was at the wheel.

"Once we drop these folks off at the hospital, we're going back for more."

"You remember where it is?"

"The hospital?"

"Yeah, the clinic. You okay?"

"Yup."

He slowly got his bearings. "The hospital…it's off to the left when we reach the plaza. I'll know the street when I see it."

"Cool."

"Where are Akil, CT, and Rip?"

"They stayed behind with Truck Two to guard the northeast perimeter. Akil's still on the roof. I think he wants to marry the 46. Refuses to come down."

He was trying to clear his head as they pressed on, the Flyer engine purring, the rest of the town quiet as though it was still asleep.

Closing his eyes, he imagined the first time he saw Cyndi poolside at Caesars Palace in Las Vegas, her toned dancer body, sweet smile, and how she put him at ease. He promised to thank her for that again next time he saw her.

"Boss?…Boss?"

He jolted awake. "Yeah."

"We're in the plaza."

Davis, to his left in the driver's seat, appeared ten years older. Deep lines creased his cheeks. His skin hung gray and lifeless over his cheekbones. There were dark circles under his eyes.

The month, date, and year were a complete muddle. Townspeople were clearing debris and assembling in clusters to exchange reports about the deaths and damage.

"Boss, can you hear me?"

"Yeah. Why do you keep asking?"

"We're here. We're in the plaza."

"I know." With the sunlight in his face, he wondered how Mayor Sabri and the rest of the militiamen had fared. The town was eerily silent. The fighting had stopped.

"Where's the hospital?" Davis asked.

He pointed. "Down there. Hang a left. Look for a blue cross."

Sheikh al-Sufi was disappointed when he heard that Qabusiye hadn't fallen, but he wasn't surprised, or particularly upset. Fate was fate, and didn't care what you wanted.

He sat in the courtyard of the mosque watching two doves feast on ants on the bark of an olive tree. Miraculously, the ancient tree and the birds were still alive. Most of the other life in this part of Raqqa had been destroyed in one way or another.

What remained were collapsed homes and wrecked buildings bristling with twisted rebar. Most of the trees shot up, shorn of upper branches, bark shredded.

As he shoveled goat milk yogurt into his mouth, he thought that there was no point dressing down or punishing Mohammad Balul. Yogurt was one of the few things he could eat, because it didn't require chewing, and chewing was painful because of the ulcers on his gums.

His aches and pains were too numerous to name, but they started with his gums, bad knees, and sore back.

Despite pains and disappointments, God's will remained irrefutable and would determine the future. He knew that. Experience had taught him that the goal of the infidel was to sow chaos in the righteous and corrupt their souls. The infidels' many tools included pornography, licentiousness, self-indulgence, idolatry, materialism, and liberalism.

All of this blasphemy advanced by the United States, Israel, and secular leaders in Europe and the Middle East was aimed at making men weak and luring them further away from God.

He'd experienced this spiritual dissolution firsthand as a junior officer in the Iraqi Army commanded by Saddam Hussein, when he spent six months training with U.S. Rangers at Fort Bragg. Many of the men he met were friendly and kept their bodies strong. But al-Sufi had observed that their minds and souls were in decay.

For one thing, they allowed women to rule their lives—women who rejected the modesty of *hijab,* and instead desired to show and adorn their bodies and brag about their accomplishments. The principle of *hijab* required modesty and humility in men, too.

In the U.S., instead of studying God's laws, men busied themselves with frivolous things and lavished time on stupid objects like cars. They turned themselves into children, spent no time in contemplation, and mistook niceness and moral ambiguity as virtues.

They worshipped Jesus without understanding his true story as explained by the Messenger Mohammad. Jesus wasn't the son of God, nor had he been crucified. Instead he had been summoned by God to rid the world of disbelievers. In this he had been only partially successful. Nor was it true that those who followed the word of Jesus, whether Jewish or Christian, would receive recompense from God.

The truth was that Jesus's teachings, and the Bible they were based on, had been tampered with by other men. The Quran, on the other hand, is the words revealed by God through the Angel Gabriel to the Prophet Mohammad. Words that were memorized by Mohammad, dictated to his companions, written down by scribes, and cross-checked by Mohammad. Not one word of its 114 chapters, or *suras*, had been altered over the centuries.

To the sheikh's mind, it was the literal word of God.

The SEALs hadn't expected this. They were grateful to have caught a few hours' sleep in shifts. But Mayor Sabri had insisted.

So here they were now standing at attention in the town hall and shaking the hands of the long line of people who had come to thank them for saving their town. Crocker reminded himself that a number of them had lost homes and loved ones. Others bore signs of physical injuries, like Mayor Sabri, who carried his injured arm in a sling around his shoulder.

Their generosity moved him.

"God…bless you, America," a young man said in broken English, squeezing Crocker's hand.

"God bless you, too, and your family."

Crocker didn't know these people and they didn't know him. The conflict had drawn them together, overcoming differences in culture, history, and language. In the end, they wanted the same things people back home in Virginia did—peace, freedom, and a good life for themselves and their families.

He was reminded of the intimacy that comes from

facing extreme danger together. How many times had Crocker attended to a wounded enemy soldier after battle? How many had he saved? And how many had thanked him afterward?

Nobody ever talked about that three years ago when he helped treat the son of an ISIS commander in Syria, who had been shot in the neck and jaw. The ISIS leader—a ferocious fighter and avowed enemy—had not only embraced Crocker for helping his son, but had also given him a gift.

"Beautiful, isn't it?" Davis, to his right, remarked.

"Sure is."

An old farmer and his wife handed Akil, who stood first in line, a platter of dates covered with plastic and tied with a red ribbon. Proximity with death made you appreciate the preciousness of life and the things shared in common.

To his left, he recognized a short woman with a long nose and a dark blue scarf tied over her head. Her son or grandson had been buried in the rubble with Akil. Hours earlier he had watched her dig furiously, then wail in agony when she found the boy's dead body. Now she held up her bruised hands to Crocker and compared them to his. Then she reached around his waist and hugged him.

"Sipas, ji were," she muttered, fighting back tears.

"I'm very sorry about your boy," he said back in English, looking into her flinty blue eyes and struggling to contain his own emotion. "I hope he's in a better place."

"Good…man," she replied, kissing his cheek.

He wanted to think so. Even though he had screwed up two marriages, and killed numerous men in battle, he had done some good, too.

* * *

The night sky was so clear that it seemed freshly cleansed, and showed off many stars. Crocker had just gotten off the phone with Colonel Rastan, who apologized for not sending relief and explained that his men hadn't been able to get past Mosul because of the fighting near Highway 47. He would be sending a platoon to relieve them in the morning, he promised.

All Crocker could say was, "Thank you, Colonel."

There were weapons to clean and reload, reports to make to the TOC in Erbil, and other chores to attend to. It was almost midnight before he and Akil gathered around Rip's DVD player in the room behind the town hall to watch the movie *Pineapple Express*.

The action on the screen was silly and outrageous—a perfect antidote to the seriousness of the day. Crocker found himself laughing at an exchange between James Franco's and Danny McBride's characters, when Rip got up abruptly and left the room.

One of Crocker's duties as team leader was to monitor the mental health of his men. He found Rip sitting on the front steps with his head in his hands. A Kurdish love song drifted from an open window across the street.

"You still worried about your dad?" A week ago, while they were in Erbil, training some of Colonel Rastan's troops, Rip had learned that his father—a Vietnam vet who suffered from Alzheimer's—had gone missing from their farm in Indiana.

"Yeah.... But he's tough. He'll be okay."

"Whatever's on your mind, it's best to talk about it."

He didn't know that much about Rip's background, except that the twenty-eight-year-old had been raised on a farm. Rip worked hard and had a ready smile and a certain innocence and decency about him. A tattoo of an eagle holding a flag with the slogan "Freedom Is Not Free" peeked from under the rolled-up sleeve on his left arm.

"Nice tat," Crocker muttered.

The young man looked up. "Don't worry about me, boss...."

"You did good today, Rip."

"Yeah...."

Crocker recognized the confusion in Rip's eyes. He'd been there many times himself. Questioning whether what he did made a difference. Doubting if he had the mental stamina to continue. Wondering if mankind was cursed by some internal devil that compelled it toward self-destruction.

"You see the gratitude on the faces of those people back there?"

"Yeah...." Rip responded, shaking his head slowly. "I almost lost it...today. I kept thinking about what those animals were gonna do to us when they captured us. I said to myself...before I let that happen I'm gonna take...my own...life."

"We all have those thoughts, Rip."

"You, too?"

"Yup."

Rip clasped his hands in front of his chest and nodded as he stared at a small crater on the opposite side of the street and the twisted remains of a bicycle.

"And...I keep thinking about what's going to happen to these people. I mean, they're celebrating now. But what happens the next time ISIS comes and we're not here?"

"We gotta take it one challenge, one mission at a time. Can't solve everything in one day."

"Embrace the suck and move forward, right?"

"Something like that." Crocker understood that the psychological scars of warfare were the hardest to overcome.

The call to *Isha* evening prayers ended with, *"Allahu akbar, Allahu akbar, la ilaha illa Allah." Allah is great, Allah is great, there is no divinity but Allah.* It signaled a time for all Muslims to remember God's presence, guidance, mercy, and forgiveness.

Sheikh al-Sufi remained on his knees on the carpeted floor of Al-Firdous Mosque, his forehead resting on his hands, feeling anger course through his body, and blood pound in his temples.

Despite what the *Isha* prayer said, he could never forgive the infidels who invaded his country, put him in prison, and killed his two sons. The best he could do was to accept his fate as presaged in the words of Allah. "Warfare is ordained for you, though it is hateful to you. But it is possible that you dislike a thing that is good for you, and love something that is bad for you. But Allah knows, and you do not."

Al-Sufi and the mosque's ancient spiritual leader, Imam Abu Anau Zabas, had argued over the nature of forgiveness many times. The thin, white-bearded imam often quoted a specific passage in the Quran: "Show forgiveness, enjoin what is good, and turn away from the ignorant."

Without a doubt, the imam was a good and deeply spiritual man. Al-Sufi could feel the spirit of God in the old man's presence. But to his mind Imam Zabas didn't heed the distinctions made in the holy book between the treatment of believers and infidels.

His journey to the hatred he felt toward them

began on a hot day in Tikrit twenty-eight years ago, when his policeman father accompanied him to the town hall to sign papers granting him permission to join the Iraqi Army.

He served proudly in the Medina Division of the Republican Guard—a Praetorian force handpicked by Saddam Hussein to provide security for his regime. Though not an ardent supporter of Marshal Hussein, he reluctantly accepted his Baathist Arab nationalist secular ideology. What it achieved was a relative peace between Sunni and Shiite Muslims—the latter group making up three-quarters of the Iraqi population.

That religious peace was shattered in March 2003 when the United States invaded Iraq and toppled the regime of Saddam Hussein. They did this, they told the world, because the Iraqi leader possessed a large arsenal of weapons of mass destruction.

When this turned out to be untrue, they told the world that they had deposed Saddam Hussein to free the Iraqi people. The real truth was that they killed them by the hundreds of thousands and divided them, pitting Shiite against Sunni.

Allah said of infidels: "Slay them wherever you catch them, and turn them out from where they have turned you out; for tumult and oppression are worse than slaughter."

At the beginning of the occupation, al-Sufi, like many Iraqis, remained hopeful that the Americans would take what they wanted—namely petroleum—and leave Iraq alone. In April 2003, as Major Abu Samir al-Sufi, he joined a delegation of Iraq's Republican Guard officers that met with U.S. CIA and military in Baghdad. The CIA official they spoke to was an open-minded Lebanese American; the U.S. general happened to be Mexican American.

Major al-Sufi explained to these Americans that he and other members of the Medina Division of the Republican Guard were professional soldiers and loyal Iraqis, who hadn't been paid in months. In return for a portion of their back pay, they were willing to help police the country, pick up garbage, or perform any other tasks the Americans wanted. Major al-Sufi and other Iraqi officers told them that they believed many other Republican Guard units would do the same.

The two American officials seemed to welcome their proposal. But when these men tried to get approval from their superiors in Washington, the proposal was rejected. Instead the U.S. ordered all Republican Guard units to turn over their weapons and disband. They also outlawed the Sunni Baathist party, which had ruled Iraq for decades.

They did this on the advice of Shiites allied with Iran, and without understanding the consequences— which included the empowerment of Shiite militias that began attacking Sunni neighborhoods and mosques.

In return for meeting with Americans and dealing with the infidels in a straightforward manner, Major al-Sufi was thrown in a U.S. detention center located outside of Baghdad. He spent four years there studying the Quran, praying, reading, and meeting with jailed Sunni officers like Colonel Haji Bakr, Lt. Colonel Abu Ayan al-Iraqi, and others. It was during his stay in Camp Bucca that the idea of creating an Islamic state to extend through the Sunni areas of Iraq and Syria was born.

Kneeling in prayer, he recited verse 33:35 of the Quran:

> For the men who acquiesce to the will of God, and the women who acquiesce,
> the men who believe and the women who believe,
> the men who are devout and the women who are devout,
> the men who are truthful and the women who are truthful,
> the men who are constant and the women who are constant,
> the men who are humble and the women who are humble,
> the men who give charity and the women who give charity,
> the men who fast and the women who fast,
> the men who are chaste and the women who are chaste,
> and the men and women who remember God day and night,
> God has arranged forgiveness for them, and a magnificent reward.

CHAPTER SEVEN

*I attribute my success to this—I never gave
or took any excuse.*
—Florence Nightingale

NO WAY Crocker could sleep. Not after a day like that. With his HK416 slung across his shoulder and SIG Sauer P226 pistol tucked into the waistband of his desert camo pants, he crossed the town square, turned right, and stopped when he found the blue cross beside the doorway that led to the basement hospital. A portion of the top story of the building had been sheared off, something he hadn't noticed before. He wondered if the damage was recent and the facility had moved.

That's when a familiar-looking man wearing a light-blue medical gown emerged smoking a cigarette.

"The hospital's still open?" Crocker asked.

"Yes," the man with the bushy black hair answered, placing his cigarette between his teeth and offering his hand. "Dr. Housani. We met before...."

"Yeah. I remember...."

"Terrible day..." The doctor looked at the damaged buildings and sighed. He had heavy bags under his eyes. "I was raised Muslim, and I don't know how real Muslims can justify something like this. The Quran I know talks about love, forgiveness, and peace."

"Maybe the guys who attacked us didn't read that part," Crocker said, as the moon shone in his eyes. "I came to see a friend of mine…named Dilshad. You know if he's here?"

"No, but…come look for yourself," Dr. Housani gestured, dropping the cigarette to the ground and crushing it out with the heel of one of his dirty white shoes. Crocker noticed that the toe of one of them was spattered with blood.

As they ducked inside, an explosion detonated several blocks away, sending a shiver up Crocker's spine and causing him and Housani to kneel in the doorway and take cover.

Expecting another rocket attack, Crocker retrieved the radio from his back pocket and said, "Davis, that sounded like it was coming from your direction. What's going on?"

"UXO, we believe," Davis responded. *Unexploded ordnance*. "CT's checking on it now."

Crocker turned to the doctor. "Could be a grenade, mortar, or rocket round that landed earlier and didn't go off."

Housani nodded. "Come…." He led him down dark stairs, to a corridor and through double doors. The large room they entered reeked of alcohol and iodine and was crowded with beds and mattresses— some of the patients on them slept, others moaned and called for nurses. Crocker counted three exhausted-looking attendants, one man and two women, scurrying about.

"Doctors?" Crocker asked.

"Only one and a half. Me, an obstetrician, and an epidemiologist from France. You a doctor?"

"Medic. Corpsman, we call 'em in the Navy."

"Then...welcome."

The basement room, lit as it was by bare overhead bulbs, reminded him of a scene from a painting or a movie. Picasso's *Guernica,* sort of, but in murky shades of brown and gray interrupted by slashes of white and red. A short, dark-haired nurse hurried over and spoke urgently into Housani's ear.

He turned to Crocker. "Some people were wounded from the recent explosion....They're arriving now. When did your friend get here?"

"This afternoon."

"If he's still here, you'll find him in this room."

"Thanks."

Crocker squeezed past hampers stuffed with bloody towels and bandages, and mothers and fathers sleeping beside the beds of children with missing limbs. He scolded himself for not coming earlier and bringing his medical bag.

To his right, he saw a man with a dark mustache lying on the floor with a dirty towel over one of his legs. He didn't moan or complain, but his teeth were clenched tight and he appeared to be in tremendous pain.

Unable to locate a nurse, Crocker knelt beside the man and lifted the towel. The wound consisted of a two-inch avulsion, or tearing away of the skin and tissue above the knee. Bleeding had stopped, but the tear hadn't been cleaned properly and the skin around it had started to darken, which wasn't good.

"I'll clean this up," Crocker whispered to the man, before getting to his feet and searching for medical supplies. He needed pain medication, disinfectant, gauze, dressings, sutures, bandages. He also needed to wash his hands.

On a metal cart, he found nitrile medical gloves and an empty box of cotton gauze. An arched passageway clogged with stretchers stood two beds away. A woman in a dark-green hospital tunic and jeans leaned over one of them. On it lay a boy whose face looked ashen and drawn. A piece of dirty canvas covered his body. His breathing appeared weak and shallow.

The nurse said something to Crocker in what sounded like Farsi spoken with a foreign accent.

"I don't understand," he responded.

She turned to him, and the space between them seemed to stand still for a moment. She appeared to be in her late twenties or early thirties and was probably European—light-brown hair, almond-shaped dark eyes, long, full lips, freckles across her nose.

"You're American?" she asked in a French accent.

"I'm part of a military team. There's a man on the floor back there with a leg that needs to be attended to."

"It is an emergency?"

"Not yet, but will be."

"Help me with this first." She had a smooth, confident voice and manner. "Grab the other end. I need to get him into that room."

She looked too refined to be in a grisly place like this. Crocker was about to ask which room, when he saw the open door behind her.

"You're the epidemiologist?" he asked. "Have you taken his pulse?"

"Yes, and no. Not yet."

"The patient appears to be in the latter phases of traumatic shock."

She was thin, but strong. They maneuvered the stretcher inside and set it on a long wooden table that looked like it had come from a dining room. The room was maybe ten by eight with a simple globe-type fixture overhead that didn't give off sufficient light.

"We're gonna need a task light of some sort," said Crocker.

She shook her head, as if to say, *That's impossible.*

"We must be very careful," she said, pointing to the canvas tarp that covered the boy's body.

Together they lifted it by the ends and set it along the wall.

He watched her eyes as she looked down at the boy. They seemed to darken and grow still. Crocker had seen worse injuries on the battlefield. The fact that the victim was young added to the horror of seeing his stomach ripped open and his lower organs exposed.

"I'm not a surgeon," the woman whispered.

"I can do this," Crocker whispered back.

He didn't have time to explain that he wasn't a doctor or a surgeon, but had been trained in combat medicine, and had sewn up wounds and delivered obstructed babies in conditions inferior to this.

The radio he'd stuffed into his waistband beeped.

"Deadwood, it's Romeo. We had a single UXO. No follow-up attack."

"Good," he grunted back, his eyes never leaving the Frenchwoman.

"Where are you?"

"I'm at the clinic. I'll call you back."

He glanced back at the boy and wondered how all the red organs and purple-tinged intestines would fit back into his stomach. Then assured himself they would.

The woman waited. He said, "I'm gonna need sutures, disinfectant, antibiotics, anesthetic, clean towels."

"We ran out of general anesthetics an hour ago," she answered.

"Bring me what you have. I'll watch the boy and check his vitals."

"Bien."

Soon as she turned to leave, the radio beeped again.

"Deadwood, Romeo...."

"Romeo, what's up?"

"Davis just reported people moving near the north perimeter."

"What kind of people?" Crocker asked.

"Militants...he thinks. With at least one truck."

"He sure it's not Rastan's men arriving?"

"We called Rastan. His men won't be here for another hour or so."

"Fuck."

This isn't where he wanted to be—in a drainage ditch 500 meters north of the town's perimeter, locating the gunner of the Russian-made 9P135 launch tripod through his ground-panoramic NVG-18s. Crocker's mind remained on the boy with his guts spilled out in the makeshift hospital and the attractive woman from Doctors Without Borders whose name he didn't know yet.

He had to force himself to focus on the situation in front of him, and move quickly through the OODA loop (observe, orient, decide, act). It was imperative. Because he could see standing behind the gunner the silhouettes of two more insurgents carrying 1.7kg high-explosive 9M111 missiles, capable of striking targets up to two thousand meters away. The 9M111 was an antitank weapon, but capable of inflicting massive damage on a hard target with more than three times the explosive power of RPG-fired rockets.

The effect of even a handful of them on the concrete walls and tile roofs of Qabusiye could be devastating—a final punch in the gut from Daesh; a warning not to resist next time, or welcome members of the Coalition.

Resistance in other towns in Iraqi Kurdistan and Syria had resulted in beheadings, rapes, and mass executions. As a Coalition soldier, sometimes by defending a town, you put it in jeopardy. He didn't want to leave Qabusiye that way, and hoped that the Peshmerga unit on its way would stay awhile. But that wasn't under his control, nor was the fate of the rest of western Kurdistan.

In an eerie shade of light green he saw what looked like a new Toyota Land Cruiser parked behind the three-man team. Where ISIS got its arsenal of military equipment was a subject of controversy. The White House wanted the public to believe that most of it had been seized from the Iraqi Army in cities like Mosul, Ramada, and Tikrit. But a lot of the ISIS equipment Crocker and his men had seen appeared brand new, and was rumored to have been supplied by Sunni supporters on the Arabian peninsula from countries like Qatar and Saudi Arabia.

It continued to be a clear, beautiful night with a temp in the mid-fifties. He scanned left and right, and didn't spot other teams—not in the vicinity at least. Akil and Davis, who were patrolling west and south, hadn't encountered additional militants, either, or he would have been alerted.

They appeared to be facing a lone demo team bent on terrorizing an already traumatized town. Rip on his belly to his right. Both of them were armed with MK 11 Mod 0 semiautomatic sniper rifles fitted with Leupold sights and QD suppressors. Crocker held up three fingers and pointed left, indicating that he would take out the gunner.

Rip nodded. Crocker flipped the NVGs to the top of his helmet, located the gunner in the crosshairs, exhaled, then gently squeezed the trigger. The 7.62mm x 51mm rounds made a muffled spitting sound as they flew out the front of the barrel. A split second later, Rip fired. Six rounds each was all it took to put down the three insurgents.

They watched and waited, but the jihadists didn't move.

"Done," Crocker whispered into the radio.

"Copy."

Three minutes later, the two men joined CT in the Flyer-60 and a few minutes after that they joined Davis on the roof of the building at the northeast perimeter where he kept watch on the field through a pair of Steiner Nighthunter XP binos.

"See anything?" Crocker asked.

"All clear," Davis reported back. "One truck, three insurgents, all down."

"Keep looking. I've got something to take care of at the hospital."

"What's her name?"

"Call me if you need me."

He left the MK 11 Mod 0 in the Flyer, grabbed his 416, and sprinted the ten or so blocks to the hospital. Glanced at his watch before he entered—0546. Rastan's men were scheduled to arrive at dawn, less than a half hour. If all went according to plan, they'd be back in Erbil by noon.

Back at base, he'd do some PT to burn through the residual tension, shower and shave, grab a hot meal, Skype Jenny and Cyndi back home.

He hurried down the hospital steps and arrived at the door of the makeshift operating room out of breath. Ran into Dr. Housani, who was backing out and looking at his phone.

"How'd it go?" Crocker asked.

Housani shook his head. "Not good."

"Why? What happened?"

"The boy started having convulsions. As soon as we applied pressure to his organs…well…He went into a deeper state of shock. We lost all vitals. Heartbeat, breath…"

"Oh…"

"Sorry."

Crocker pushed by Housani to check for himself. The boy had no pulse.

"I left a man in the other room with a wounded leg."

"We took care of that."

"Where's the epidemiologist?" Crocker asked.

"My colleague from Doctors Without Borders? Séverine?"

"Yeah."

"Maybe out there," said Housani, pointing to a doorway that led outside. "She needed a mental health break."

Crocker stepped outside through an archway and found her sitting on a plastic crate, staring at the ground, holding a bottle of water.

He crouched in front of her and said, "I heard what happened. It's not your fault."

She didn't look up.

"I had to go take care of something," he continued. "I ran back as soon as I could…"

A tear fell from her eye and hit the concrete. He felt awkward crouching in front of her, his HK416 casting a shadow over her face. In the light from the lamp on the opposite wall, she was prettier and softer than he remembered, and gave off a pale glow.

"I came to help," she said softly, "but feel so useless sometimes…"

"I know how that goes." He checked his watch again, found a wooden folding chair near the wall, moved it beside her, sat, removed his helmet, ran a hand through his thinning hair and over the beard on his face.

She looked into his blue eyes, smiled. "I don't know your name. Mine is Séverine Tessier. I'm French." She offered a delicate hand that trembled in his.

"Tom Crocker. Most people call me Crocker. I live in Virginia."

"You know Thomas Jefferson's home? Monticello?"

"I know it, yeah. But I'm on the east coast, maybe three hours away by car."

"It was so peaceful there," she said. "I visited three summers ago. Very interesting man…this Jefferson…this friend of France, author of the Declaration of Independence, inventor, architect, expert on the Quran, and owner of slaves. He believed that God created the world and then abandoned it."

"I didn't know all that," Crocker offered.

"Maybe he was right."

"About God abandoning the world? I don't think so."

"No, Tom Crocker? Not after what you've seen here?"

"Nope."

She studied him carefully.

"Can I get you something?" he asked.

"No," she answered, leaning her head on his shoulder. "Just stay with me awhile, if you can."

He caressed the top of her head. "Of course."

She fell asleep on his chest. Then he drifted off, too, and dreamt he was standing on the shore of a lake waiting for someone. Tall pines rose to his left and sunlight streamed through the trees and hit his eyes. He raised his hands to shade them and a dog started barking, causing him to wake. His radio was beeping. He retrieved it from his back pocket and glanced at his watch. 0723.

Akil's deep voice reverberated in his ear. "Deadwood, Rastan's men are here. Ten of them with six volunteers from the YPG. Interesting cats…One's an Italian anarchist. There's a California kid who doesn't speak.…"

He lowered the volume.

"Is there someone in command I can talk to?" Crocker asked.

"A major named Ardalan. Nice guy."

"Is that his first name or last?"

"Fuck if I know. He's a major. You want to hang here awhile, or return to Erbil?"

Crocker looked down at Séverine, who was starting to open her eyes. "Tell Davis to check if Highway 47 is open," he said softly.

"He already checked. The road is open. Why are you whispering? You with someone?"

"Tell the guys to get ready to deploy. I'll be there in ten."

*   *   *

He walked with her to the building next door, and down a hallway crowded with bicycles, to the room where she was staying—small, with a window, and two mattresses on the floor separated by a purple sheet that had been hung from the ceiling. A blue backpack leaned against the wall.

She reached into it and removed a laptop. "I'll make some tea, if you have time," she said, looking up at him.

"Thanks for the offer, but I have to go."

"You leaving town?"

"Yeah, heading back to Erbil."

"You think you'll return?" she asked.

"Probably not, but you never know...I'd like to stay in touch, if that's okay."

"Me, too."

He handed her the little pad he kept in a pocket of his combat vest, and a pen. "Write down your e-mail, or your Skype, or Viber."

"Be safe, Crocker," she said sweetly, writing down her contact info, then shielding her eyes from the sunlight that slanted through the window.

"You, too. And be strong. Here's hoping our paths cross again."

"They will if we want them to."

CHAPTER EIGHT

If I got rid of my demons,
I'd lose my angels, too.
— Tennessee Williams

HE COULDN'T get her out of his head as he sat in the lead truck with Akil at the wheel, humming the theme to the movie *Gladiator* as the sun rose behind them.

"What's on your mind, boss?" Davis, in the back-seat, asked over the low roar of the engine. "You thinking about the town?"

Crocker shook his head. "Nope. All good."

"Francetti…that Italian kid back there….Told me he's as opposed to the ISIS caliphate as he is to capital-ist modernity."

"What's that mean?"

"He favors something he calls a stateless democracy."

"How does that work?" asked Crocker.

"No national borders. People come and go as they please. Individual liberties are guaranteed."

"Here…in the Middle fucking East?" Akil asked.

"Yeah."

"Good luck with that."

Crocker noticed that they were passing cars and

trucks leaving town. Apparently, some residents had little faith that Rastan's men would stay long enough to defend them from the next Daesh attack.

He wondered if they would be staying with relatives in more secure locations farther east? Or were they leaving Iraqi Kurdistan completely to join millions of other refugees who occupied the massive temporary camps in Turkey? Sheep and goats grazed on the field to their right. The crisp beauty of the day almost lured him into accepting that life had returned to normal. Meanwhile, drivers of the passing Nissans and Toyotas honked, and their occupants waved, and Crocker wondered if his neighbors in Virginia Beach would be as cheerful if forced to abandon their homes.

Sheikh al-Sufi had moved from the Al-Firdous mosque to a room under the Raqqa Museum that had once been part of an Assyrian temple. While Coalition drones and military jets buzzed the city, he spent most of the night quietly chanting the name of God in an attempt to ward away the *jinn*—demons—he saw waiting in the corners.

They weren't something he ever talked about with Yasir Selah or anyone else. He never confided that the *jinn* had first appeared during his detention in Camp Bucca, Iraq, at a time when he was convinced the oppressors were trying to break his will by playing loud music that sounded as if it was coming from inside his head.

"How do they do that, brother?" al-Sufi had asked one of the Iraqi workers who came to clean his cell.

"Do what?"

"Put this music in my head. All day, all night…it plays over and over."

"What music, brother? What does it sound like?"

"Men and women screaming like demons. Metal pipes slamming into one another, breaking glass…"

The young man had looked at al-Sufi like he was crazy.

"If you hear music, my brother, it's your imagination."

Then one day while showering, he saw a demon—a large naked woman with horns on her head. She was a foul creature with gray whiskers, hot stinking breath, and saliva dripping from her mouth, and looked as real as the cinder blocks that formed the walls. He named her Ibah.

When he shouted for the guards, the demon bounded out the door and ran. Two nights later, she appeared in his cell with another demon—a thin man with a bald head covered with dozens of eyes.

The *jinn* had harassed him ever since and appeared at night when he was alone. He was sure they were a trick devised by the infidels to drive him crazy. Sometimes they would throw things at him; other times they would spit, or emit noxious black smoke. A few times they appeared with other demons and ghosts.

The only way he knew to get them to leave was to stay calm and pray to Allah.

He saw Ibah now, leering at him from the ceiling, beckoning him with her long, dirty finger to join her in what he imagined would be some form of fornication that would turn him into a demon as well, and put him in opposition to God.

He thought of calling Yasir Selah on the radio, but didn't want his aide to see him like this—scared and trembling like a little girl.

Clutching his Kalashnikov rifle to his chest, he said,

"*Jinn,* what are you going to say to Allah? One day you will face Allah!"

Ibah sneered at him and laughed in a way that made him nauseous.

He prayed, "Allah, give me the strength to send these demons away. Put me on the right path, and make me your faithful servant, now and forever. *Inshallah.*"

The SEALs had spent three days at the Coalition base in Erbil, resting, reading, playing video games, and doing PT. Tonight they were celebrating Akil's thirty-fifth birthday at one of the new hotels. They entered Superclub Bardo in the best civilian clothes they had with them—in Crocker's case, black jeans, a black t-shirt, black hoodie, and boots.

The club was dark with lots of blue glass and chrome, strobe lights, and slashing red-and-white lasers. A DJ in a black muscle shirt stood in a booth above the dance floor swaying to the music with eyes closed as though in a trance. Packing the dance floor were men in expensive-looking jeans and suits with open shirts and a few young women dancers, who Crocker thought looked like hookers. One with short white hair and a red micro-skirt twirled with arms overhead to the music—a deafening blend of electronic beeping sounds—while men took pictures and videos of her with their iPhones.

"Weird scene," Crocker shouted over the pounding bass line.

"You're looking at the hottest club in Erbil, bro," Akil answered. He wore tight jeans, a white muscle tee, and an unbuttoned glittery black shirt. "Reputedly owned by Russian gangsters."

"Great. I meant the music."

"EDM," Akil answered. "Perfect for grinding and getting your groove on."

"What's EDM?"

"Electronic dance music."

"Where'd you get the outfit?" Crocker asked.

"Swag, right?"

"Whatever that means."

"You need to relax, bro. Let the groove move you." Akil spun and showed off his dance moves.

A dark-eyed girl with white streaks in her straight black hair and a very prominent nose led them to the back of the club. Akil whispered something in her ear. She smiled and whispered something back, then escorted them down a mirrored hallway.

"She's into me," he whispered to Crocker.

"Yeah, so are the guys standing by the bar. Look."

"Where? They looking at my ass? I'll fuckin' kill 'em."

"Relax, bro. You merked."

"Merked?" Akil asked. "Where'd you learn that?"

Crocker was busting his chops. They entered a room that was dark and decorated in shades of red. An old black-and-white gangster movie was projected on one wall. An Asian man in a light-blue suit stood on a little round stage doing karaoke, singing "My Way," off-key.

"What's this?" Crocker asked. "The torture chamber?"

"You got your funny on tonight," Akil remarked.

Their terp, Zumar, who had just returned from his honeymoon, sat waiting at an oval banquet table that faced the stage. Man hugs were exchanged. Beers and shots were ordered. Toasts were made to Akil's health and longevity.

Rip, CT, and Akil got up to sing "Uptown Funk" by Bruno Mars. The former two actually had decent voices, but Akil sang completely off-key. His dance moves were a scream, complete with karate kicks and a spin.

More drinks were ordered. Toasts were made to Mancini, former teammates, other buds, girlfriends, and wives. More songs were sung.

"Come on, boss. Let's hear you sing 'Sweet Caroline,'" Rip said, busting Crocker's balls.

"In your dreams." His young teammate appeared to be in a much better mood.

"All good?" he asked.

"Yeah, they found my dad. He decided to spend a couple nights at a friend's house without telling anyone. Typical."

"Glad to hear it."

Three of Akil's friends—Dez, Oliver, and Rollins—joined them, the last two former British SAS commandos, now working as military contractors. Heavily tatted, muscular dudes, who seemed tightly coiled and dangerous.

Dez was their leader, a former Delta operator and bullrider. Oliver, the most talkative of the group, confided that they were fresh from a very difficult mission inside Syria, but couldn't say what it was or who had hired them.

He sat next to Crocker as Zumar regaled them with horror stories about the atrocities Daesh was inflicting on his Yazidi people.

"They're gang-raping women, man. Kidnapping girls, and if they don't convert to Islam, they sell them into slavery," he said. "Sometimes for like…fifty dollars. My wife has a friend who was taken away by them. It's disgusting."

CT asked, "You listening to this, boss?"

Actually, he'd been hoping to avoid talk about the military situation for one night.

"Real nasty business, mate," Oliver interjected.

"Colonel Rastan know about this?" Akil asked.

"Yeah. Everyone does," Zumar answered.

"You know where these camps are located?" Crocker asked out of curiosity.

"Fuck yeah," answered Oliver. "Most of them are in the foothills of the Sinjar Mountains near the Syria border."

"You think you can lead us to them?"

"In my spare time. Sure, mate."

Zumar was growing agitated. "We need to do something! Those are my people who are being slaughtered and raped."

"I'll talk to Colonel Rastan," Crocker offered.

"Will you?"

"I said I would."

Suddenly, it felt strange to be celebrating while people were suffering nearby. But the guys were in the mood to party and blow off steam.

Oliver lightened the mood with a joke. "How do you make a hormone?"

"How?"

"Don't pay her."

"That the best you can do?"

"Who is the most popular man in a nudist colony?"

"Me?" Akil asked.

"The guy who can carry two pitchers of beer and a foot of onion rings."

The karaoke machine was shut down, the house lights dimmed, and five young women in matching glittery red dresses appeared on the stage. They started lip-synching and doing a dance routine to a Lady Gaga song.

> "I wanna roll with him
> A hard pair we will be
> A little gamblin' is fun when you're with me."

"You can roll with me anytime," Akil remarked, getting up and grinding his hips.

"You look like a gorilla with a bug up his ass, mate."

"Sit down. You're making us look bad."

"Me?" Akil boasted, sticking his chest out. "I lend you all some swag."

The women looked Russian and Tajik, ranging in age from about eighteen to thirty-five, and were all some variation of attractive. The most striking shook her booty in the middle of the group, a head taller than the rest, and looked strong enough to pull a plow. She was clumsy as hell, too, but determined and energetic.

She spun, almost lost her balance, and Crocker had to bite his knuckles to keep from cracking up.

She focused her heavily mascaraed eyes on him, dipped forward to reveal her ample cleavage, and, pointing a long red fingernail at his chest, shouted, "Poka face…Poka face."

He was about to bust a gut.

"Boss, the big one's got the hots for you," Akil announced.

"Likes the salt-and-pepper thing you got going on," added CT.

"She looks like she could break me in half."

"Looks like she might be packing something else," Rip said.

They laughed. The routine ended to applause and

hoots from the Asian and Russian contingents at tables behind them. Then a delicate, very young-looking woman came out carrying a birthday cake with sparkler candles. The women sang an off-key version of "Happy Birthday" to Akil.

Afterward, the Russian dancers sat with them. They didn't speak English, so the conversation was awkward, but everyone seemed to have a good time.

CHAPTER NINE

Write on my gravestone: Infidel, Traitor.
Infidel to every church that compromises
with wrong; traitor to every government that
oppresses the people.
— Wendell Phillips

FROM HIS position high atop the reviewing stand, Sheikh al-Sufi looked over the heads of the thousands of residents of Raqqa who had been summoned to the traffic circle in front of the Raqqa Museum in the city's al-Mukhtaita industrial district. The three-story museum had once housed antiquities from the region, including a large collection of pottery from the Ayyubid dynasty of the twelfth century led by Sultan Saladin.

Months ago, the sheikh had ordered the destruction of much of the colorful underglazed painted ceramics and inlaid metalwork, because he viewed them as the idols of devil-worshipping Assyrians and Akkadians, who made sacrifices to the gods of rain, agriculture, and war. He was following the example of Mohammad, who after capturing the holy city of Mecca in 629, ordered the demolition of the cult statues kept inside the Kaaba—"reducing them to fragments," according to the Quran.

Today's assembly wasn't about history or destroying statues and idols. It was about punishing activities that shamed Allah.

Hundreds of ISIS militants, dressed head-to-toe in black, waited in the adjoining streets and alleys in case of a Coalition or Assad government air attack. They manned Russian-made DShK and ZU-23-2 Sergey antiaircraft guns, Russian-made shoulder-fired 9K32 Strela-2 missiles, and American-made FIM-92 Stinger surface-to-air missiles. Lookouts searched the skies for drones and jets.

Meanwhile, ISIS special religious police checked to see that all females in attendance were accompanied by male escorts and wore the required two black gowns to hide their body shape, black gloves, and three black veils. Those who didn't or smelled of perfume were led away to a nearby prison for punishment.

The crowd faced a platform that had been erected in front of the five-story Governant Building cater-corner to the museum. That's where al-Sufi stood with his lieutenants listening to a speech by Imam Abu Anau Zabas, who recited the seven articles of faith (*imān*): belief in the Oneness of God, the angels, the Sacred Scriptures, the messengers of God, the Last Day, destiny coming from God—whether good or bad—and resurrection after death.

The imam explained passionately that God (*Allah*) was the sole creator of the universe and its absolute controller and regulator, and how everything in the universe had a predetermined course (*al-qadar*). "Nothing can happen without God willing it and knowing it," he said.

Then he related the story of the city of Sodom on

the western shore of the Dead Sea, whose residents robbed and killed travelers, and the men had sex with men instead of women.

"At the height of their crimes and sins," Imam Zabas said, "Allah revealed himself to the Prophet Lut and told him to summon the people to give up their indecent behavior. Lut warned them of Allah's punishment. He asked, 'Will you not fear Allah and obey him?'"

As the imam spoke, al-Sufi's thoughts drifted to his two deceased sons—Mustafa and Jamir. Both died before they reached the age of twenty— Mustafa as a result of a U.S. air strike on their hometown of Tikrit during the invasion, and Jamir while fighting U.S. Marines during the Battle of Fallujah in 2004.

He remembered two dark-eyed boys chasing each other across the red tile floor of their house and sitting in his lap as he told them stories about their grandfather—a hero of the 1980 war with Iran.

They were good boys, filled with spirit, and both loved chocolate ice cream. Now they were martyrs living in the gardens of heaven.

A profound sadness came over Sheikh al-Sufi as militants fired guns in the air and all attention turned to the roof of a five-story building behind him. A hush came over the crowd. Militants wearing black hoods escorted four young prisoners in orange jumpsuits onto the flat roof. The men's heads had been shaved and black bandanas tied over their eyes. One, with long legs and narrow shoulders, resembled Mustafa.

Crows cawed from rooftops. Pigeons circled in the air.

"Nothing is lost. Nothing is forgotten," Imam Zabas declared. "Allah sees and is all."

Large black Islamic State flags flapped in the breeze as militants led the prisoners to the edge of the flat roof and forced them to their knees. All of this was captured on videotape by other militants with cameras—footage that would later be distributed through ISIS propaganda networks and posted on jihadist websites.

The imam, his voice cracking with emotion, read a passage from the Quran through the PA system. "'As a prophet of God, Lut said to his people: Will you commit lewdness such as no people in creation ever committed before you? For you come to lust in men in preference to women. No, you are indeed people transgressing beyond bounds.'"

There was a long moment of silence. The old imam's knees started to buckle and he was helped into a plastic chair. Sheikh al-Sufi thought he could hear the thousands of hearts beating together like a single drum.

Two militants came up behind the first kneeling prisoner and pushed him off the roof. The sinner pitched forward, flipped over twice, and hit the pavement with a violent snapping sound. The thousands of men and women applauded and cheered in triumph as though they were at a soccer match and their team had just scored the winning goal.

The rapturous applause filled al-Sufi's chest with pride. Tears filled his eyes as he remembered his sons and longed for the day they would meet again in the gardens of paradise. "'For those who have faith and work righteousness, they are the companions of the

Garden. Therein shall they abide forever…'" he muttered.

Three more times, a condemned man was pushed over the roof, and three more times the crowd exploded with applause and al-Sufi's chest filled with pride.

Then at the moment of sunset (*Maghrib*), everyone in the plaza turned to face Mecca, went to their knees and prayed, ignoring the four twisted, broken bodies that would later be picked apart by rats and vultures as a reminder of their indiscretion to God.

Crocker sat in a little room in the base communication center talking over a secure line with his commander, Captain Sutter, who was at ST-6 HQ camp in Dam Neck, a few miles south of Virginia Beach. A cold wind howled outside.

"I think you know what this is about," Sutter said.

Crocker saw a prompt on his cell phone indicating that Séverine was calling. He wanted to talk to her, but couldn't now.

"In case you've forgotten, you and your men have been in the field more than three months without a break," his commander continued. "I assume you know what that means."

Before this assignment to Kurdistan, Black Cell had spent six weeks in Yemen training forces from Saudi Arabia and units from other Arab countries who were fighting al-Qaeda. There they had tested a new JSOC data collection program known as SKOPE, which predicted insurgent movement. Prior to that they had been in eastern Afghanistan going after HVTs (high-value targets) including Ahmed Sufredi

Khan, one of the top military commanders of the Taliban. The latter had been a success; the former not so much.

"Sir, another four to six weeks should give us enough time to wrap up our missions here," said Crocker.

"Not in the cards, Chief Warrant," Sutter countered. "Your time's up. You're headed west for R&R and training, now."

"Colonel Rastan just informed me that he needs our help in Mosul. The situation there is desperate."

"Dammit, Crocker...." Sutter started, his Kentucky accent sounding thicker than usual. "When are you gonna get it through your thick head that we're all accountable to rules and regulations that are put in place for a purpose?"

"What purpose is that, sir?"

"To keep guys like you from crossing the line and wandering into stupid and self-destructive situations. Bottom line, you and your men need a break and are coming home."

"Sir, with all due respect, I know my men better than anyone and they're good for another four weeks," Crocker argued. "Besides, what about the mission to eliminate Abu Samir al-Sufi, the Viper? We haven't started to move on him yet."

"The intel on him has never coalesced. He's somewhere in or around the city of Raqqa, right in the middle of Islamic State headquarters. They're dug in deep; he's heavily guarded."

"I'll sit down with Rastan and his men tonight and make a plan," Crocker countered.

"Mosul's the main focus right now."

"Then we'll go to Mosul."

"No, you won't."

"Maybe we hit the Viper now when he doesn't expect it."

"No, get your asses on a plane and come home! An order's an order. Besides, you need to get acquainted with your new intel team back here, BC/2."

"What? We're not taking our orders from the Agency anymore?" Crocker asked, referring to the CIA.

"You will continue to receive your missions primarily from them, yes. But the daily stuff…Briefings and updates will be handled differently. When you get here, I'll explain."

Crocker didn't want to go home, not because he didn't need the rest. But because home was complicated, and the transition from field to pre-phase (a.k.a. R&R and training) was always a bitch. Besides, he liked the Kurds and wanted to help them.

"Sir, you hear about all the Yazidi women and children Daesh is holding in prison camps in eastern Syria? Apparently, it's a real human rights nightmare. Colonel Rastan is planning a raid and wants our help."

"Not now!"

"Sir, is there any way I can talk you out of this?"

"No, Crocker."

"Anything you want from Erbil? A carpet, silver jewelry, a Russian hooker?"

"Your presence in my office in two days."

"Yes, sir."

First call Crocker made was to his girlfriend, Cyndi. Calling her a girlfriend could be an exaggeration, because although they'd met a year ago in Las Vegas, he and she had only been together twice since then.

Crocker Skyped her whenever he had a chance, and tried to stay involved in her life, even contributing $300 a month to help pay for her daughter Amy's treatments for a rare blood disease known as Diamond-Blackfan anemia.

"I hope you'll find time to visit," Cyndi gushed upon hearing that he was returning soon.

"You know I will."

Cyndi was a beautiful, talented dancer who usually sounded upbeat, even when she was dealing with problems that included serious knee pain that she was afraid might require surgery and could jeopardize her dancing career with Cirque du Soleil, an alcoholic mother, and a musician ex-husband who was currently in rehab.

"How's everything with you? How's Amy?"

"Okay. I'm so excited to see you, Tom."

He'd researched Diamond-Blackfan and found out it was a genetic abnormality that could result in serious organ damage and delayed growth.

"Just okay?" he asked, sensing worry in her voice.

"Well, sorry, but today was kind of…challenging," Cyndi answered. "Hearing from you—"

He cut her off. "No reason to be sorry. What's up?"

"I saw Amy's hematologist, who told me the monthly blood transfusions and steroid therapies aren't working. We'll find another way."

"Not working? What does that mean?"

"I hate to lay this on you, Tom. You've got your own problems."

"Tell it to me straight."

"It means her body's still not producing enough healthy red blood cells. And the steroids are messing with her appetite, so she isn't getting the proper nutrition. She's supposed to start kindergarten in September, and…"

Cyndi had the heart of an angel, and the tenacity of a pit bull.

"Are there any other courses of treatment besides blood transfusions and steroids?" Crocker asked.

"There are, but they bring…other…problems."

"What?"

"Seriously, Tom, don't worry about it. Get home safe."

"Tell me."

"All right, the treatments are expensive, and my health insurance doesn't cover them."

"What kind of treatments?"

"The doctor says she might need a bone marrow transplant."

"Oh…"

"And the transplants don't always work. So before I try anything I want to consult this other hematologist I've heard about."

"Sound thinking."

"Except he isn't in our network."

"Go see him, Cyndi. I'll pay for it."

"That's so sweet, Tom, but—"

"Schedule an appointment tomorrow. No excuses."

Next, he called his father, who seemed to have recovered fully from the triple bypass surgery of nine months ago. After that, his daughter, Jenny, told him that she'd just moved in with her boyfriend.

"How's that going?" Crocker asked.

"It's kind of an adjustment for both of us. He's more of a neat-freak than I am."

"That's good, isn't it?"

She laughed. "Thanks, Dad."

He was proud of her. At twenty, she was assistant manager of a restaurant and taking business management classes at junior college. It seemed like a month ago when she was in his lap, asking him to read *Goodnight Moon* for the ten thousandth time.

The challenges and concerns of home crowded his head as he sat on the bunk in his wet hooch, checking his e-mail for the first time in a week and a half. An invitation to a Frogs with Hogs motorcycle rally in March, an ST-6 colleague's wedding in June, a notice about a memorial service for his buddy Suarez, who had died on the mission to North Korea last year, various solicitations from veteran charities and purveyors of ED medication.

SOS…same old shit…

He was about to close his laptop when his Viber app starting pinging. Though he didn't recognize the number, he accepted the call anyway. Séverine's smiling face appeared on the screen of his laptop with his grizzled visage in the corner. With his salt-and-pepper beard he thought he looked like he could be her father.

"Hey, Séverine," he said. "Great to see you. Sorry I didn't pick up earlier. Where are you camping these days? What's up?"

"Am I interrupting something? Is it too late?"

"No, no.…Not at all. What's going on?" He saw light curtains in the background and a painting of some kind on the wall.

"I'm in Istanbul," she answered. "Luxuriating in a four-star hotel. Please don't tell anyone, okay? It doesn't fit my image." Her French accent was charming. She looked more relaxed than last time he had seen her in Qabusiye.

"Istanbul...nice. One of my favorite cities." The last time Crocker was there, he got involved in a firefight with some of Assad's agents near the Blue Mosque. Taken one out, sent another two to the hospital. He wasn't sure Turkish authorities would welcome him back.

"I hitched a ride here with some colleagues," Séverine explained. "I decided I needed some time off, and some of...what you call...personal care."

He wasn't sure what she meant by that. "Good for you. You deserve a break."

"I arrived yesterday, you know," Séverine continued. "Spent the day sightseeing and shopping. I never shop!" She laughed, then covered her mouth. "Maybe I'm a little drunk. Where are you?"

"Erbil. We leave tomorrow for the States."

"That's good, yes? You like it there?"

"Erbil or the States?"

"Erbil."

"Yeah....I mean, it's changing all the time. New shopping malls, new restaurants, a brand-new airport...Séverine?" The line went dead.

She called him right back.

"It's so nice to see you again," she joked.

"What's it been? Five seconds? It's good to see you again, too." He meant it. She was pretty in an unconventional way, with dark, soulful eyes and a longish nose.

"I called because I want to thank you again. You were really kind to me in Qabusiye."

"You're welcome."

He flashed back to the town, the survivors at the town hall, the boy on the stretcher.

Tonight, Séverine didn't seem to want to talk about

Qabusiye. Instead, she wanted to tell him more about herself. How she'd learned English while living in New York City, moved there with a girlfriend at seventeen, later attended Columbia University and majored in European History, and then she switched to pre-med.

"You're way more educated than I am," Crocker admitted. "I barely made it out of high school. Graduated last in my class. Something I'm not proud of."

"But you've got real life experience and knowledge, yes?"

"I guess."

"*Alors*.... You were probably more interested in girls and sex."

"Girls, motorcycles, and generally raising hell. Not in that order."

"Are you married?" she asked, apropos of nothing.

"No. But I'm twice divorced."

"I was married once, too," she said, pushing her straight hair off her forehead. "It lasted less than a year. I was completely unhappy. The sex...was terrible."

He started to imagine how she'd feel in his arms, then stopped.

"If the sex was lousy, why'd you bother?" he asked, figuring she was probably fifteen years younger than him.

"Guilt, naiveté, lack of confidence..." Her smile conveyed a beguiling mix of sadness and longing. "You have to be ready. And you have to be with the right person. *N'est-ce pas?*"

"I'm still not ready." He wasn't sure where she was going with this, or whether she viewed him as colleague, friend, or possibly something else. "How long have you been with Doctors Without Borders?"

"Two and a half years, since my divorce from Alain. It feels like longer.... You live alone?" Séverine asked. "I'm sorry.... Am I being too forward? If I am I blame it on the rosé."

"I don't mind."

"That I'm flirting? That I'm acting like a silly girl?"

"I like talking to you," he admitted. "I wish I was with you in Istanbul right now."

"Me, too."

"To answer your previous question, I'm not alone. I'm sharing a hut with four smelly teammates. Two of them are snoring. Why?"

"I mean...when you're in the States, do you live alone?"

"Yes, but I'm not there much."

"You have family?"

"A daughter who just turned twenty. My father's still alive."

"My mother is alive, too. She lives in Paris. My father was from Aix-en-Provence in the south. You know France?"

"Parts of it, yeah."

"Which parts?"

"Paris, the Riviera, the Loire Valley...."

"The good ones."

"Yeah. Paris is one of my favorite cities...." He remembered the terrorist attacks there in November 2015 and stopped.

"I'm not pure French," Séverine added. "Because my grandmother on my mother's side was from Morocco."

"That explains your eyes. I've never thought of Moroccans as Arabs."

"Some are, some are Berbers. Maybe half and half.

You think you'll be returning to Kurdistan later?" she asked.

"Probably, at some point."

"Then you must read *Seven Pillars of Wisdom* by T. E. Lawrence, if you haven't already."

"T. E. Lawrence…Is he the same as Lawrence of Arabia?"

"Yes. Yes. That was the first book that helped me understand something of the Arab mentality."

"I'll read it. Thanks."

CHAPTER TEN

This above all: To thine own self be true.
    —William Shakespeare, *Hamlet*

ABU SAMIR al-Sufi completed his evening prayers and remained on his knees, entreating Allah to calm his unsettled mind, which roiled with confusion and anger. Foremost, he was searching for the best way to address what he considered a very troublesome situation that had resulted from the serious injury to Caliph Ibrahim Muhammad al-Badri (a.k.a. Abu Bakr al-Baghdadi).

Sheikh al-Sufi had been at al-Baghdadi's side in a mosque in Mosul in 2014 when he announced *The Promise of Allah,* and said that the "long slumber in the darkness of neglect" had ended. "The sun of jihad has risen. The glad tidings of good are shining. Triumph looms on the horizon. Infidels are justifiably terrified for, as both East and West submit, Muslims will own the earth."

His friend al-Baghdadi was announcing the return of a single caliphate, like the one that had ruled all Muslims until the year 750, when provinces broke away to pursue their own political agendas.

Naming himself Caliph Ibrahim, al-Baghdadi asked for the allegiance of Muslims everywhere, urging them to throw out "democracy, secularism, nationalism, as well as all the other garbage and ideas from the West."

It had been the most significant day in Sheikh al-Sufi's political life. Now, three years later, he hadn't had any communications from the caliph in more than three months. Even though al-Sufi was a member of the Islamic State's Military Council, and therefore one of three top commanders appointed by the caliph himself, he wasn't sure if his leader was alive or dead. And the military commanders below him in rank and rumored to be with Caliph Ibrahim in Mosul—including Abu Wahib, also a former officer in Saddam Hussein's army and prisoner in Camp Bucca, Saddam Jamal, and red-bearded Omar al-Shishani (a.k.a. Omar the Chechen)—remained closemouthed.

Why? What are they trying to hide from me?

Although al-Sufi understood the need for vigilance and secrecy, he considered this a sign of disrespect. Part of him suspected a power play. None of those three commanders were members of the Military Council, whose role was to plan and supervise all military leaders and operations in the field. Instead, they were part of the lesser Defense, Security, and Intelligence Council responsible for the personal security and safety of the caliph, and the collection and dissemination of intelligence.

A few days ago, Sheikh al-Sufi—a member of the Military Council—had ordered a new assault on the town of Qabusiye, only to learn that his units had been called away by Saddam Jamal—a former drug dealer and member of the Free Syrian Army who had only joined the movement in 2014—to help defend Mosul. Not only had the sheikh been countermanded by someone below him in the chain of command, the young Saddam Jamal didn't even have the courtesy to call him and explain.

This made him furious. To his mind, Saddam Jamal was an opportunist and unqualified to determine military strategy. Qabusiye should have been subdued while it was vulnerable.

The Islamic State had to be feared to be effective. This was an important component of its central strategy established by the Military Council and approved by the caliph. If the Kurds in Iraq and Syria believed that the American Coalition would stand by them and protect them, ISIS's objective to conquer all of Iraqi Kurdistan and make it part of the caliphate would be lost.

The Silent Sheikh prided himself with being a ferocious warrior, learned military tactician, and sage advisor. He had been appointed to the Military Council in part because of his extensive studies of battlefield tactics.

To prevail in this war against the powers of Satan, the forces of the Islamic State had to be disciplined and true to the word of God. In the battlefield, they had to keep the enemy guessing, and hit him on multiple fronts much the way the North Vietnamese and General Võ Nguyên Giáp had in the war against the American imperialists fifty years ago.

When he rose to call Saddam Jamal to tell him he had overstepped his authority, he saw the demon Ibah squatting naked in the corner, licking her lips with expectation. He interpreted this as a sign that excessive pride was goading him in a dangerous direction.

Returning to his knees, he bowed his head and

prayed: "In the name of Allah, the beneficent, the merciful. All praise is due to Allah. Thee do we serve and thee do we beseech for help. Keep us on the right path—the path of those upon whom you have bestowed favors. Not the path of those upon whom your wrath is brought down, nor of those who go astray."

The C-17 the SEALs flew in passed over the island of Crete. Almost a hundred years earlier, in June 1919, T. E. Lawrence had stopped in Crete on his way to Cairo. A month earlier, the Handley-Page bomber he had been flying in crash-landed in Rome. Two of his fellow passengers died, but Lawrence escaped with a broken arm.

Earlier that year, Lawrence attended the Middle East Peace Conference in Paris as an independent delegate and lobbied for Arab independence.

Lawrence of *Lawrence of Arabia* had fascinated Crocker since he watched the movie with his father in a cold theater in Methuen, Massachusetts. As a kid, he both admired Lawrence and was confused by the hints of masochism and homosexuality that ran through his story. He had no idea how active a life he had led as a British intelligence officer and liaison to Emir Faisal, who headed the Arab revolt against the Turkish Ottoman Empire.

Lawrence, he read now, helped the Arabs plan their military strategy and had actively participated in numerous battles, including attacks on Ottoman military camps in Hejaz and Tafileh, and the liberation of Aqaba and Damascus—currently the capital of Syria.

For his bravery, he was awarded the French Légion d'Honneur even though he was accused of stirring up the Syrians to revolt against French rule. And though he was considered one of Britain's greatest military heroes, he declined an appointment to Knight Commander of the Order of the British Empire.

In Crocker's opinion, he was an honest man and a visionary thinker. As Séverine said, he understood and admired the Arab character. Crocker underlined a passage in Lawrence's book *Seven Pillars of Wisdom*, regarding Arabs: "Their mind was strange and dark, full of depressions and exaltations, lacking in rule, but with more of ardour and more fertile in belief than any other in the world. They were a people of starts, for whom the abstract was the strongest motive, the process of infinite courage and variety, and the end nothing. They were unstable as water, and like water would perhaps finally prevail."

It was raining when he arrived in Virginia Beach. From the airport, he called Jenny, who didn't answer. Then hopped a cab to Dam Neck, found his truck in the ST-6 HQ parking lot, and drove to his apartment—a garden-variety mid-'70s one-bedroom off Grant Street. The place smelled moldy, and looked like it hadn't been visited in months.

Jenny had stacked his mail on the kitchen counter, in two piles—obvious solicitations and personal. The former stood four times taller than the latter. The electricity and cable still worked, which meant that she had paid his utilities. Aside from that, it appeared as though she hadn't done much, or used the apartment herself.

The first thing he did was open all the windows to air the place out.

Then he checked his phone messages. Most were solicitations of some sort. One, from two months ago, was from his buddy Stevie, inviting him on a bicy-cling/camping trip to the Shenandoah Valley. Two were from his ex-wife Holly.

Both messages simply said, "Tom, call me when you get back. I need to speak to you about something important."

Her words conveyed the gravity of a warning, and most warnings from her these days had to do with money. Between helping Cyndi with doctor bills and paying his and his dad's rent, car payments, insurance, et cetera, he was pretty tapped out.

Still, he called her cell and left a message. Then he telephoned his dad in Fairfax, Virginia, just outside DC.

"Hey, Tommy boy, welcome home!"

His father sounded chipper, in fact, the most energetic he had in years.

"Thanks, Dad. How you doin'?"

"Good, very good. Still getting around despite my sore hip. Doc says I probably need a new one. Don't think I'm up for that. Haha....Seeing a new lady...a younger woman...seventy-six-year-old divorcée with two grown girls. She's hot...."

"Hot?"

"The sex is great. The best."

"Good for you, Dad, but too much information."

It was hard to think of his father with a woman besides his mother. They'd been married for more than forty years before she died when their house was struck by lightning and caught fire. Crocker had left hours earlier, and his dad had been where he often was—hanging at the local VFA with his buddies.

"Everything okay with you?" Crocker's father asked. "You still in one piece? That legal difficulty you were involved in completely over?"

He was referring to the breaking-and-entering and assault charges that had been filed against him in Fairfax County court. Involved a police officer and a young woman friend of his father's who had been ripping him off. He'd found the two of them smoking crystal meth together, just after the woman had solicited money from his father to pay for rehab.

"Yeah, Dad. Over and done with....You still talk to Clara Ruiz?" That was the name of the female leech.

"Nope, haven't spoken to her in months," his father answered. "Nancy doesn't trust her."

"Nancy your new girlfriend?" Crocker asked.

"Yes."

"I like her already."

Just before midnight, after a trip to the supermarket and Italian takeout from Luigi's, he started to feel disoriented. Like he didn't belong in this artificially ordered world, where actors on the late-night talk shows talked about themselves as though they were the center of the universe. As though their opinions about things like global warming and refugees made a difference.

He stopped himself. He was already starting to get angry, and feel he belonged with the people of Qabusiye, who were just trying to survive, and humanitarian workers like Dr. Housani and Séverine, who really did help people and didn't ask for anything in return.

Over the years, he'd gotten better at making the transition from the battlefield to civilian life. No more getting drunk out of his mind and getting into stupid fights. Still, it was a challenge.

Three hours past midnight and many hours since he left Raqqa, Abu Samir al-Sufi sat in the lead technical, his Kalashnikov AK-74 clutched between his knees, fingering the wooden beads at his waist, and praying to himself: "Oh, Allah, give victory to our brothers, the Muslims, the oppressed, the tyrannized, and the muja-hedeen who fight the jihad throughout the world."

A dozen more Toyota trucks and captured Iraqi Army Humvees packed with ISIS militants followed, all at high speed, with their headlights off.

No stars were visible tonight, and very little moon-light made it through the thick canopy of clouds. The growl of engines excited him as they approached their target. His purpose was clear and he imagined future battles—and victories—against the infidels. As always, Allah would lead the way.

Pushing the button on the radio in his lap, he raised it to his mouth and said, "Brothers, now is the time to fight. Now is the time to put our fates in the hands of God! Repeat with me this prayer with courage, and belief:

> *"A'uzu billahi minashaitanir rajim.*
> [I seek refuge in Allah from the outcast Satan.]
> *Bismillahir Rahmanir Rahim.*
> [In the name of Allah, the Most Beneficent, the
>   Most Merciful.]
> *Allahu Akbar, Allahu Akbar, Allahu Akbar!*
> [Allah is the Greatest, Allah is the Greatest,
>   Allah is the Greatest!]
> *Allahu Akbar, Allahu Akbar, Allahu Akbar!*
> [Allah is the Greatest, Allah is the Greatest,
>   Allah is the Greatest!]
> *Allahu Akbar, Allahu Akbar, Allahu Akbar!*
> [Allah is the Greatest, Allah is the Greatest,
>   Allah is the Greatest!]

Al-hamdu lillahi rabbil 'alamin.
[Praise be to Allah, the Lord of the worlds!
    God calls us to this glory.]
Inshallah!
[If Allah is willing!]"

Sheikh al-Sufi felt the words resound in his chest. He raised his right arm, and directed the trucks to peel off left and right, producing twin columns of dust. Like the armies of the Messenger during their liberation of the holy city Mecca, they attacked the town of Qabusiye simultaneously from all sides.

Al-Sufi led the first group east to west like the great Az Zubayr had on Wednesday, November 29, 629, entering the town before its defenders knew what was happening. While the Messenger had commanded his followers to refrain from fighting until the enemy attacked, the Viper ordered his men to kill everyone—even in their sleep.

It was time to punish those Muslims who didn't adhere to Sharia law and served the infidels. It was time to show the power of Allah.

They entered furiously, mowing down everything with their AKs and machine guns—Peshmerga soldiers, YPG militiamen, dogs barking, women shuttering the windows of their homes, half-dressed young men running for cover, even children. The speed of the assault exhilarated the sheikh. He imagined he felt the spirit of Allah coursing through his veins.

His men went house to house, rousing all male residents from their sleep, beating them, and binding their wrists together with plastic ties. They led them at gunpoint into the central plaza, past buildings in flames.

Al-Sufi stood in the bed of the Toyota, his beard and black robes blowing in the wind, counting the prisoners as they arrived. "Forty-eight…fifty-three…sixty apostates."

He shouted an order and his men lined up the prisoners and pushed them to their knees. Other soldiers held back the pleading women, some half-dressed, others clutching sheets and bedclothes, as they tried to enter the plaza.

One of the sheikh's men helped him down from the truck and led him over to a short, stocky man with a bushy gray mustache who waited on his knees with his wrists bound behind his back. Al-Sufi grabbed Mayor Sabri's face by the chin and pulled his head up.

"Where are the Americans?" he asked in Arabic, glaring into the mayor's eyes.

"They left days ago, you son of a whore," Mayor Sabri spat back.

"When you see them again, give them this message…*Allahu akbar!*" Al-Sufi pulled the trigger until the mayor's face and head were almost completely obliterated.

Terrible wails and screams echoed through the plaza.

ISIS militants drowned them out with a chorus of *Allahu akbar*s followed by the blasts from their rifles as they executed all the men. Then they turned and unleashed their fury on the women who had come to plea for their husbands' lives. Then they killed the children hiding under their beds. Finally, they spread gasoline everywhere and set what was left of the town on fire.

Less than an hour after the assault began, it ended, and the Silent Sheikh and his men were back in their trucks racing toward the Syrian border. The words of

Allah's Apostle echoed in the sheikh's head: "Know that paradise is under the shade of swords."

Crocker was dreaming of his stepson, a strong, athletic, good-looking twenty-year-old who had started hanging out with the wrong people in college and dealing drugs. He sat across from him pleading, "Christian, listen.... You need to turn your life around...go to the police and give them the names of the punks you've been hanging with. They're not your friends. They don't deserve to live in our society. Save yourself."

He heard the phone ring and sensed what was coming: news from the local hospital that Christian had been shot in the head and was dying.

He picked it up and braced himself for the feelings of guilt and sadness that were about to overwhelm him.

"Tom?" It was a woman's voice.

"Yes…"

"Tom, did I wake you?"

"Are you calling from the hospital?"

"I'm sorry, Tom. I'll call…later."

It took him a couple seconds to recognize Séverine's voice. And another few seconds to realize where he was—in the bedroom of his apartment in Virginia Beach, surrounded by things his mother had left him.

"Wait."

"Tom, if this is the wrong time…"

"No. Séverine…It's okay." Christian's framed high school graduation photo hung on the opposite wall. On the chest of drawers beneath it sat the alarm clock his grandfather had carried during World War II.

"Tom, I don't know if you heard the news."

"What news?"

He heard a catch in her throat, then, "Qabusiye was

overrun this morning. The mayor and lots of other people were killed."

He felt as though someone had kicked him in the chest. "Daesh?" he asked.

"Yes." He heard her weeping on the other end.

The faces of Mayor Sabri, Dilshad, and other townspeople flashed before his mind's eye. They felt close and at the same time very far away. Anger spread through his mind and body. Suddenly, he was completely awake and looking for his HK416.

"Tom?"

"Séverine, it's awful. I don't know what to say." He'd left his 416 in his team locker at ST-6 headquarters. All he had with him was a Glock and two mags.

"They were farmers, housewives, children… innocent people. How can other human beings, other Muslims, do something like that? I don't understand."

"You can't….It's sickness. Evil."

"Yes."

"Where are you?"

"I'm still in Istanbul. I leave for Paris tomorrow to visit with my mother. Then maybe I'll take a new assignment."

He didn't catch all she had said. His mind was focused on Qabusiye and its residents, and calculating what he had to do to return there to punish the bastards who attacked them.

"When did it happen?" Crocker asked.

"The attack? This morning. Several hours ago." Istanbul and Qabusiye were something like eight hours ahead. It was 0543 in Virginia Beach according to the clock on the dresser.

"There was no one there to defend it?" asked Crocker.

"What, Tom?"

"It's not important."

"I don't know how to deal with this....I'll try....I think of all those people...the ones who struggled to get by...and the wounded ones we tried to save. They slaughtered all of them."

"Séverine, don't." He knew what she was doing: drifting into guilt where reason was of no help.

She didn't hear him. "I think of that boy...Omar— the one we tried to save. I felt so bad about losing him. That means nothing now...."

"Séverine, stop." The savagery of Daesh was hard for Crocker to comprehend, too. He understood killing enemy soldiers in battle. But slaughtering civilians just because they didn't share your beliefs...

"It's strange, because I've been dreaming of him every night. Me and Omar....We're walking, or we're sitting somewhere talking. There are people around. I ask for his forgiveness. He tells me he misses his family, but likes where he is now."

"Séverine, I've got to go. I have to call Colonel Rastan."

"What does it mean? I wake up trembling. You're the first person I've told....Then this....Oh, Tom...."

"Séverine, forgiveness isn't necessary. Wherever he is, he doesn't blame you. You're a good person. A beautiful angel. Go for a run; go visit friends. Find a way to clear this out of your head. Sometimes there's no rational explanation. I've got to call Colonel Rastan now."

"Who is he?"

"A friend. I'll call you back, Séverine. I promise."

"Thank you, Tom."

CHAPTER ELEVEN

One cannot step twice into the same river.
— Heraclitus

CROCKER SAT in a red booth at Pocahontas Pancakes on Atlantic Avenue in Virginia with Jenny and her boyfriend, Bogart, who also went by "BD." Crocker stared at the large laminated menu, trying to decide between the multigrain pancakes and a California omelet, his head a muddle of confusion, anger, and guilt.

His messages to Colonel Rastan hadn't been returned. Like Séverine, he needed answers. He wanted to go back. He needed to clear his head.

"So good to see you, Dad. Feels like you've been gone…forever." Jenny gushed, her skin glowing in the morning light that filtered through sheer curtains. She wore sweatpants and a VIRGINIA IS FOR HATERS t-shirt.

BD had tattoos of stars on his neck, and elaborate depictions of saints and historical figures like Poe and Lincoln on his arms.

"Three months, yeah….Almost four." He wanted to

be present, but was struggling. "You look beautiful… happy." His words sounded hollow to him.

"I am," she responded, reaching over and draping an arm over BD's shoulder.

A product of his first marriage, she'd arrived at his doorstep six years ago, a confused, angry teenager who didn't get along with her mother. Since then, she'd managed to adjust to a new environment, make friends, and graduate from high school with little help from Crocker or his second wife. Now she was on her way to making her own life.

"I'm so proud of you," he said. "I really am."

A Hispanic waitress in a tight skirt smiled at him as she passed, holding plates stacked with pancakes and French toast smothered in whipped cream.

"Good morning, sir. I'll be back."

"Take your time. We're still deciding." He couldn't remember when he'd had his last meal, or what he had done yesterday.

"We are?" Bogart asked.

"I am."

Crocker didn't know what he expected Rastan to do. He just wanted to talk to him and get more details.

The pancake house was bustling like it always was on weekend mornings. The sounds of forks clanging, and chairs scraping against the floor echoed in his head.

"People seem to like this place," he said as he tried to calm his nerves and focus.

Bogart agreed. "The blueberry cakes are total bliss."

Crocker had been living on hummus, falafel, salads, goat cheese, bread, and MREs for the last three months. He wasn't sure if his stomach could accommodate a meal this rich. Not now; not first thing in the morning.

"BD's a talented artist," Jenny announced, proudly. "He's into all kinds of things. Tattoo art, auto detailing, murals, signs. Super versatile." She squeezed BD's forearm as if to prompt him.

"Yeah, I've been building a clientele on the body art side of things. I'm like a hair away from opening my own place."

"Good...."

He seemed like a nice kid with big ambitions. As long as his daughter liked him and he treated her well, that's all Crocker cared about. No way *he* was qualified to give advice about relationships.

"I wish you luck."

"Thanks."

The rich, sweet smells and the chatter of the many customers crowded into the tight space started to make him feel uncomfortable. He couldn't reconcile the tragedy in Qabusiye with the casual frivolity surrounding him. It was as though the scene he was seeing wasn't real.

"You okay, Dad?" Jenny asked. "You decide yet?"

"Yeah. Yeah."

To his right sat a big family—father, two sons, and their wives, several young kids. All of them were enormous and self-satisfied, except for one boy of about six, confined to a wheelchair, his neck held in a metal brace.

He was the only one who seemed to hold himself apart from the madness and to possess an inner life. The pained expression in the boy's eyes spoke to Crocker, and sent him back to the wounded kid in the Qabusiye hospital. He caught a whiff of alcohol, decay, and desperation.

His throat tightened to the point where he had trouble breathing.

"Dad, you all right?" Jenny asked.

"Excuse me," he said, rising to his feet. "I'll be right back."

A day and a half later, Séverine was still haunted by memories of Qabusiye. It had been difficult to discuss her feelings with her mother, or her Parisian friends. Most of them thought she was crazy to have been working in a war zone in the first place, and used her mention of the recent tragedy to remind her that she had no business being there and shouldn't return.

All that accomplished was to make Séverine feel that the place where she didn't belong was Paris, surrounded with bourgeois comfort and staying in her mother's one-bedroom apartment in the 3rd Arrondissement, near the Pompidou Center.

For some reason, she felt closer to her Moroccan Jewish grandmother Zohra, who died when Séverine was seven. A kind woman with dark eyes who was constantly in the kitchen producing amazing treats like harira soup and b'stilla—a pie made with almonds, eggs, sugar, cinnamon, and layers of paper-thin pastry. In the old days, her grandmother said, the pie included pigeon meat.

What had it been like for her, a Jewish Moroccan woman living in France right after World War II?

Séverine contemplated this question as she walked through the light rain down Rue St. Denis to the Pont Neuf. The tourists she passed from all over the world provided no distraction. Nor did the self-satisfied hipsters sporting face jewelry and tats, and fashionable girls in tight, low-cut sweaters and form-fitting jackets—none of which would be appropriate in Erbil, Baghdad, or Amman.

She was so occupied with thoughts of her grand-mother that she almost forgot she was on her way to meet her university friends Axelle and Christine. They greeted her with hugs and kisses in front of Lapérouse, a landmark restaurant on the Left Bank with a view of the Seine.

"So good to see you, Séverine!"

"Wonderful to see you, too!"

She was under-dressed in jeans and a t-shirt, sweater, and boots, with her hair pulled back in a simple ponytail as the hostess led them up a winding staircase to one of the private rooms on the second floor. Elegant and beautifully preserved with hunting pictures on the walls and lots of red velvet brocade that made it look like a high-end brothel, which it reputedly was at one time. Founded in 1766, the restaurant had hosted the French literary greats Victor Hugo, Émile Zola, and Guy de Maupassant.

It was hard for Séverine to imagine that she had once felt comfortable here during romantic dinners with her ex-husband and friends. Only eight years had passed since her last time here, savoring the *soupe de homard* and *côte de veau rôtie* with a bottle of Côtes du Rhône. Yet it felt like another life….

She didn't want to judge. That wasn't the purpose of this lunch. She was here to spend time with Axelle and Christine, whom she'd met while studying at the Sorbonne during the difficult years after she separated from her husband and was waiting to get divorced.

Trying years of self-doubt and guilt made worse by accusations from the Delage family lawyers and her despicable mother-in-law.

"It's so good to see both of you," Séverine said as

they settled into plush brocade chairs. "You look so glamorous. I'm afraid I haven't had much time for myself...."

"You're thin and tan," Axelle said. "You spend a lot of time outdoors?"

"Yes."

"Very healthy."

"Thanks." Both friends were super thin and chicly dressed. She saw signs of strain under their eyes and along the sides of their mouths, but thought she must have looked appalling to them since she wasn't wearing makeup and had barely slept.

"Are you here long?" Axelle asked. She was a dark-haired beauty with high cheekbones and sparkling blue eyes. At the Sorbonne, she had studied Buddhism and human rights law. Now she was engaged to a twice-divorced man who ran a hedge fund and collected abstract art. Kandinsky and Rothko were her fiancé's favorite painters, and their work hung in his penthouse apartment overlooking the Luxembourg Gardens and estate in Rémy.

That meant that Axelle was soon to become a member of the *bon chic, bon genre* (Parisian upper class) and could no longer say *de rien* for *you're welcome,* but had to use the much more formal *je vous en prie.* This was one of the many affectations of the *classe supérieure.* Séverine knew them well, and had always found they had an obnoxious way of creating barriers.

"A week, maybe less," Séverine answered, hiding her rough leather bag under the table. Axelle's had been recently purchased at Fendi on Rue du Bac for $3,000. A dozen years ago she lived in a tiny flat on the Left Bank and dressed exclusively in sweaters and jeans purchased at one of the city's flea markets.

"You will be seeing Alain?" Christine asked. She was the more reserved of the two friends, with an aristocratic manner that lent her a certain formality even in the most casual circumstances. She possessed a bony face with a long nose, and dressed fashionably, but conservatively. Shorts to show off her toned legs, loose sweaters, and long coats.

"I haven't thought about it," Séverine answered. Mention of her ex brought back memories, some pleasant, others not so much. She still admired his wit and intelligence, but had learned to despise his superior manner. They'd met in New York City when she was an undergrad and he was completing a training assignment at the Banque de France.

"Alain never remarried," Christine added. "I'm sure he'd love to see you and hear about your adventures."

Séverine smiled. She harbored no enmity toward her former husband, and wished him well. But she had no real interest in hearing him talk about his family coat of arms, or the people he had socialized with last summer at the Yacht Club de Monaco, or how much money he made last year, or the modern updates he was making to the family estate in Montpellier.

None of this interested her anymore, and she knew him well enough to know that he hadn't changed. Men like Alain dedicated themselves to preserving the manners and stations of the past.

"Does Alain know you're in Paris?"

"Not as far as I know."

"Then we must tell him!"

Axelle changed the subject. "Tell us about your life, the places you've been, the interesting people you've met...."

*   *   *

Constant threat had made Abu Samir al-Sufi a light sleeper. Now he drifted in and out of consciousness.

He saw names and prayers scratched into the wall of his cell at Camp Bucca. He focused on one of them…Fatima—the name of one of his wives. He saw her smiling face.

Then a white horse galloped past the jeep he rode in; a cloud of red dust parted and he saw a row of beautiful maidens washing clothes along the banks of a river. Doves fluttered overhead. One of the women slipped and fell. The others laughed. He ordered the driver to stop.

Everything turned silent. Thick fog moved in. He thought he heard a woman weeping. Then realized something was moving in the courtyard outside. He opened his eyes suddenly, rose out of bed, and reached for the AK-74 propped against the wall, chambered a round, flipped off the safety, and hurried down the hallway and up three steps.

The cold tiles stung his bare feet. Through a hole in the plywood over the window, he saw the silhouette of a figure in the moonlight.

Looked to be a woman seated by the fountain with her head down. Like she was praying. As peaceful as she appeared to be, she startled him. Could be an illusion, or a demon, or a trap.

Sheikh al-Sufi didn't trust anyone. Not even his closest aide, Yasir Selah. He lived in a world of danger and treachery with enemies on all sides. There were savage, ambitious men in his ranks. He suspected some of them were psychopaths.

The brutal dictator Bashir Assad waited to the south and west, the al-Qaeda allied Al-Nusra Front directly east, Free Syrian Army and Coalition units north and west. All poised to destroy him and the jihadists under his command. Deadly bombers and drones could strike him from the sky at any moment.

Allah remained his sole guide. Caution, intelligence, and courage were his only weapons. Now they were pulling him in different directions, with some voices telling him to call his guards to arrest the woman, others urging him to confront her himself.

Something about the delicate way she held her head, and her perfect stillness, drew him closer. He crossed the hallway to the door that would allow him to come up behind her. Quietly, on tiptoes, his heart humming in his chest.

His gums and feet sore; his mouth sour; yet filled with curiosity.

He crossed to within six feet of her, the AK-74 pointed at her head. Heard her weeping softly as hard, cold air filled his lungs.

"Woman, who are you? Where do you belong?"

His voice sounded harsh, and he held his breath as she slowly turned toward him. Her weeping seemed to have stopped. He couldn't see her features because of the shadow cast by her scarf. But he had the impression that she was older, maybe middle-aged.

"What are you doing here?" he asked. "You should be inside."

"I came to grieve for my sons. *Inshallah*."

"Here? In the middle of the night? You're not afraid?"

She shook her head.

"Don't you know you should be indoors? That there are guards nearby with orders to shoot?"

She remained still.

"What's your name, woman?"

"Khadijah."

Khadijah was the name of the Prophet's first wife—the most revered woman in Islam. The Prophet had been married to her for twenty-five years. About her he wrote: "God Almighty never granted me anyone better in this life than her. She accepted me when people rejected me; she believed in me when people doubted me; she shared her wealth with me when people deprived me; and God granted me children only through her."

Twice a widow before she met the Prophet, she became a successful merchant, and fed and clothed the poor. In need of a new agent to travel with her trade caravan to Syria, she hired a young man who had been recommended to her, named Muhammad ibn Abdullah. They soon married and remained so monogamously for twenty-five years.

"Why are you crying, Khadijah?" Sheikh al-Sufi asked.

"Only you can answer that, Sheikh."

It was an odd answer from a mysterious woman, and delivered without insolence. It made him pause for a minute and remember his own wife, Fatima Sadir—named after the Prophet and Khadijah's daughter—and the many sacrifices she had made on his behalf, and the tragedies she'd been forced to endure.

She'd been a vivacious and sly young girl of nineteen with sparkling dark-brown eyes when they married. The last time he'd seen her she looked like an old woman, even though she had just turned forty-three.

Sheikh al-Sufi's heart opened for a moment, and tears flooded his eyes as the woman who called herself

Khadijah watched. As he cleared his eyes with the sleeve of his robe, she stood with her back toward him, and headed for the gate.

"Wait," he said. A bird called from the roof of the mosque.

She continued silently and disappeared into the darkness, and he realized that he had never seen her face.

CHAPTER TWELVE

The nation that makes a great distinction
between its scholars and its warriors will
have its thinking done by cowards and its
fighting done by fools.
—Spartan king, quoted by Thucydides

CROCKER HAD spent a week at ST-6 headquarters
meeting with members of the new intel team—BC/2
—and Black Cell's CIA liaison, Jim Anders, going over
new protocols. Anders would continue to define the
missions Black Cell would carry out for the CIA and
White House. BC/2 would provide daily intel support
for the team while it was deployed overseas, and facilitate all communications to Anders when it was on a
mission.

Lt. Colonel Barbara Smithson from Naval Intelligence had been selected to head BC/2. Other members
included a Major Assad Hussein from SOCOM, and
Crocker's old ST-6 teammate, comms expert, and favorite surfer, Warrant Officer Davis. Davis had decided to make the move from combat team to HQ staff
in order to spend more time with his wife and kids.

BC/2 met for the first time on a Friday afternoon in
a conference room in ST-6 headquarters. Represent-
ing Black Cell were Crocker, Akil, CT, Mancini, and a

new breacher and assistant comms man named Danny
Chavez. Rip, who was out of town attending a friend's
funeral, was absent.

Crocker had driven directly from the meeting to
the airport, where he boarded a Southwest Airlines
flight to Las Vegas. Now, the next morning, he was
walking with Cyndi's four-year-old daughter, Amy,
down the Strip. It was a dry, cloudless afternoon, and
they'd already stopped at the Mirage Casino to see the
white Bengal tigers, lions, and leopards in the special
habitat created by magicians Siegfried & Roy. After
that he'd taken her on a gondola ride through the
Venetian across the street, and been serenaded with
"O sole mio" by the gondolier.

Now they were crossing the boulevard again, for ice
cream at Serendipity 3 near Caesars Palace.

Amy pointed at the greenery in the shape of a giant
sundae complete with a blue straw and cherry on top
in front of the twin-columned restaurant/ice cream
parlor across the street.

"Look."

"You think you can drink all that?" Crocker asked
as the light changed and they moved hand-in-hand
with a rainbow tribe of tourists.

"That's not real…you silly!" she squealed back.

"It's not?"

Being with a young child was a strange experience
for Crocker, but one he enjoyed. Instead of being
hypervigilant to everything around him, he had to
force himself to focus on the young girl with blond
pigtails who called him Uncle Tom.

Cyndi had given him that ridiculous name. She was
currently rehearsing with Cirque du Soleil in a studio
somewhere nearby. The two of them had barely had a

chance to talk since he arrived late last night. Shared some laughs and kisses, and then made love. She fell asleep before he did.

Cyndi seemed overwhelmed, which is why he'd volunteered to take Amy this morning while Cyndi's mother was away.

Amy was super cute with brilliant blue eyes like her mother's and a slight craniofacial malformation that looked like an indentation between her eyebrows. She also had oddly shaped thumbs. She didn't suffer from the more serious symptoms of the disease, including urogenital and heart defects.

But she looked slightly odd and undersized. Like a doll, Crocker thought.

Cyndi had told him that getting her to eat anything was a good thing. So he was excited that Amy wanted to order a large mint chocolate cone half as long as her arm.

"Good?" he asked, as he held the giant cone and she shoveled ice cream into her mouth with a pink plastic spoon.

"Del-i-cious," she pronounced, her lips turning green from the artificial color.

Her smile caught the attention of a middle-aged woman with a boy about Amy's age. Introduced herself as the boy's grandmother. They were visiting from Missouri for a family wedding.

The boy asked to taste Amy's ice cream. She let him.

"So sweet," the woman gushed. "You from around here?"

"No. No, but she is," said Crocker, whose eyes drifted toward two young men huddled together near some steps at the other end of the plaza. They looked like hawks watching the stream of tourists.

"Oh....Where are you from, if you don't mind me asking?"

"Virginia," Crocker answered.

Out of the corner of his eye, he saw the kids pounce. One with a shaved head stepped in front of an old couple shuffling along, and offered a newspaper to the man. As the elderly man and woman looked down at it, the second kid, wearing a black hoodie, swooped around behind the woman and grabbed her purse. As he ripped it off her shoulder, the woman spun, lost her balance, and fell.

Crocker instinctively jumped to his feet.

"Watch her for a minute, please," he said to the grandmother, nodding toward Amy.

"Yes, of course. But—"

"I'll be right back."

He was gone before the words were out of his mouth, dashing across the plaza, past the old woman who other passersby were helping to her feet. Down the steps. He spied the two guys with the purse getting into a black VW Tiguan stopped along the curb on Flamingo Road. The car sped through the intersection, barely beating the red light.

When Crocker saw that the SUV was momentarily stuck in traffic, he gave chase, darting through vehicles coming from both directions.

Cars honked and skidded to a stop. A woman leaned out of a vehicle and shouted, "You crazy asshole!"

It occurred to him that maybe she was right. But he couldn't help himself. It was as though he needed this, or some basic sheepdog instinct had taken over. In very simple terms, people were divided between sheep and wolves. Protecting the unsuspecting sheep were sheepdogs like himself.

He bounded through traffic to the other side, arriving just as the black Tiguan darted in front of another car and around a worksite, separated by traffic cones and yellow tape. The engine revved, and he saw that once it got around a parked dump truck, it would have a clear path to escape. No law enforcement in sight.

So he pushed himself hard, arriving at the back of the car just as the engine revved again.

Stupid punks!

He saw the car had a sunroof, which was open. Lunged forward and clambered up the back to the roof and went in, head first, just as the driver hit the gas.

He landed partially in her lap. His knees slammed the steering wheel. His feet pushed the shaved head of the kid in the passenger seat against the side window. The female driver hit the brakes and screamed, "What the fuck!"

The car skidded left, slammed into the back of a van, and stopped. Crocker felt someone punch him in the back as he twisted his body up, blood oozing from a cut to his forehead. He turned and shoved the butt of his palm under the shaved guy's chin, so that his head flew back and shattered the side window.

The female driver screamed, "You fucking madman! What are you doing?" He turned and reached for the kid in the black hoodie. A sharp pain erupted from his forearm and stunned him for a moment. The kid had stabbed him with a pencil, the tip of which had broken away and was still embedded in his forearm.

Slippery pissant used that moment to try to escape out the side door. But Crocker squeezed through the middle console, gave chase, and grabbed him hard by the back of the hoodie, taking the kid's feet out from under. Scrambled on top of him. Readied his fist.

"The purse or your face, motherfucker!"

"Take it, man. Fucking take it! Who the fuck do you think you are? Rambo?"

A decade earlier, Séverine's then-husband, Alain, was at the wheel of his silver Citroën DS—a creepy-looking car in her opinion, and one she described as a "slithering amoeba"—talking about his great-uncle Maurice Delage, a famous pianist, who had studied with Ravel and became one of the top French composers of his time.

"He was an amazing man, you know. A world traveler...In 1900 he helped form a group of very esteemed artists known as Les Apaches that included Ravel, Manuel de Falla, and Igor Stravinsky. I believe I get my appreciation of music from him...."

It was a beautiful afternoon in late March and they were on a twisting mountain road outside Aix-en-Provence headed for an inn Alain had discovered on a previous trip. "So you believe that traits like musical appreciation are passed through DNA?"

"Oh, yes," Alain responded. "It's been proven there's such a thing as the biological transmission of memory."

She always thought that he drove too fast, but usually kept her mouth shut. Alain was a skilled driver. But the speed at which he was taking the blind curves of this road made her chew her bottom lip.

"I've read research that claims traumatic experiences like phobias and severe anxiety can somehow be passed from the brain into a parent's genome, allowing them to be passed on to later generations, but never anything as complex as artistic appreciation," she said, bracing herself for the next sharp turn.

"Yes, but if that's so, doesn't it follow—"

"Watch out!"

A few feet ahead the road was blocked by a truck.

"*Salaud!*" Alain exclaimed as he applied the brakes and turned into the oncoming lane to try to pass. *Bastard!* When he saw that lane was blocked as well, he braked to a stop. "*Merde!*"

Several vehicles had stopped and a small group of onlookers had gathered along the right side of the two-lane road. Alain slammed his hand on the wheel and got out to take a look. "Wait here. I'll go."

But Séverine didn't wait, and followed. The driver of the truck, a heavyset man with a thick black mustache, was waving his thick arms and explaining that he hadn't seen the bicycle.

"I was going slow. In second gear, you know, to make the incline. The boy was in the lane. Right in the middle of the lane! I honked and tried to turn, but he didn't move!"

Séverine leaned forward and saw the boy on the ground past the crumpled green bike. His eyes were rolled back in his head and he appeared to be choking. The skin around his mouth had turned bluish green. Two men knelt beside the boy but looked as though they didn't know what to do.

One, wearing a pink shirt, shouted, "Call a doctor!"

A woman in the crowd of maybe ten people answered, "I already called for an ambulance. It's coming."

The bluish-green color spread to his cheeks. Séverine had no medical training at that point, but intuited that the boy was choking on his tongue. She stepped forward, only to be stopped by a hand that grabbed from behind.

It was Alain. "No," he whispered.

"But...I think I can help."

"No!" he said more emphatically, holding a finger up to her face, his other hand tightening around her arm.

He pulled her back to the car. "You're not a doctor or a nurse. Nor am I.... Then we get into areas of liability and such..."

She felt angry, humiliated. By the time the EMT workers arrived in an ambulance, the boy was dead.

Cyndi stood behind Crocker in the bathroom as he washed his face, checked the superficial cut over his brow, and swallowed two Motrin. Parts of him were sore, but otherwise he was fine.

"What the hell, Tom? I don't understand!" Cyndi shouted, her face red and strained with anger in the bathroom mirror.

There appeared to be no need for stitches to his forehead, or to close up the puncture to his arm, which had been cleaned and bandaged by the EMT workers who had arrived to tend to the muggers and the girl. They were later arrested and carted off.

"You just leave a four-year-old and run off?" Cyndi continued. "Why? Because you saw a woman being robbed? Of what? A purse that probably contained less than a hundred dollars and some credit cards that could have easily been canceled?"

He toweled his face and hands. "I'm sorry, Cyndi. Everything happened so fast."

"Do you realize what you did? Do you know how freaked out Amy is now? Tom, do you understand what could have happened?" She was getting louder and more worked up.

"Amy is fine. Calm down."

"Calm down? ... Goddammit, Tom! Look at me!"

He turned and took her by the shoulders. "I saw the woman get thrown to the ground. I reacted. It's over."

"Get your fucking hands off me!" she shouted at the top of her lungs.

Their eyes met. He saw fury in hers, like that of a mother bear protecting her cub. He didn't feel like arguing or being attacked, so he let go of her shoulders and took a step around her.

"I'll go apologize to Amy now."

She spun and struck him with her fist at the base of his neck. "No, you won't! Don't you dare!"

It was approximately the same place he had been grazed by a bullet ten years ago in eastern Afghanistan. That time he'd been lucky. This time his entire head went numb for a second and he thought he was going to collapse.

Through the mental fog he saw Cyndi coming at him again with clenched fists, shouting, "I trusted my daughter to you. You animal. You ... asshole."

"Cyndi. ... Stop."

"You have no control of yourself, do you?"

He brushed her away with his left arm, and steadied himself on the side of a dresser. "You must be talking about yourself, Cyndi. Go see a shrink."

He sat with a beer in his hand, gazing out the window of the room he'd booked at the Mirage. Artificial blue, green, red, and yellow lights sparkled in the distance. The windows of the tower across from him sparkled gold. He rubbed his tired eyes and the lights seemed to meld into a nebula-like glow.

He wanted to be in the field, assigned a mission, away from the emotional confusion of civilian life.

Hell...I try to help an old woman and this shit happens...

Caesars Palace had offered him a complimentary room because the woman whose purse he retrieved was one of their guests. But he'd turned it down. A year ago, he and Mancini had gotten involved in a confrontation with some North Koreans who were staying there posing as Chinese diplomats. A friend of his, who was the casino's head of security at the time, had been fired as a result.

So this wasn't the first time his impulse to do the right thing had gotten him in trouble, or caused complications.

I wonder where Jeri is now?

A sassy African American lady with a great sense of humor and formerly a member of the U.S. Secret Service. Even though she'd been let go by Caesars, she didn't blame it on him. She understood. Appreciated the fact that he was wired to act. Not sit around licking ice cream while some North Korean assholes got away with ripping off the casino, or some old lady was mugged.

The adrenaline had subsided, but thoughts hadn't stopped cycling in his head. His phone vibrated on the glass-topped table beside him. Cyndi. He pushed "Reject."

He downed the beer and a soft numbness came over his neck and shoulders. *I don't belong here.*

He got up to get a pillow, and when he returned to the armchair, his phone was dancing on the table. Cyndi again. This time he accepted the call and put the phone on speaker.

"Tom?"

"Yeah…" He stretched his legs out. His left knee barked.

"Tom, I'm sorry." She sounded like the sweet person he'd known before.

"Yeah…"

"Is that all you have to say?"

"You and me are different.…"

He'd already decided to leave in the morning, and would figure out something to do over the last two weeks of R&R. Maybe go scuba diving in the Caribbean, or climb a mountain, or run with the bulls in Pamplona. Figured he needed to get away and clear his head.

"Tom, I said I'm sorry. I've been under a lot of pressure. I know that's no excuse. I get super protective when it comes to Amy, and I think you know why."

"Yeah."

"She's so precious to me. You have no idea what I've been through."

"I get it." Crocker twisted open another St. Pauli Girl and took a long swig. "She was never in any kind of jeopardy. I would never let that happen."

"Really?"

"Yes, really. Listen, Cyndi—"

She cut him off. "As her mother, I feel that you shouldn't have left her. That's my opinion."

"Fine. How is Amy?" Crocker asked.

"She's okay. Before she went to bed, you know what she said to me?"

"No."

"She told me you're a hero."

"Sweet kid."

CHAPTER THIRTEEN

Life is pleasant. Death is peaceful. It's the
transition that's troublesome.
—Isaac Asimov

SHEIKH AL-SUFI sat with his top lieutenants in a room on the bottom floor of Raqqa Museum watching the ISIS propaganda videos that had been sent by a representative of the Islamic State Institution for Public Information. They did this at least once a month to boost the morale of frontline fighters, especially the new recruits from places like Libya, Qatar, Kuwait, Pakistan, Yemen, Nigeria, the UK, the Netherlands, and France.

A young jihadist faced a camera and said, "My message to my brothers who are stationed on the front lines: Remain steadfast and resolute. Allah is with you. Present your severed limbs, bodies, and blood, and sacrifice them to Allah. Do not be weakened. Do not grieve, as you are superior."

The camera followed him as he climbed into a specially modified Nissan, whose rear seat and trunk were packed with explosives. An ISIS surveillance drone followed the car as it wound through the streets of Mosul, slammed into an Iraqi Army checkpoint, and exploded.

The men and women seated around al-Sufi jumped to their feet, cheered, and shouted. The sheikh himself was less demonstrative. Despite the successful attacks shown on the propaganda videos, he knew the war wasn't going well. Every day the Islamic State was losing more militants and land. Leaders were being targeted in drone strikes. Because of their deaths, the executive military structure of the State was falling apart.

When the video presentation ended, he was ushered into the basement of the building, where he was greeted by a Kuwaiti-born engineer named Jaber Sami al-Sabah from the Al-Bara' ibn Malik Brigade—the aviation sector of the State's Committee for Military Manufacturing and Development. Jaber had traveled from committee headquarters in Fallujah, Iraq, to demonstrate new drone capacities developed by State engineers and how they might aid the sheikh and his officers in the battlefield.

The sheikh and his men had been using surveillance drones for almost two years—cheap DJI quadrotors the size of small boxes equipped with high-resolution cameras. These remotely piloted devices were useful as artillery spotters and for locating targets, and correcting the fall of mortar and rocket fire. Recently, they'd switched to X-UAV Talon drones, which were also hand-launched, but had a longer range and because of their six-foot wingspan could be equipped with better cameras.

They were assembled from kits purchased on Amazon.com and cost about $100 USD.

Now Jaber al-Sabah started to brief the sheikh

about a new generation of offensive drones, which were entering the State's arsenal.

"These are offensive drones?" he asked.

"Yes, Sheikh," Jaber answered, firing up a Dell laptop and showing him a spreadsheet of drone missions launched, type of mission (surveillance, support, bombing, explosive plane, or rocket launch), the names of the drone pilots and militants involved, the location of the attacks, the waypoint coordinates of the flights.

"Excellent work...." Sheikh al-Sufi commented.

"The second and third pages are pre- and post-mission checklists for the drone operators."

"Very professional."

"My engineers are in the process of assembling two hundred new and more sophisticated drones now."

He pointed to pictures of the various models on the screen. "Skywalker X7s and X8s, AeroVironment Switchblades, even Israeli Hero 30s. They come equipped with jam-proof communications, terminal guidance, and advanced weapons, including missiles."

The sheikh's attention perked up. "Missiles?" he asked. He'd heard about primitive ISIS drones dropping 40mm grenade rounds on Iraqi Army targets in Mosul and Fallujah, but never missiles.

"Yes," Jaber answered. "The Hero 30 weighs only 3 kilos, and can be operated by a single soldier. It's designed as a suicide drone that can be launched from an air-pressure canister. It has an electric, battery-powered engine that can fly at up to 185 kph for thirty minutes, and it leaves no acoustic or thermal signature, so it's very hard to trace."

"What kind of weapon does it fire?"

"Commander al-Sufi, Hero 30 *is* a weapon. It

attacks a target like a missile and can carry a half-kilo warhead."

"Half a kilo? Any kind of explosive? TNT, C-4, Semtex, even a nuclear bomb?"

"Maybe a bomb is too heavy, but a small nuclear weapon, yes.…One Hero 30 armed with .45 kilograms of Semtex can destroy a truck, or a house, or kill a bus full of people. The Hero is so light that one militant can carry three of them and launch one at a time."

"It had to be Zionists who would create a thing like this," the sheikh said, thinking of its possible uses on the battlefield and as a terrorist weapon.

"Sheikh, these new technology weapons will change everything."

"By the will of God."

Crocker wanted to get this over with quickly, return to ST-6 HQ, and tell Captain Sutter to send him back to Kurdistan ASAP.

He had the driver drop him off a block from Cyndi's house, a modern ranch on a cul-de-sac in a sprawling development in North Las Vegas. It was a relatively new sand-brick structure with an old silver Streamline Duchess mobile home parked in the driveway, along with a car under a weathered canvas cover. Gravel and various cactuses covered the front yard. A FOR SALE sign leaned against the side of the garage.

With backpack and duffel slung over his back and shoulder, Crocker knocked and glanced at his watch. He had an hour to spare before going to the airport for his flight to DC. The man who answered looked like Tommy Lee from Mötley Crüe.

Must be Cyndi's ex.

"Yeah?" the man asked.

Tattoos covered his thin arms and neck. He wore a single large silver skull earring and his hair was spiked and dyed black.

"Tom Crocker. I'm a friend of Cyndi's. I came to say goodbye." Cyndi had told him that her ex-husband was in rehab. Apparently he got out.

Her ex mumbled back, "She went to the drugstore, dude. Will be back soon....My name's Crash." He leaned outside and looked to see if Crocker was with anyone. "How'd you get here? You get dropped from the sky?"

"Uber." Crash seemed like a strange name for someone who used to be a drummer and whose hand had been destroyed in a car accident.

"Come in. I'm watching our kid."

Crocker hesitated. He wasn't sure this was a good idea. Cyndi had given him the impression that her ex was no longer part of her life.

Crash squinted into the sunlight. "You coming in, or not?"

"Yeah. Thanks."

He sat at the kitchen table sipping rusty-tasting water from a glass. Crash stood at the sink washing dishes, humming to himself, and simultaneously letting ashes drop from the cigarette clenched between his teeth to the kitchen floor.

Felt like death to Crocker. "Everything okay with Cyndi?" he asked.

Crash's mind seemed focused elsewhere.

Crocker focused on the care she'd put into the place—curtains over the windows, family photos on the walls, everything neat and in its place.

"Cyndi okay?" he asked again, louder.

Maybe his eardrums are fucked up, too.

"She had to pick up something at the drugstore," he said laconically. "Maybe stopped at Starfucks. Doesn't clear her schedule with me, dude. I help her out when I can, especially till her mom gets back."

Cyndi had told him that her personal life was complicated. Until now he didn't realize to what extent. "She on vacation?" he asked, referring to Cyndi's mother.

Crash chuckled. "You could say that....Currently in a state-ordered alcohol treatment program at the Samaritan House. You know it?"

"No."

"Down the road, dude. Old lady's there now. Drove her car through a red light and crashed into a service station while totally blitzed on booze. Her second strike. She's got one left."

"When did that happen?" asked Crocker as he glanced again at his watch.

"A week or so ago. Broad's got anger issues. Seems to worsen as she ages. That's not supposed to happen, right?"

"Depends on the person," he answered, thinking of himself.

"I mean, you're supposed to mellow with age, right? Not her....She can be perfectly...like... normal, okay, then something sets her off...and this fucking Satan demon comes out of her!"

"I've known people like that."

"Explains why she's in and out of sobriety like a bouncing ball. She's got what they call...underlying issues. You don't deal with them, you're just jerking yourself....Hell, I should know."

Crocker wasn't interested in hearing about Cyndi's mother's sobriety or her ex's problems.

Through the beaded curtain, he saw Amy sitting on the rug in the living room watching *SpongeBob SquarePants* on TV. He considered joining her, when his phone rang to the opening chords of "Start Me Up."

"Rad ringtone, dude," Crash commented over his shoulder. "Them old Stones still rock."

Crocker pointed to his cell phone and said, "I'm gonna take this outside."

"Be my guest."

It was Séverine, calling from the Charles de Gaulle Airport in Paris. He heard a woman announcing a flight to Athens in French and English in the background.

"Tom, I was hoping to catch you before I leave. Is this a good time to talk?"

"Yes, yes. Good to hear your voice." A week ago, she'd invited him to spend a couple days with her in Paris. He'd decided to come to Las Vegas instead.

"You've been well?"

"Yes. You on your way to Athens?"

"No...we have a stopover there on the way to Istanbul."

"You mean...you're going back?"

"Yes, Tom....It happened fast. I found out yesterday. I'm joining a special team from Médecins Sans Frontières. Then we're traveling to Aleppo."

Alarms sounded in his head. "Aleppo?" He'd been in the area around the city two years ago and had barely made it out alive. He doubted it was safer now.

"That's what everyone asks. Aleppo? Just like that," she continued. "But we go where we're needed. That's what we do, yes?"

He couldn't help feeling protective of her. "Yeah."

"The UN observers assure us that the major fighting is over and there's a cease-fire in place between Assad government forces and the various rebel groups who are holding parts of the city. Besides, we'll be on a humanitarian mission, and all the parties have guaranteed our security."

He wasn't sure that meant much, or that anyone really understood the ever-changing situation on the ground. According to the intel briefing he had read recently, the Assad regime had reestablished control of the airport and the center of the city and was surrounded by various rebel groups to the west, including the Fatah Halab, al-Nusra Front, and the al-Tawhid Brigade of the Free Syria Army, Kurds and YPGs to the north, and ISIS to the east.

None of them loved Westerners. All of them would probably love to get their hands on a vulnerable Frenchwoman like Séverine.

"How long you staying?" Crocker asked.

"That depends on how long it takes us to stop the outbreak."

"What outbreak?"

"It's something called *cutaneous leishmaniasis,* also known as 'Aleppo evil,'" Séverine answered.

He knew from medical training that cutaneous meant relating to the skin. "What's that?"

"It's a flesh-eating boil that causes painful lesions and can lead to permanent disfigurement. It's spread by a particular kind of female sandfly that thrives in sewage and garbage."

"Sounds nasty." Last time he was in Aleppo, raw sewage ran throughout the city, and garbage was piled everywhere. It was hard to imagine that people still lived there and militants were fighting over the ruins.

"It's extremely nasty."

"How do you treat it?"

"First, we have to isolate the particular organism and identify the species," Séverine answered. "That's my job. Once we know exactly what we're dealing with, we will probably treat it with some form of sodium stibogluconate, which is applied topically. It enables the lesions to heal faster and prevents relapse and transmission."

He saw Cyndi's dark-blue Elantra turn into the cul-de-sac. "Séverine, I've got to go. I'll call you after I land in DC. Maybe you'll be in Istanbul by then, and I can meet you there."

"I hope so."

"If not, I'll call later."

"Please. Stay in touch."

"I will. Of course. Be safe."

"Au revoir…"

Sheikh al-Sufi sat in a ground-floor room in a building across the street from the mosque surrounded by members of his staff at laptops monitoring developments in the war. Russian airplanes had dropped bombs earlier that morning in the center of Raqqa, leveling several buildings, one of which had earlier housed an Islamic State communications center. Dozens of civilians had been killed and injured, but so far there were no reports of military casualties. The Syrian Tabqa airbase, 140 kilometers west, which ISIS had captured two years ago, was also under air attack by the Russians. Rocket and artillery exchanges between ISIS and Assad forces continued around the town of Dayr Hidr, on the western perimeter of Aleppo. The coordinated Coalition air assault on western Mosul entered its seventh day and showed no signs of letting up. They were also receiving reports of fighting around Ramadi, Karbala, and Kirkut in central Iraq.

Every day was like this, an intense buzz of reports of assaults and counterassaults. And every night, he shuffled his headquarters and communications hubs to another location in Raqqa without telling anyone ahead of time. Given the threat of treachery, the constant electronic surveillance and hacking, the drones overhead, and the almost constant movement of foreign fighters in and out of the city, vigilance and security were a priority.

He remained behind his folding desk, stroking his beard as the two aides seated across from him gave updates on recent purchases of weapons and ammunition from stocks of NATO material that had been left behind in Libya. They had arrived in Turkey and would be smuggled across the border at night in trucks.

"The roads have been secured?" al-Sufi asked.

"We have our routes, Emir," one of his aides answered. "Turkish border guards have been paid off."

"This is good."

Because of the sale of crude oil from fields captured around Mosul and elsewhere in Iraq, and donations from wealthy Sunnis in Qatar, Kuwait, Oman, and other Arab countries, money wasn't a problem. But transporting weapons systems into Islamic State territory was becoming increasingly challenging by the day.

As the sheikh listened to the difficulties his men were experiencing, he kept thinking about the Hero 30s and other attack drones Jaber Sami al-Sabah had briefed him about that morning. He imagined hundreds of them raining down on Coalition airbases, and crowded soccer stadiums throughout Europe, and even airports and targeted buildings in cities throughout the United States.

The prospect filled him with excitement. *The infidels kill our civilians, now we will destroy theirs!*

His chief aide, Yasir Selah, arrived to remind him of a prearranged encrypted Skype conference with Sheikh al-Athir, of the State's Defense, Security, and Intelligence Council, to discuss troop deployments and strategy. Four heavily armed men kept guard as they moved quickly from the building across from the mosque to another temporary communications site in a bakery three blocks away.

Al-Sufi arrived there out of breath, but bristling with ideas and excitement. The armed men led the way down a corridor, past ovens and sheets covered with freshly baked bread. Before they ducked under the low arched door to enter the communications room, Yasir Selah pulled the sheikh aside.

"What is it, Yasir?" the sheikh asked, as he noticed the strange pained expression in his aide's eyes.

"Sheikh," Yasir whispered. "It's with a heavy heart that I tell you this news from Tikrit."

"What news?"

"Your wife, the most noble and holy Fatima Sadir…is now a martyr. She was killed several nights ago by a U.S. drone.…"

The sheikh's head and body went numb. He leaned against the wall to hold himself up, and was quickly filled with sadness and anger.

"When exactly?" he asked, remembering the strange woman who had appeared in the courtyard of the mosque.

"I don't have that information."

"Find out."

"Inshallah," was the last word Yasir Selah said before he bowed his head and entered the room.

Sheikh al-Sufi stayed behind a minute and prayed silently. He had lost two other wives in his twenties—one during childbirth and another to illness—but Fatima remained closest to his heart.

These were the days of Fatima's judgment—a time when no soul could help her; a time when all decisions regarding his dear wife's future belonged to God.

"My beloved Fatima…this life is but a passing trial and comfort. The Hereafter is the enduring home. And on the day my soul is called, may God select me to join you. *Inshallah*."

CHAPTER FOURTEEN

No struggle can ever succeed without
women participating side by side with men.
—Muhammad Ali Jinnah

CROCKER LOOKED out the window of the United
Airlines 737 as it began its descent to Norfolk International Airport, reminding himself how under
different circumstances he could have ended up like
Cyndi's ex. One or two stupid decisions or bad luck
and he could have been like many of his childhood
buddies from Methuen who became drug addicts and
spent time in the pen.

As a wild high school kid he'd been involved in one
scrape with the law after the other. One night when
he was fifteen, his dad had to bail him out of jail for
trying to outrun the cops on his motorcycle, before
crashing it into a fence. During the ride home, his
father had told him a Cherokee story about a grandfather and his grandson.

It went something like this: Seeing that his grandson had been self-destructive, the old man sat him
down and said, "Son, there's a battle between two
wolves that goes on inside all of us. One wolf is evil

and filled with jealousy, greed, resentment, inferiority, lies, and ego. The other wolf is good and filled with kindness, hope, joy, humility, and truth."

The boy thought about it and asked, "Grandfather, which wolf wins?"

"The one you feed," answered the grandfather.

For more than twenty-five years, he'd been feeding the good wolf. But all the while he felt the bad wolf's hunger. Everybody did.

He deplaned, reminding himself not to be judgmental and to have sympathy for Cyndi's situation and the pressures she was under. She wasn't a bad person; she was trying the best she could.

In his head, he composed a list of things to do — stop for groceries, call Mancini and see if he wanted to go for a run through the woods, try to reach Séverine via Skype or Viber, take his Harley out of the garage and check to see if it needed servicing before he wound it through the Shenandoah Valley and into the Blue Ridge Mountains.

Once he returned he would sit with Captain Sutter and demand — yes, demand — that he be sent back to the Middle East.

Right now, he so badly needed to clear his head, order his priorities, plan for the future. What was his future? Who would he spend it with?

These questions lingered as he entered the arrival lounge and saw a man in civilian clothes holding up a sign with his covert name — Al Swearengen, after his favorite character in the TV show *Deadwood*.

"Yeah, I'm Swearengen. Who are you?"

"Ensign Wallace. Captain Sutter sent me."

"Good."

He checked his phone just to make sure the man

with the sign was who he said he was. There were two encrypted text messages from Sutter's deputy, Corporal Jackie Calderon, telling him to call or report to HQ upon landing. He did.

A short drive later, he rolled into the ST-6 compound wishing he had time to take a shower and change. He was directed to a secure conference room on the second floor of Team Command. The first person to greet him as he entered was Jim Anders from the CIA Special Activities Division—a muscular, clean-cut man two or three years younger than Crocker. He looked like a middle manager of a finance company except for the dark circles under his eyes from focused intensity.

His presence meant something was going on.

Anders and Crocker had worked numerous difficult missions together—from Yemen, to Syria, to Somalia—and shared a deep respect for each other.

He squeezed Crocker's hand and slapped him on the shoulder. "When I heard you were in Vegas, I worried you'd won big at the craps tables and wouldn't come back."

"I'm not that type of gambler."

"Yeah. You get your thrills elsewhere. Welcome back."

Familiar faces were already seated at the table, sipping water and coffee. All of them a blur as he set his duffel and backpack in the corner, grabbed a bottle of water off the credenza, and took a seat.

"Crocker's here. Let's get down to it," Captain Sutter started, then cleared his throat.

Crocker almost didn't recognize Davis with his blond hair neatly trimmed and wearing a clean uniform. Crocker was dressed head to toe in his usual black. His hair curled over his ears and he hadn't shaved in a week.

All attention turned to Anders and Lt. Colonel Smithson at the head of the table. She stood a few inches taller than him at six-four. Dark hair, attractive with wide shoulders. Looked like she could handle herself in a fight.

"You ready, Crocker?" she asked.

Ready for what? A mission? Fuck yeah, he wanted to say back. Instead, he answered, "Yes, Colonel."

"Listen carefully, because what we're looking at here is a quick multiple strike."

He liked the sound of it already.

"We're calling this MK Doubletap," Anders said. "The object is to cut off the supply of NATO weapons left behind after the war against Qaddafi that are currently going to ISIS. We're talking large stocks of RPGs, MANPADS, Stinger missiles, grenades, .50 cal and AK rounds, et cetera."

"Left behind or seized?"

"Both."

"Large stashes of them, mostly in A-plus condition, that are now in the hands of radical Islamic militias."

Who was the brains behind that? he asked himself. From everything he'd seen and heard, the overthrow of Qaddafi had been a fiasco.

"Crocker, you know Libya," Anders said, "so I'm sure you're jacked to be going back."

"One of my favorite places." He was being sarcastic. Four years ago he and his teammates had been in Tripoli searching for chemical and nuclear weapons developed by Qaddafi that Iranian officials were trying to get their hands on. During that time his wife and one of her colleagues from State Department

Security were kidnapped by radical Islamic militia-men. His wife's male coworker was tortured and killed in front of her, which threw her into an emotional tailspin that Crocker believed killed their marriage.

So, yeah, he knew Libya. But, no, he wasn't real thrilled to be going back.

"You and your men will fly to the USS *Theodore Roosevelt,* stationed in the Mediterranean," Anders continued. "From there you'll launch a night raid on a compound in al-Marj, an hour outside Benghazi. Lt. Colonel Smithson here will give you the specifics."

She nodded. "That's correct."

"When?" Crocker asked.

"When will she give you specifics or when will the mission launch?"

"When do we launch?"

"You and your men should report here at 2200 geared up and ready to deploy," Sutter answered.

"The first phase of the mission will launch the night after tomorrow, depending on weather, and logistics," Anders interjected.

"The object is to destroy the compound, and the weapons stash?"

"No, we can do that with air assets," Smithson objected.

"Then what do you need us to do?"

"We want you to grab ISIS's chief arms procurer first. Goes by the name Abu Omar. Real name, Nasir Abu al-Asiri. We believe he was born in Iraq, but usually travels with a Pakistani passport."

Davis slipped several surveillance photos of Abu Omar in front of him. Showed a middle-aged businessman, slightly overweight and balding with a close-cropped beard, getting into an SUV and in the company of other men.

"He's key to their operation. We want him," Anders declared.

"Alive, I assume."

"Yes, that's important. We need him in our custody so we can break him down and roll up his network, which extends from the dark net to suppliers all over the globe."

"The dark net?" Crocker asked. "They're involved in that, too?"

"Of course. The hidden underbelly of the Internet is designed for organizations like ISIS, other terrorists, criminals, perverts, hackers, and credit-card scammers to cloak themselves in obscurity and exchange services and buy illegal arms. Only accessible using special software and with encrypted passwords. Clandestine networks like Onionland."

"Never heard of Onionland," Crocker said.

"Not important," Sutter replied. "Let's focus on the mission."

"We want Abu Omar in our possession. He's critical."

"Got it."

"Method of infil?" Crocker asked.

"Helicopter....Blackhawks, most likely."

"Method of exfil?"

"Same."

"I'm assuming the compound is guarded," Crocker said, thinking ahead to the challenges.

"Affirmative. Heavily. Lt. Colonel Smithson has the full surveillance package."

The half-bird Smithson looked up and nodded.

"You and your men ready?" Sutter asked.

Crocker nodded. "Always."

"Good answer."

"You said there's a second part of the operation," said Crocker, planning the six hours until departure in his head. "What's that?"

Anders cleared his throat. "We've got our eye on a couple of transport ships sailing east from Libya that we believe are headed to Turkey. We're pretty sure they're carrying weapons bound for ISIS. So you should expect to do an intercept or two as well."

"When?"

"When, what?"

"Will the intercepts take place before or after the attack on the compound?"

"After."

"We going in military or black?"

"Third option; zero footprint." That meant nothing that could ID them as American mil.

"Third option" was CIA SAD's motto. When diplomacy fails and military is not an option. There seemed to have been a ton of that since 9/11. Whether in or out of uniform, it was all the same to Crocker. Eliminate the bad guys, rescue the hostages, rid the world of those who threaten our freedoms and way of life.

Afterward, he sat in Sutter's office going over personnel, when Anders slipped in and shut the door behind him. "The compound is owned and operated by a militia group called Ansar al-Sharia. Expect them to be nasty and heavily armed. By the way, they're the bastards who attacked the embassy compound and CIA Annex in September 2012, killing Ambassador Stevens and three other Americans. So don't be nice."

"We won't be," answered Crocker.

*   *   *

The Doctors Without Borders (DWB) team had stopped in a refugee camp in the Turkish border town of Suruç to lend help for the day before crossing into Syria. "A trial run," their coordinator, Per Mikkelsen, called it, "to practice teamwork before we arrive in Aleppo."

The vast, hastily erected tent city spread across flat barren land and housed nearly fifty thousand refugees who had escaped recent fighting between Islamic militants, Kurdish forces, and other militia groups in Kobani. Infants, children, and men and women of all ages, minus young men between fifteen and thirty-five. Most of the latter were either militants of some kind, or had been killed in the fighting.

The round-bearded Turkish man named Özgün who ran the camp explained that several million Syrians had been displaced since the civil war broke out in March 2011. More than two hundred thousand civilians had been killed. Turkey's thirty camps housed more than three hundred thousand refugees. Another two million lived on the streets and in shantytowns.

As he spoke, humanitarian workers came up to him with an assortment of urgent requests—an argument had broken out between two families in Sector 103, supplies of bottled water were running low, three unregistered men snuck into camp last night, et cetera.

The need for food, doctors, and medical supplies was enormous, Özgün explained. "We feed and clothe them today, but nobody knows what will happen to these people in the future. They're trapped in no-man's-land. One refugee said to me the other day,

'We are dying here, just like we were in Syria, but slower.'"

Per, a hospital administrator from Denmark, divided the nine nurses, doctors, and public service workers into three teams and dispatched them to different sectors of the vast camp. Özgün assigned each an interpreter, jeep, and driver.

Séverine sat in the back, a black scarf tied over her head, struggling with familiar feelings of displacement, sadness, and futility. The irony was that the more you tried in places like this, the more you realized your efforts were just a drop in the huge bucket of needs to be filled.

Maybe that's why the burnout rate in DWB was so high, and why every time Séverine volunteered she ended up working with new people, most of whom were on their first assignment, or had been with DWB for less than two years.

Her thirty-eight months of service made her a veteran, but she didn't feel that way, remembering her friends Axelle and Christine in Paris as though they were from another galaxy, and wondering what they would make of the camp and its residents. The strange thing about it was that as primitively functional as the camp was, wherever she was in the company of refugees she felt a kind of hope.

She sensed it in the eyes of the children as they chased a ball made of rags tied together, or made circles in the red dirt. She saw it in the tired eyes of the women who lugged buckets of water and went about their chores.

Before Séverine and her colleague Nabhas—a young medical student from the UK—met their first patient, they could hear his desperate screams coming from the white medical tent. A Syrian nurse explained to their female interpreter that the man was twenty-two and named Hamza. Had just arrived in the clinic, carried by four young men in a dark thermal blanket.

Séverine instructed the young men to place their friend on the assessment table so she and Nabhas could attempt to make a diagnosis.

The young man's agonized screams and thrashing didn't stop.

"Did he suffer a head injury?" Séverine asked his friends through the interpreter.

"No."

"Is he intoxicated?"

"No."

"Does he have a history of mental problems or seizures?"

They didn't know.

Nabhas said, "This has to be a surgical problem like a kidney stone or a perforation of the stomach. Let's sedate him and cut him open."

"Not yet," Séverine pronounced, noting some symptoms in common with the boy she'd seen dying on the road near Aix. Particularly the discoloration around his mouth and eyes.

When she used her gloved finger to clear the young man's airway, she realized that he was trying to swallow his tongue and hold his breath at the same time. As a result, his oxygen levels were falling, producing pain in his head and the muscles throughout his body.

"But why is he doing it?" Nabhas asked. "And how do we get him to stop?"

"I don't know."

Through the interpreter, Séverine instructed his friends to hold Hamza's limbs. When they did, he just became more agitated. One of his kicks hit Séverine in the chest, causing her to fall back and lose her balance.

Nabhas said, "We need a strong sedative, like diazepam, or he'll choke to death."

"There's some in the truck."

"I'll go quickly. Wait here."

Nabhas ran off, and one of Hamza's friends explained through the interpreter that Hamza had just been informed his sister had been killed in an air strike in Syria. He was so stricken with grief that he was trying to kill himself.

Séverine applied jaw-thrust pressure to keep Hamza's airway open until Nabhas returned with the diazepam, which quickly took effect.

The Syrian nurse explained that she had witnessed similar extreme psycho-physical reactions to the violence and killing—a middle-aged woman who experienced fainting spells following the death of her sister in Aleppo. A seven-year-old boy who couldn't urinate for four months after witnessing his father being shot and killed by a rebel sniper.

The nurse said, "People don't leave these experiences behind when they flee. The traumas follow them like shadows."

CHAPTER FIFTEEN

*I accept chaos, I'm not sure whether it
accepts me.*

—Bob Dylan

CROCKER SAT with the rest of his Black Cell team in
the operations room of the USS *Theodore Roosevelt*
(a.k.a. The Big Stick)—a Nimitz-class aircraft carrier
more than three times longer than a football field and
home to eighty-six fixed-wing aircraft and helicopters.
They were currently located a hundred and ten miles
southwest of Tripoli, Libya.

Crocker, Mancini, Akil, CT, Rip, and Danny
"Tiny" Chavez were in various states of disorientation
following their fourteen-hour journey. Hours from
now they would be deploying on an op against an
HVT, the details of which still hadn't been communicated to them. Careful planning and precise execution
were paramount to mission success.

So they all felt a sense of urgency as they focused on
the satellite images of their target, an Ansar al-Sharia
compound thirty-two miles southwest of Benghazi on
the big screen in front of them. Other screens featured
projections of local maps and a live feed of Lt. Colonel
Barbara Smithson from ST-6 HQ.

"First, a little background," Smithson started. "Ansar al-Sharia translates to 'Partisans of Islamic Law,' and they were founded in 2011 during the Libyan Revolution. As the name suggests, their goal is to establish the rule of strict Sharia law throughout North Africa and the Middle East and remove U.S. and Western influence. As you might imagine they're closely allied with ISIS and have helped supply them with militants and arms."

"Nice."

"Their logo is a pair of AK-47s, a clenched fist, a Quran, and a black flag."

"Pretty much says everything we need to know," offered Akil.

"Who said that?" Smithson asked.

Akil raised his hand. "I did."

"Did you know that they're based in the western Libyan cities of Benghazi, Darnah, Sirte, and Ajdabiya, and also have an active branch in Tunisia?"

"Thanks for filling me in," answered Akil.

"They're the ones who directed the Benghazi attacks in 2012 that resulted in the deaths of J. Christopher Stevens, our ambassador, and three other U.S. officials, including two former Navy SEALs."

"That makes me hate them even more," Akil groaned as he looked across the table at Crocker. Both of them knew one of the men who had died defending the CIA compound in Benghazi, former Navy SEAL Ty Woods.

"Ty was a good man, a hero," Crocker commented. "What's our time window here?" he asked, shifting to the current mission. The history of Ansar al-Sharia could wait until later.

"Our source on the ground tells us that the target,

Abu Omar, is there now and will be until noon tomorrow."

"In the compound?"

"Correct."

"Where specifically?"

"In the main house. Second-floor bedroom is where he sleeps."

A close-up of the house appeared on the screen. Looked like a new, modern structure with balconies, columns framing the entrance, and a red-tile roof. A house you might see in the upscale suburbs of Istanbul, Beirut, or even LA. Surrounding it were high walls topped by razor wire, and guard towers. The compound also featured several satellite dishes, parked military vehicles, technicals, and two one-story structures along the back wall.

"Which bedroom?"

"Unclear. According to our source there are four bedrooms on the second floor."

A schema of the house appeared on another screen.

"The big one on the northwest corner belongs to the house's owner, militia leader Ahmed Tamin al-Ghazi. The one to the left of it is occupied by one of his wives. The other two on the south side of the building are reserved for guests. We assume Abu Omar is in one of them."

"But you don't know."

"No."

"How good is your source?"

"Very good. The Agency has used him before."

"These pictures we're seeing are live-feed?"

"Correct. The ones on your right are from a surveillance satellite. The left...those are from a high-altitude drone."

He saw two guard towers on the northwest and southeast corners of the wall surrounding the compound, and another several guards stationed in front of the main gate.

"What's in the other two structures at the back of the compound?" Crocker asked.

"The one on the right, facing you, contains living quarters for various guards. The one on the left is where al-Ghazi's chief aide, Hassan, stays. It also houses a dining room and game room."

"Are Hassan and al-Ghazi there now?"

"Hassan is. According to our source, al-Ghazi's in Sirte."

"You have a picture of Hassan?"

"No."

"What can you tell me about him?"

"Older man in his late fifties. About five-seven. Speaks some English."

"How many guards should we expect, and are they heavily armed?"

"I'll have to get back to you on that," Smithson answered.

Crocker said, "That information is critical."

"Just a sec."

She left and came back a minute later.

"No more than eight to ten," Smithson answered. "Usually there are at least a dozen. Tonight is Friday, which is a holy day. Some of the guards have the day off."

"How will they be armed?"

"The usual: AKs, RPGs, grenades, machine guns. But none in the house. According to our source the guards are stationed outside."

"Thanks."

*   *   *

He felt a buzz of adrenaline as the radar-evading MH-60 Black Hawk stealth helicopter, like the one first used in the bin Laden raid, passed over the dark Mediterranean and entered Libya. A few lights sparkled along the coast and disappeared as they proceeded farther into the desert.

For some reason, he pictured his old teammate and friend Ritchie in his head. Ritchie had died on a secret mission in Venezuela, the focus of which was another HVT.

He chased away the memory, replaced by the strange muffled sound produced by the helo. Strange to his ear, because it had been specially modified to dampen rotor noise and reduce infrared signals. The latter accomplished with the help of a high-tech exhaust system that injected fresh air to lessen the aircraft's heat signals.

Out the side window, he saw the dark outline of Bravo Two, the second helo with Mancini, Rip, and Chavez aboard, following slightly to their left. The redesigned nose made it look like a blue whale.

Crocker checked his watch and held up his hand to indicate they were getting close. CT, on the bench across from him, nodded back and started to slip on his gloves, and check his gear for the tenth or eleventh time. Then used gaffer's tape to secure everything to his combat vest and belt.

MK141, M18, M32, and M67 grenades...all check. Extra mags for HK416 and SIG Sauer pistol...check. Medical kit, VIP in-flares, SureFire strobe lights, light sticks...check. Quad-tube NVGs...check.

Akil, next to CT, cool dude that he was, continued bobbing his head to EDM through earphones like they were on their way to a club. Crocker kicked his boot.

"What?" Akil shouted over the noise from the engine.

"Check your shit!"

"I don't need to.... As long as I've got this bad boy, I'm good." He patted the German-made MP7 with Airsoft suppressor clenched between his knees.

The SOAR Night Stalker pilot's voice came through the bone phone taped along his cheekbone. "Deadwood One-Zero, Bravo Alpha here. Five minutes to ready. Ten minutes to launch."

"Copy, Bravo Alpha."

"Godspeed down there."

"We'll see you in a few. You want us to get you a falafel sandwich?"

"I'm good. Thanks."

The helo banked sharply left, then eased right as it circled around the back of the compound. Crocker took a series of deep breaths. With each beat of his heart, time seemed to slow. The helo turned abruptly and started its descent.

Fifty feet, forty, thirty, bouncing. Hovered at twenty. He exhaled fully and the cabin light illuminated, turning Akil's bearded face green.

"Go! Let's go!" he shouted.

Akil and CT were already on their feet, boots thumping on the metal floor. The hatch opened. Warm desert air filled his lungs. His nose picked up a hint of frankincense mixed with exhaust.

Akil took the rope first. Then CT. He slipped his NVGs in place, grabbed the rope with both hands, and jumped.

Touched the ground, knees bent, as the helo engine

whined higher and faded. He loved the synchronicity of machines and men moving together, the thrill of being on their own in enemy territory.

Mancini's husky voice came through the earbuds. "Deadwood, all clear, section two."

Crocker was pleased his teammate's foot had healed quickly and he was good to go. "Big Wolf, section one clear. Deploy to vector two-zero and wait."

"Copy, Deadwood."

Crocker raised his arm—the prearranged signal to deploy. Akil split off left. He and CT circled the compound wide right over sand, dirt, and rubble, lights from several adjacent properties in the distance glowing light-green through his NVGs.

He noted that there was scant ambient light and barely any from the sliver of new moon, which hung beyond the compound like a crooked smile.

All good.

A breeze stirred, whipping sand across his chest. In a crouch, they came in close along the concrete wall and directly under the northwest tower up front. His heart thumping hard, Crocker waited for the signal from Akil, before he turned the corner to look for targets.

A moment of silence passed before all hell broke loose.

"Now!" his teammate's whisper came through his earbuds. Seconds later, Crocker heard something crash into a vehicle parked in front of the gate. The shatter of glass. A man shouting a warning. Men running.

Trying to decipher the sounds, he raised his left arm to CT, and with the suppressed 416 in his right, turned and immediately started picking out targets— a bearded man with an AK. Down! Another militiaman with a cigarette in his mouth, ripped across the chest.

He watched them fall, heard the sound of more rounds like loud spitting. Boots pounding the ground. Taking in dozens of impressions in split seconds—the tower above them silent so far, two technicals parked near the gate, militants running for cover.

CT pointed to the technicals, as if to say, What about them?

Crocker held up a hand. Wait.

No need to rush things. Wait for events to unfold in a Zen warrior way, and react.

The right move always presented itself…until it didn't and your ticket was punched.

"Romeo…Gate clear!" Akil said urgently through the radio.

The three of them met at the gate. Huddled. CT had strips of C-4 ready. They weren't needed, as Akil indicated with a wave of his hand and a sideways grin.

Crocker relayed to the other team leader, Mancini. "In, Big Wolf! We're in! Sector One."

"Copy, Deadwood."

They crouched behind the inside wall as the M33s CT tossed into the technicals detonated and lit up the sky. Debris rained down, then Akil ran to the back corner of the house and covered the two structures in back until the three operators from Bravo-2 arrived.

Meanwhile, Crocker and CT went for the front door, which was locked. A little C-4 punched it open. Crocker ducked in first and hurled himself left as bullets rained down from the second floor. Somersaulted sideways through an archway into a large room and took up position behind a wall, with an upholstered chair behind him. A PlayStation on the seat.

Smithson had said to expect little resistance inside the house. Wrong! Now another shooter joined in and pinned Crocker. He wanted this over fast.

"Two-four.... Two-four."

Where the fuck is CT?

"Deadwood here. Two-four...come in!"

He heard the crackle of AKs firing outside as he loaded a grenade into the XM320 launcher on the rail of his 416.

Whoosh...*Bam!!*

It tore into a balcony above the staircase. Plaster and part of the rail tumbled down. A man screamed, "Allah....*Allahu akbar!*" as Crocker loaded another round and fired.

Boom!!!

Take that!

He jumped to his feet, paused to fire a third grenade, AK rounds glancing off the tile floor and tearing into the walls. Hurried through the living room, into another room, and a kitchen, to another set of steps. His heart pounded in his throat.

"Deadwood, two-four...." It was CT.

"Two-four, Deadwood. Where are you?" Crocker asked as he heard more firing from the balcony and men calling to one another in Arabic. He took the stairs two at a time, his weapon ready.

"Deadwood, I'm stuck in front. More militants coming through the gate! Need support."

A quick call to Mancini. "Big Wolf, can you respond?"

"Boss...."

He almost ran into a man in a white robe looking

behind him as he hurried down the steps. Crocker couldn't tell from this angle if he was Abu Omar or maybe Hassan. All he knew is that the dude held a pistol in his left hand, and started to raise it when he saw Crocker and opened his mouth to gasp.

Keeping in mind the instructions from Smithson and Anders, he turned the 416 around and drove the butt stock into the man's chest. Heard bones snap and saw the man's bare feet go out from under him, and his head hit a step. Knocked him out cold.

Crocker slapped the pistol out of his hand. Checked quickly to see if the dude had a pulse. He did.

Fuck, he said to himself. *This is taking too much time!*

Gun battles raged at the front and back of the house. Akil, on the right corner, facing the back wall, raised his MP7 and cut down a militant who made a dash for a Humvee with a .50-cal machine gun in back. The bearded jihadist was so jacked on something he kept coming even though Akil had shredded his torso. He quickly reloaded as the militant fell face forward a few meters from his feet, close enough that he could see the blood seeping out of the hole in his back.

"Need support...at the..." someone shouted into his earbuds as bullets whizzed toward him and ricocheted off the bricks to his left.

"Who? Who? What location?"

Akil was confused. He spit the dirt out of his mouth, took cover farther down the wall. Used the cover of a smoke grenade that someone had tossed to dart right and climb into the desert camo–painted Humvee.

"Big Wolf. Romeo here...Who needs support?"

Part of his brain waited for a name. The rest of it

focused on getting into the turret and looking for an ammo box. Found a full one. Shit operational security, but his good luck.

An incendiary grenade slammed into the one-story structure forty meters in front of him and exploded. Militants started running out, firing wildly, and shouting. Bullets glanced off the metal shield around the turret like crazed bees.

Akil lifted the ammo in place, fed the belt into the chamber, quickly rotated the turret with the crank on the left, cocked the action, gripped the handles, and started firing. The .50 rattled and clanged like a mofo, but ripped the militants apart.

Power surged from the .50 into his chest. Jihadists screaming and falling, his forearms shaking, he cracked the turret and focused on the front door of the structure to his left. Fired and tore the door apart until only fragments of wood hung from the hinges.

Sweet!

"Romeo, hold your fire! *Hold!* It's Big Wolf. Look left!"

Saw Mancini at the other side of the backyard, raising his left hand to indicate he stop shooting.

Akil raised his fist back. Understood.

Both structures turned silent. Dust and smoke hung in the air. He took a deep breath and kept watch as Mancini and Tiny Chavez went in to clear the building on the left. Came out a minute later leading two militants with their hands over their heads. The taller one had a stream of blood from his nose down to the front of his white robe.

That's when he heard CT screaming in the radio. "Two-four! Two-four. Situation critical. Need help at the gate!"

CHAPTER SIXTEEN

The ethical warrior must avoid getting crushed
between falling in love with the power and
thrill of destruction and death dealing and
falling into the numbness of the horror.
—Karl Marlantes,
What It Is Like to Go to War

CROCKER PUSHED through the smoke-filled darkness on the second floor toward the front of the house. Reached the stairway balcony, which looked like a couple maniacs had gone at it with sledgehammers. Saw a dead man sprawled against the wall, his left arm up above his head like he was reaching for something. Part of his right shoulder and chest were missing. Spotted a second militant halfway down the stairs dressed in a t-shirt and underpants, his Kalashnikov held high like he'd watched too many action movies.

Had to make a quick read if it was Abu Omar or wasn't. The jihadist moved like a young man, paused and started to turn. Wasn't Omar in Crocker's opinion. He aimed and raked the man across the chest.

The terrorist fell, glanced off the railing, and slammed into a potted plant on the ground floor. The house turned quiet; dust and smoke gently settled.

"Two-four, Deadwood. Report."

CT responded, "All good, DW. Need help up front.

Took out several militants coming in the gate. Machine gun fire coming from guard tower one."

He wanted to ask, *Why gunfire from the tower now and not before?* but stopped himself. Wasn't important. Besides, he had already turned back and was entering the first bedroom. A dirty mattress on the floor with a laptop beside it. Otherwise empty except for some framed Islamic scripture on the wall; nothing in the closets. Slipped the laptop and some thumb drives into the bag on his combat belt.

The other front bedroom was completely bare except for a barbell in the corner and a flat-screen propped against the wall. Grabbed a handful of DVDs, stuffed them in the sack. Then turned with his 416 ready, and hurried toward the back of the house.

Twelve minutes....

Somebody was trying to communicate through the radio, but the voice was garbled.

"Two-four, Deadwood. You copy? You hear me?"

No answer.

Women's stuff filled the rear right bedroom. He saw a white bed, a framed painting of a unicorn on the wall, white phone, journal, glass bottles of perfume all through his NVGs. Probably cost a fortune at some mall in Dubai. Slipped the phone and journal into the sack on his belt—could be useful—cleared the closet and bathroom. Empty. Looked like no one had been here in weeks.

Quickly checked the timer on his watch. The Black Hawks were scheduled to land in six minutes if he didn't call them off.

"Big Wolf, Deadwood here. We're fourteen minutes in. Six minutes to exfil. Gotta wrap this up. Respond!"

Again, no answer.

The last bedroom, the one Smithson said belonged to al-Ghazi, was a total mess. Radios in the corner, papers scattered everywhere, the king-sized bed disheveled, mattress…warm.

He's here…somewhere.

Crocker hurried down the back steps to check on the man he'd encountered there. Breathing, but unconscious, blood gurgled through broken teeth. He pulled off the black cap he was wearing. The man had a full head of close-cropped white hair.

It's not Abu Omar.

Snapped three quick photos, and then pumped two rounds into his head.

Sorry.…

Eighteen minutes.…They were running out of time. He dashed for the back door when he heard a tremendous firing outside and to his left. Ducked his head behind the window.

Who the hell is that?

Seconds later, he heard Mancini through the radio. "Big Wolf here. We got a man down! Man down!"

"Where? Where?"

"Left front! Left…" The rest was garbled.

Crocker kicked through the back door. Saw that the fighting had subsided in back. Light from the moon reflected off shell casings on the ground. Smoke drifted out of the structure along the back right wall. He turned toward a continuous rip of automatic fire and went down.

It wasn't his men. They didn't waste ammo like that.

From the rear corner of the house, he looked ahead

and quickly appraised the situation. Two team members pinned behind a four-foot cement planter alongside the house. Another sprawled on the ground. Militants firing multiple machine guns from the guard tower, front left corner.

Not good.

"Big Wolf, Deadwood. That you behind the planter?"

"Check."

"Who's been hit?"

"Rip."

"Hold on."

Fighting to not lose his cool, he unleashed a salvo at the guard tower, and decided to circle around the house for a better angle. As he did, he ran into Akil pushing a Humvee backward on the cement driveway toward the front of the house.

"Boss!"

"What the fuck...."

"Help me!"

Soon as he saw the .50 cal he intuited the rest. Lowered his shoulder and pushed with Akil until the Humvee reached the front driveway and militants from the gate and guard tower started directing their fire at them. Crocker jumped in the driver's seat and applied the hand brake as Akil climbed into the turret.

"I hope this baby functions."

"Do I look stupid?"

Akil grinned and started firing. Screamed, "Say hello to my little friend!"

Crocker couldn't help smiling in spite of the fact that fire from the tower slammed into the hood and windshield and glanced off the pavement. Death and mayhem dancing all around him, he took cover behind one of the front wheels, aimed his 416, and returned fire.

Fucking Akil....

It had ended much quicker than he'd anticipated. The .50 cal had literally torn the guard tower apart, causing several jihadists to fall and hit the ground, where Akil and Crocker applied the coups de grâce. Now they were hustling out the gate toward the SOAR Black Hawks waiting in a dry riverbed approximately two hundred meters away. Crocker ran awkwardly because he was holding the back end of the medical litter with Rip on it. Basically a heavy-duty PVC tarp with a torso-stabilizing strap and nylon web loop handles. Not ideal under current conditions.

Looking back to see if they were being followed, he shouted, "Hurry!" His arms and shoulder barking.

Saw nothing to be concerned about, but knew that could change in a second. The taller of the two men they'd captured tripped and fell. Because his wrists were zip-tied together, CT had to stop and help him up.

The tall man, with a prayer cap on his head, spit some curse of disgust.

CT responded with a growling "Shut the fuck up!"

They continued running as fast as they could; a gust of wind threw up a curtain of sand, so the helo disappeared for a moment. Crocker hoped one of the prisoners was Abu Omar, but had his doubts. Something always went wrong on every mission. The injury to Rip concerned him more.

He'd taken an AK round into his right upper hip. Crocker had applied QuikClot to the back entry point and sealed it with an Israeli pressure bandage. Luckily the bullet hadn't ruptured the femoral artery or Rip would have bled out by now.

Last time Crocker checked, Rip's blood pressure and heart rate had stabilized, and his body temp was a little lower than normal. All good. They were drawing close. He'd require surgery to clean the wound, deal with the likely fracture to the ilium bone, and make sure any bone fragments hadn't pierced the stomach or other organs.

Crocker was trying to keep his mind off the aches in his arms, quickly approaching unbearable. Reminded himself that pain was weakness leaving the body, and they'd be out of there soon.

"Stop a second," Akil gasped, holding the front of the makeshift stretcher.

"No can do!" Crocker responded. "Suck it up!"

Akil groaned and picked up speed. "Yo momma so fat, I took a picture of her last Christmas and it's still printing."

Crocker pushed harder. "Yo momma so fat her belly button gets home fifteen minutes before she does."

"Yo momma so ugly that when Santa came down the chimney he said, 'Ho! Ho! Holy shit!'"

It hurt to laugh, but he couldn't help it.

Sixty more meters.…Behind them, he saw headlights wash across the side of the compound.

"Push, guys! Push hard!"

Every part of Crocker's body was screaming now—especially his lungs, shoulders, and calves. He tried recalling the lyrics of "House of the Rising Sun" to stave off the pain—so intense that he was on the verge of losing consciousness. Refused to stop.

"'Mother tell your children, not to do what I have done…'"

He used to pump iron to the Animals' version in his dad's garage. Dozens of reps at a time. Never tired.

Now he made out the outline of rotors of the Black Hawks, spinning over the embankment like in a dream. Akil caught his boot on a rock, started to trip, grunted, and at the last second recovered his balance.

"Clumsy fuck."

Rip groaned. "I'll get you back for that."

Crocker wanted to laugh again, but his body had turned numb. He struggled to stay conscious.

"'I got one foot on the platform...the other...on the train....'"

The next thing he remembered was one of the Night Stalker copilots helping him load in Rip, and then the sensation of lifting off, like rising on a magic carpet. Stars sparkled through the window. He thought he recognized Orion's belt.

CT, on the bench beside him, had his face in his hands.

"You okay?"

CT looked up and nodded. "'No more than eight to ten' guards...Bullshit."

He'd spent the night running through the streets of Tikrit with his deceased wife Fatima, being chased by demons. The horrid-smelling Ibah multiplied by three, sometimes four. Hand-in-hand with Fatima he ran along the banks of the Tigris River, through the ancient stone gates to Old Town, where the two of them first met more than twenty years ago. Memories returned of a cool evening in May before the summer heat. The town safe and quiet then.

He didn't mind that Fatima's great-grandmother on her father's side had converted to Islam from

Christianity. Or that the town had once been the center of Assyrian Christianity.

All he cared about were Fatima's dark beguiling eyes, and the way they gave him confidence, and the strands of black hair that blew out from under her white scarf. She represented hope, strength, and a kind of intuitive wisdom.

All things he longed to use to fill a space inside himself. Imagined his needs were simple as they ran together up a hill toward the ruin of the Assyrian Green Church—family, work, children. Like the three stately archways gleaming in the moonlight—the ones President Saddam Hussein had restored before the wars. When life made sense. When all he wanted was simple happiness.

Thoughts filtered through his head as they ran with the demons on their heels. At some point he knew they would grow tired and have to give up. Fatima, beside him, showed no fear. When he turned to her she smiled as if to say, *It's okay, Abu Samir. You're safe with me.*

Just as he smiled back, the multiple Ibahs snorted and lunged, one of them knocking her to the ground, and, as he stood helpless, devouring her in the most disgusting manner until all that remained was red slime and bones.

His whole world stopped. His insides turned numb. He wanted them to kill him, too. In weakness and shame, he begged them.

"Take me, too!" he shouted. "Don't leave me here… alone!"

Instead, the three beasts turned into the night and disappeared.

Now it was morning. Feeling like an old man, he

descended the narrow stone steps at a snail's pace, all the time praying under his breath and asking Allah to give him strength. What awaited him in the low-ceilinged basement beneath the mosque, he didn't know or care.

The news of Fatima's death had sent him into a terrible emotional spiral. Grief and anger fed each other as he imagined her shattered body, the violence that had been visited on his favorite wife, their house, and their few family mementos. From the air, no less, borne by a diabolical unfeeling machine.

"The devils," he muttered under his breath. "Godless cowards."

"Who?" asked Yasir Selah, at his side.

Fingering the wooden beads at the side of his robe, he remembered the words in the Quran about revenge. "If you punish, then punish them with the like with which you were afflicted."

He wanted the drones he had heard about to rain destruction down on the infidels, to attack their women and children in their beds, to feel his pain and hatred, so they knew how he felt to have his homeland, his dreams, and his family violated the way they had been.

He stopped three steps from the bottom and looked up at his aide. "Yasir," he said, "when the Lord spoke to His angels about the *kafir,* what did he say?" *Kafir* were infidels, or literally "concealers of God's word."

"He said they were hated by them for their arrogant, disdainful hearts."

"And he said, 'I will send terror into the *kafirs'* hearts, cut off their heads, and even the tips of their fingers.'"

CHAPTER SEVENTEEN

A bone to a dog is not charity. Charity is the
bone shared with the dog when you are just
as hungry as the dog.
——Jack London

THE SUN shone on the five-vehicle DWB convoy as it passed over green fields on its way east into Syria. Aside from the garbage and burnt-out vehicles alongside the road and occasional crater, it was hard for Séverine to tell that they were approaching the most destructive war zone in the world.

She felt emboldened with a sense of purpose as she rode in the backseat of the first Mercedes Sprinter with a UN jeep escort in front of them. This is where she belonged. Not planning social dinners at the Delage estate, or choosing fabric for new curtains.

"If you want to be Mother Teresa," her mother had said before her departure, "you must surrender your pride."

The words still stung. Drawing within fifteen kilometers of Aleppo, she realized this might be the last time she could be honest with herself, and questioned the reasons she had left her mother in Paris.

Am I still mad at her for scolding me when I filed for divorce?

In her opinion, her mother had always been too impressed with the Delage family name, and had fawned over Madame Delage, Alain's mother. Séverine didn't mind that her mother enjoyed the regular visits to the Delage estate in Rémy, and other privileges.

Do I still hold a grudge for the way my mother put her petty self-interests above mine, when I'm the one who had married Alain and took on the burden that came with that? Did I want to elevate my position in society, too?

Maybe…yes. To be perfectly honest, she had thought in the beginning that his social position and money would give her freedom. And, yes, she had loved Alain in certain ways and still did.

She'd quickly realized she made a mistake and ended their marriage. She wanted nothing. She held no grudges. She wished Alain and his family the best.

Alain had moved on. He was dating other women and had started a successful new business. It was her mother who mourned the most and expressed bitterness, as though she was the one Séverine had hurt.

That was understandable in a way. Her mother was a sixty-year-old woman suffering from arthritis and living alone in a one-bedroom apartment, surviving on her husband's pension as a train conductor with the SNCF.

So, yes, she is limited in what she can do and what she can accomplish. But aren't many of her limits self-imposed?

It was an old quarrel. The truth was that mother and daughter had never gotten along so well. Séverine's independent nature and rejection of conformity clashed with her mother's belief that there was a proper way to behave in all social situations and it was necessary to compromise one's pride in order to advance, and moving up the ladder of society was the key to achieving the only kind of happiness one could rely on.

She accused her daughter of excessive pride, ignorance, and even disliking men. Or, at least, expecting too much of them.

But why should I have to settle for a man I didn't love and respect, and a life that didn't excite me? If that's what my mother considers excessive pride, I'll live with it. Or maybe not...

Séverine wrestled with her conscience as the convoy wound up a particularly scenic hill. She leaned out of the side window to let her hair blow freely and fill her lungs with fresh air.

"Look," said Marku, their Hungarian driver, pointing left.

"What?" Per asked beside him.

Séverine couldn't see past their big shoulders at first. When she craned her neck, she was blinded momentarily by sunlight slanting through the windshield. She felt fear and excitement stir in her colleagues seated around her.

"What is it?"

Shielding her eyes, she made out a mass of people moving quickly across the green hilltop about a hundred meters away. Because of the beautiful setting, she thought it was some kind of happy group excursion at first.

Then she heard Marku mutter the word "refugees," and looked more closely, and the reality hit her.

"From Aleppo most likely," Marku commented. "Headed to Turkey."

"I thought that the people who wanted to leave had already been bussed out," someone said.

Séverine estimated about two hundred men, women, and children. The red sweater of one young boy, being carried on his father's back, stood out in the morning light.

"Why are they walking so fast?" Séverine asked. They seemed to be carrying only basic possessions in suitcases and backpacks.

"They're afraid of something," Per answered. "Let's find out."

The vehicles rumbled across the field and stopped. The refugees seemed apprehensive until they saw the DWB logos on the sides of the trucks and relaxed.

A thin, long-faced man explained to an Arabic-speaking doctor that they had remained in Aleppo through the ISIS occupation and many years of fighting, but were forced out by recent Russian and Assad air strikes.

"We were under the impression that the bombing had stopped," Per said.

Séverine, who had been studying Arabic, tried to follow as the man explained.

"He says that ISIS and the other rebel groups are gone. All the government is doing now is killing Sunni civilians. That is their aim, he says. They're savages and cowards who drop bombs and rockets from the sky on houses and apartments."

"Disgusting," Séverine said in Arabic.

"Disgusting, yes," the Syrian man responded. "Why does God allow this?"

Séverine shook her head. While she had been talking to the man, she noticed a bruise on the face of a girl wearing a Teenage Mutant Ninja Turtles sweatshirt.

When she knelt to examine her, it looked like a lesion caused by *cutaneous leishmaniasis*.

She pointed this out to Per and suggested that the rest of the team examine the other members of the group for lesions, so she could conduct biopsies.

"How?" he asked.

"A skin scraping with microscopic analysis is best," she answered.

"You can do that quickly? Because these people seem to be in a hurry."

"I can."

"All right, let's move fast."

The lesion, on the girl's right cheek, was the size of a coin. The girl's mother held her hand while Séverine gently did a scraping, and hurried to the lab truck to examine it.

Indeed, it was a case of *cutaneous leishmaniasis* parasitic disease. Two dozen other cases were found. Séverine stopped at each infected person and used a needle to aspirate tissue fluid from the margin of the lesion, which she would later use to isolate the organism and identify the particular species.

There was no time for that now. Instead, she cleaned each lesion thoroughly and applied a coat of sodium stibogluconate.

"That's the best we can do for now," she explained to Per. "I imagine there's nothing we can do to alleviate the stress and bad nutrition that helps the parasite spread. And there's no way we can eradicate it completely until we develop a vaccine, which will take time."

"We can only do what we can."

While Séverine attended to those with signs of the disease, her colleagues spent the hour treating people for tooth- and muscle aches, sprained ligaments, diarrhea, incontinence, and other minor ailments. The worst case involved a three-year-old boy—the boy she'd seen wearing the red sweater—suffering from an infection caused by a recent shrapnel wound to the back of his neck. The infection was advanced and though they lanced, cleaned, and bandaged it, and administered antibiotics and ibuprofen to relieve the pain and swelling, the three-year-old's condition remained serious.

Per explained to the boy's father that he really should rest in a hospital for a few days. There was a risk that the infection could spread and the boy could die.

"Which hospital?" the father asked.

Per, through a translator, offered to take the boy and his father with them to a special DWB clinic housed in a guarded UN compound on the outskirts of Aleppo. But the father balked. He was leaving his dead wife and five other deceased members of his family behind in Aleppo, and had no interest in returning.

All the DWB doctors and nurses could do was give him antibiotics to administer to his son, and advise him to take the boy to a hospital as soon as they reached Turkey.

Séverine stood beside Per, watching as the boy with the red sweater climbed on his father's back, and smiled back at them as he left with the rest of the refugees.

As she waved and prayed the boy would survive, tears gathered in her eyes.

We can only do what we can....

"Where exactly did you find these men?" Lt. Colonel Smithson asked from the video screen in the operations room of the USS *Theodore Roosevelt*. Crocker sat with his feet propped up on the chair in front of him to relieve the pressure in his lower back. The two Advil he'd swallowed recently hadn't taken effect.

Crocker didn't hear her at first, though he was aware of the massive vessel creaking in the background, and rocking him to sleep. His mind was on Rip, who had just been medevaced to the Landstuhl Regional Medical Center in Ramstein, Germany. When Crocker spent time there two years ago, a nurse had told him that on a typical day the hospital accommodated twenty-three new patients and nine acute emergencies—more than many civilian hospitals admitted in the space of two months. He wondered about the damage the AK round had done to Rip's hip.

Will he ever be able to run again? Or bicycle long distance, which he loves to do? Or rejoin the team?

"Crocker? Crocker, can you hear me?"

Her voice jarred his attention. He focused on her dark eyes on the screen. She seemed to be scowling. "Yes, Colonel. I'm sorry. What was the question?"

His mind was numb with exhaustion. The last six hours had been a blur of downloading photos from the compound, filling out reports, processing the prisoners, and watching them being loaded onto a Gulfstream with two men from CIA Ground Branch, who would escort them to Bagram Airfield in Afghanistan to be interrogated. He'd managed to catch a couple hours' sleep and a quick breakfast of ham and eggs with a few cups of coffee.

Even so, he could barely focus. Now he was thinking ahead to the next target, a Greek freighter sailing east through the Mediterranean on its way to Turkey.

"I asked you about the two prisoners, who we're calling Benji One and Benji Two. Benji One being the older and taller with the short white beard."

"Yes."

"You should be able to see their photos on the screen. Can you confirm that?"

He didn't want to concentrate, but did. Neither appeared to be lighthearted fellows. Maybe he wouldn't be, either, if he lived in the post-Qaddafi chaos of Libya.

"Crocker, you see them?"

She seemed impatient. It was 0923 where he was, and 0323 in DC. "Yes, I can."

"I believe these are pictures you took shortly after you seized them at the compound."

He was trying to remember. "Yeah....My teammate Akil took the photos. That's correct."

"My question to you, Crocker: Where were these militants when you captured them?"

The questioning annoyed him. He'd already been debriefed twice, and didn't want to go over the op again. It hadn't been a great one from his point of view. One of his men had suffered a serious injury. They hadn't found a weapons cache. Nor did it seem as though the arms dealer who had been the target of the mission had been on-site.

"Crocker, did you hear the question?"

"Yes, I'm trying to recall....I wasn't there when they were captured, but I believe they were found in one of the one-story structures at the back of the compound. The one on the left."

He wanted to move on, to get some sleep, to check in with Jenny, Séverine, and maybe Cyndi. To reconnect with his ex-wife, Holly, and see what she wanted.

To summon the team together and plan for the next mission.

What's the value of going over this again?

"As far as we're able to determine at this time, neither of these men are Abu Omar," Smithson said.

His head pounded. His back hurt like hell. The Advil still hadn't taken effect. "I'm sorry to hear that."

"Excuse me."

"We did the best we could based on the intel provided. If Abu Omar was there, we would have grabbed him. Apparently he wasn't."

"Can you state that with a hundred percent certainty?" Smithson asked.

That struck him as a ridiculous question. "We went through the entire house and property, and we didn't see him. Nor did we see anyone leave the compound. A number of militants were killed. I think it was fourteen in all. All we had on Abu Omar was a single photo, so maybe we shot him in the heat of battle, or maybe he wasn't there."

"Our local informant claimed he was."

"Maybe your informant was incorrect. In my experience, they often are. Are we done here? Because I got other shit to take care of."

"Crocker, there are other things I'd rather be doing, too!"

"Understood."

"We're not assigning blame. We're just looking at what we did and didn't accomplish, so we can plan steps going forward."

"Okay." She was right. He was tired and upset about Rip.

"You sent us a dozen photos of dead militants."

"Yes…"

"You just told me you killed fourteen in all. So where are the photos of the other two?"

He wanted to tell her to go fuck herself, or get up and drive his fist through the screen. But reminded himself that she was doing her job.

"We photographed all the dead militants. If I sent photos of a dozen, that's the true number and I misspoke before."

"Benji One and Benji Two are on their way to Bagram?" asked Smithson, referring to the prisoners.

"Correct."

"Hopefully we'll be able to get some intel out of them."

"Yes."

"The tall one, Benji One, we believe is al-Ghazi's chief aide, Hassan. Benji Two, we haven't been able to identify as of yet, but he's too young to be Abu Omar."

The rocking of the boat combined with his lack of sleep and the Advil were making him nauseous. "What about the guy on the stairs...the one I took the picture of? Short, kind of heavy, close-cropped white hair?"

"We're not sure, but we suspect he could be al-Ghazi."

The picture of al-Ghazi they'd been shown before the mission was of a much younger man.

"Al-Ghazi, the leader of the militia group and owner of the compound?" Crocker asked.

"Correct. You weren't able to capture him alive?"

"No. He died in a gunfight." Not exactly true, but he didn't feel like explaining and being second-guessed.

"His death could create possible complications in Libya."

"Why?"

"He was an influential man in that part of the country. His death could compromise some of the things we're trying to do there."

"Your local informant told you al-Ghazi wouldn't be there, correct?" asked Crocker.

"Yes, that's correct."

"Like I said before, your source is shit. Now excuse me, because I've got to throw up."

Halfway through the silent prayers for her mother, relatives, and friends, Séverine fell asleep. She dreamt she was floating above the clouds. She saw a field below. Next thing she knew, she was tossing an inflatable ball to the Syrian boy with the red sweater. His neck had healed, leaving a crescent-shaped scar. His father, who leaned into the picture, said in broken English, "Look....It's...good...luck."

She smiled. The boy smiled back, and the ball sailed over his outstretched hands and struck him in the face. He let out a delayed scream that echoed.

Séverine awoke, surrounded by thick darkness. The wool blanket chafed her arm. Another blood-curdling scream filled her ears. She sat up, disoriented.

"Séverine! Séverine!" a girl screamed in English. "Rats! Oh, my god! We have rats! Big rats!"

She switched on the flashlight on the floor beside her. Saw her new roommate Dayna standing in shorts and a Texas Longhorns t-shirt near a mattress on the floor of the metal pod. It was really a shipping container with a window cut into it, containing two mattresses, two blankets, a desk, a space heater, and a plastic bucket. No sheets, no rug, no chairs. The bathroom was somewhere outside.

Dayna jumped up and down with her arms clutched over her chest. "Séverine. Oh, Séverine…. I'm afraid to move. One of them crawled over me. What should we do?"

She remembered that Dayna was a twenty-one-year-old nurse from Savannah, Georgia, who had discovered Jesus while attending the University of Texas in Austin. She also recalled that rats usually didn't bite humans.

Séverine said, "Dayna….Dayna, calm down. It's okay. The rats won't hurt us."

Dayna had straight shoulder-length reddish-blond hair, high cheekbones, and a slight overbite. She reminded Séverine of the actress Erika Christensen in one of her favorite movies, *Traffic,* and spoke with a Southern drawl.

"How can you say that?" Dayna shouted back. "They're rats, Séverine! They're disgusting!"

She heard a rustling sound and saw two rats with long gray fur trying to hide in the corner. A chill ran up her spine. She knew she had to be the strong one.

"Calm down, Dayna," she said. "They'll go away. They're looking for food. We don't have any food here, do we?"

"No!"

"I'll talk to the camp administrator in the morning."

"You can't talk to him now? I mean what happens if they…attack us?"

"They won't attack us. I don't know where the administrator sleeps. I don't even know his name. Come here."

Kneeling on the mattress, she held out her arms. Dayna crossed the metal floor and the two women embraced.

Séverine felt the young American trembling in her arms like a delicate bird, even though she was broad-shouldered and tall.

"I hate rats, Séverine. They disgust me."

"They disgust me, too."

"Séverine....I came here to spread God's love. I asked him to send me to the hardest place. To send me where others do not want to go."

"You got your wish."

They laughed together. "You know the words of Luke from the Bible, 'From everyone who had been given much, shall much be required'?"

"I've heard them, yes."

"That's why I'm here."

CHAPTER EIGHTEEN

We only have what we give.
—Isabel Allende

CROCKER HAD just gotten off the phone with an aide at Landstuhl Medical Center who told him that Rip was in emergency surgery to repair damage to his intestines and spleen caused by bone and bullet fragments when the AK round ripped into his pelvis.

He said a silent prayer for his teammate as he climbed up to the flight deck of the USS *Theodore Roosevelt,* his fully rigged HK416 slung over his shoulder, Mancini, Akil, and CT following, Tiny Chavez by his side. They called him "Tiny" because of his massive shoulders and chest, made stronger through endless reps of presses and lifts.

He was showing Crocker a picture on his cell phone, taken at his son's first birthday. Showed a round-faced kid licking a plate of chocolate ice cream that was smeared all over his face.

"Look, boss, he likes to eat like me."

"He just turned one?"

"Yeah."

"Big kid."

Tiny grinned with pride.

They reached the massive flight deck and were hit by a blast of ocean air, laden with the smell of salt and slight decay. Over his left shoulder, he saw an F-18 Super Hornet coming in for a landing, engines screaming, tailhook deployed.

He shouted to Tiny, "Cover your ears!"

The F-18 hit the deck, sending up a huge shower of sparks, hit one of the ship's arrest wires, and skidded to a stop.

"Fucking epic!" Tiny remarked. "Can't be easy…"

"Not at a hundred and seventy-five miles an hour."

A landing signal officer escorted them past a row of A-63s to a spot beneath the ship's superstructure, known as the island. Waiting for them were two MH-60 Knighthawks and four SOAR pilots and copilots.

Rick "Scarface" Jameson, the lead pilot—olive flight suit, short hair, big mean-looking scar over his left eye, the result of a crash in Afghanistan—offered Crocker a fist to bump.

"You ready, Crocker?"

"Always…."

"We got some weather blowing in from southwest, so this might be a little rough."

"That's the way we like it, Scarface."

"Good."

This was going to be a bitch any way you sliced it, because they had no Zodiacs, no cigarette boats, no dive equipment. Instead they were planning to fast rope onto the deck of the HS *Star Helena* in bad weather.

Crocker revved himself up for the challenge.

Saw enthusiasm in the eyes of Akil on the bench across from him as the lead Knighthawk, "Shaggy One," pitched from side to side as it tried to push through the oncoming wind.

The big Egyptian American inspired him, though Crocker tried to hide that. Now he grinned from ear to ear and wagged a thumb at Crocker. Akil was super pleased with himself for hooking up with a pretty young aerographer from Phoenix that afternoon. They'd met while working out in one of the *Roosevelt*'s gyms. And of course he'd regaled them with all the details of how they made out in one of the ship's restrooms after dinner.

Crocker leaned into him and said, "You're sick in the head, you know that?"

"Thanks, boss. I learned everything I know from you."

He wasn't sure what he meant by that. Didn't matter. Glanced at his watch, which read 1949. They were in the Mediterranean, somewhere between the west end of the Libyan coast and the island of Crete. Naval ships had fought battles in these waters during the Trojan War in the twelfth century BC.

He remembered reading about the Turkish pirate Barbarossa, who spread terror throughout the Mediterranean in the early 1500s. In the space of three years, he and his brothers captured as many as fifty-six ships. Later he ousted the leader of what became Tunisia, and used it as a base for his raids on coastal towns in Spain, Sicily, Malta, and mainland Italy. He later became the inspiration for the pirate actor Geoffrey Rush plays in the *Pirates of the Caribbean* series.

Crocker wanted to read more history—not the long-winded diplomatic kind, but featuring real-life action heroes, like his favorite Revolutionary War general, Francis Marion, the Swamp Fox.

"Scarface, you got a ETA for us, or are you keeping that a secret?" Crocker asked via radio.

"We're looking at about twenty-eight minutes, give or take. I'll give you an update when we draw closer."

"Copy."

"Enjoy the ride."

He knew it was going to be hard to keep the helo steady enough for them to land on the *Star Helena*'s deck. According to the intel Smithson had given them, it wasn't a big ship, but apparently carried a cargo of MANPADs, Stinger missiles, and other arms bound for ISIS. Also on board, according to electronic surveillance, was notorious Islamic State arms procurer Abu Omar—the dude they hadn't found in al-Marj.

Smithson said that the NSA had picked up some cell phone chatter related to the upcoming arrival of the *Star Helena* at the Turkish port of Mersin, less than a hundred miles from the Syrian border. In these communications reference was made to sending a delegation to receive "Emir Omar."

Crocker couldn't wait to meet the bastard. If he got a chance, he'd give him a couple kicks in the ass for Rip. Having a teammate disabled or killed was the worst feeling in the world.

Hopefully, the young man was out of surgery now and resting. Crocker didn't want to jinx him.

Instead, he focused on the mission ahead. Speed and surprise would be key. Any resistance from armed militants on the *Star Helena* could present a problem, especially as they were fast-roping down. That's what the second Knighthawk, "Shaggy Two," was for—specifically its M240 machine guns and Hellfire rockets—to provide cover.

Soon as the five SEALs hit the deck, Akil and CT would clear it, while Crocker, Mancini, and Tiny went for the bridge. The object was to overwhelm the crew, take charge of the ship, stop it, inspect the cargo, and get out fast.

Crocker had led dozens of similar missions, but felt anxious about this one. Maybe it had to do with the rough weather, or the sketchy intel. He wasn't sure.

The helo pitched sharply left, then suddenly lost altitude, sending the contents of his supper into his throat.

"What the fuck!" Akil complained over the radio.

"Wind shear," Mancini countered.

"Ten minutes to target," Scarface announced.

"Copy, Scarface. Ten minutes!"

Adrenaline started to surge in Crocker's bloodstream and he did a last check of his weapons and gear.

"Tom?"

It was a few minutes past 0100. He'd been checking Harley parts for sale on eBay, because he couldn't sleep.

"Séverine, is that you?"

Though her voice came through clearly, her face didn't appear on the laptop screen. He wanted to see her face.

"Tom, the wifi in the camp isn't good. How are you?"

"Fine."

"You sure? You don't sound so good."

"I'm a little pissed.... A mission we were on tonight was aborted at the last minute."

"Aborted? What do you mean?" she asked in her charming French accent.

"I mean…canceled. The mission was canceled." Actually it had been called off just as they were getting ready to fast rope onto the deck, because someone in the White House was worried about Russian and Chinese naval ships in the vicinity.

"Where are you now, Tom?"

"I can't tell you. Sorry. But I'm not far from where you are." What Russian and Chinese ships had to do with them intercepting the *Star Helena* was a mystery to Crocker. When he had spoken to Anders and Smithson upon their return to the *Roosevelt* neither of them offered an explanation.

"You mean…Aleppo?" Séverine asked.

"Yeah."

"You can't sleep?"

"No." It angered him, because tonight was their last chance to stop the Greek freighter before it docked in Turkey and unloaded its cargo. Given the Turkish government's cozy relationship with the Islamic State, the weapons on board would soon be on their way to Iraq or Syria, and Abu Omar would fade out of sight.

"Me, either, Tom. I'm in something that they call a pod, which I share with this girl from Georgia. Maybe you can hear her snoring in the background. Last night we had rats."

"We call them pets."

She laughed.

"No, seriously. Smart little critters. Much maligned in reputation. They don't carry diseases and spread rabies, and can actually be trained."

"I'll tell that to Dayna. She hates them. She prays a lot, too. Says Jesus is her one true love and savior."

"Sounds like a lot of fun."

"No, really…I like her. She's a sweet person, a nurse who is planning to go back to school to study epidemiology. That's why they paired her with me."

"You're in Aleppo now?"

"Yes. We're living in a UNSMIS camp on the outskirts. It's considered safe. The food isn't bad. Today we made our first trip into the city, or what's left of the city, to visit one of the hospitals and treat patients suffering from the parasite I told you about."

"That Aleppo evil thing?"

"Yes."

"What's UNSMIS?"

"The United Nations Supervision Mission in Syria. The camp is guarded by soldiers from Norway, France, and the Netherlands. Today's visit was cut short because some hospitals and clinics came under air attack."

"By who?"

"The Assad air force and the Russians. That's what we were told."

"They're bombing hospitals?"

"Yes!"

"What about the cease-fire? I thought there was some kind of cease-fire in place?"

"That's what we heard, too. But the bombing continues."

"So you're leaving? I hope you're leaving."

"The UN has told Assad that we're returning to Erbil unless the bombing ends immediately. The government insists they're only targeting ISIS. But there are no ISIS or other rebels in the city anymore. There is no city. I saw it today.…Everything is in ruins."

"Then you should split."

"Before I go to sleep I wanted to talk to you. You're the only person I know who can understand."

"Understand what, Séverine?"

"Evil, Tom.... You can feel it here. It's like something dark and suffocating that hangs in the air."

"I know the feeling."

"There's so much to do. There's sewage everywhere, garbage, disease, but here's the crazy part: people still live here. It's hard to believe. The people we meet tell us that they want to stay, because this is their home. Meanwhile, their president and his Russian and Iranian friends kill more of them every day. It's genocide. It's impossible. Where do we start when even those who come to try to help are driven away?"

"Séverine, I'm ashamed that the U.S. and other countries have allowed this to happen."

"I don't mean to put this on you, Tom.... I'm sorry...."

"Don't be sorry, Séverine. You've got a beautiful heart. You haven't done anything wrong."

"What do you do when you want to do good, and the evil people in the world won't allow you to?" she asked. "If we're not careful, evil will take over. It's taken over...here."

Sporadic bombing continued in the city of Aleppo. With bombs exploding in the background, Per called the nine-member DWB team together and announced, "If the UN cease-fire inspectors don't give us an all-clear by six p.m., we'll leave. The Assad government and rebel groups promised a secure environment for us to work in, and they haven't provided that."

After what members of the team had seen yesterday—Russian jets firing rockets and dropping bombs, Assad's air force dropping barrel bombs out of helicopters, white-helmeted Syrian Civil Defense workers trying to dig women and children out of the rubble—not a single one of them protested.

Séverine wasn't the only one who'd spent a fitful night of sleep, trying to process horrifying images she'd seen the day before. Rather than passing the day in the camp playing cards, messaging friends on Facebook, and waiting for news from Per, she volunteered to visit a clinic in the largely abandoned western suburbs, which the UN had classified as safe.

It would give them a chance to resupply the clinic with much-needed medical supplies and for Séverine to collect more *cutaneous leishmaniasis* cultures to use in creating a vaccine they could administer if they returned to the city, or were allowed to remain.

Now she sat in the passenger seat of a Mercedes Sprinter with Marku at the wheel and Nabhas and Dayna in back. Escorting them front and rear were two UN jeeps carrying four "military observers" from Norway, who were armed with pistols.

It was a beautiful late-February day with a brilliant blue sky. The temperature hovered in the high sixties.

The area they drove through had once been a prosperous suburb. Now it was completely destroyed. Block after block of bombed-out houses, apartment buildings, and trees with no signs of life aside from an occasional crow or rodent. It's as though a tornado had swept through and the survivors, if there were any, had been blown far away.

As they drove, she tried to imagine what the neighborhood had been like before—children playing, music drifting out of houses, men climbing into cars on their way to work.

Dayna and Nabhas in back were discussing the challenges of being a Muslim woman. Nabhas had recently been working in Kabul, Afghanistan. He was saying, "Now that people are worried about the Taliban returning to power, you see fewer and fewer women on the street without a *burqa* or *chador*."

"What's the difference?" Dayna asked. She'd awoken early to shampoo and style her hair. She wore jeans and a Texas "Aggies" sweatshirt.

"A *burqa* is a shiny garment that fits over the head and covers the entire body with mesh screens for the eyes," Nabhas answered, scratching his scruffy chin. "In Afghanistan, they're usually light blue. The person inside is completely invisible. You can only identify her by her voice."

"How strange...."

"A *chador*, on the other hand, is a big headscarf, usually black, that covers a woman's hair, arms, and butt."

"Why do they wear them?" Dayna asked.

"Some women wear it for cultural reasons, others because the Quran calls for both men and women to cover their bodies."

That, Dayna could understand. Modesty and cultural tradition were things she clung to, too.

Last night, she'd opened up to Séverine and told her she'd always been an ambitious girl, who did well in school and wanted to be liked. She'd let dark influences drift into her life after her parents divorced when she was in seventh grade. Being shuttled back and forth between her mother and father and forced to switch schools made her feel deeply insecure.

Instead of participating in school musicals and playing on the girls' basketball team, Dayna started spending time at the mall and the skateboard park and hanging out with boys. She longed for their approval. Freshman year of high school she started drinking and going to parties. Met a rebellious boy named Raymond who introduced her to drugs and sex. Behaved in ways that felt wrong because she wanted to please him. On her seventeenth birthday, she found out she was pregnant. Afraid to tell her parents, fearing they would disown her and feeling as though she couldn't tell her friends, because she was worried about being expelled from school, she had an abortion. It was horrible.

Afterward, she felt like a stone. Like she was dead inside. She continued going to parties, drinking herself to the point of unconsciousness, and having one-night stands.

Then her father found out about the abortion. He confronted her one night at dinner. It was the most humiliating moment of her life. But instead of scolding her or rejecting her, her father looked at her with tears in his eyes and told her that he loved her.

"That was the first step," she had told Séverine, "toward accepting God into my life."

Despite the enormity of the USS *Theodore Roosevelt,* and the fact that this city on the sea accommodated 3,200 crew members and hundreds of pilots, featured mess halls capable of serving 18,000 meals a day, communication centers, gyms, shooting ranges, banks, stores, game rooms, a library, doctor and dentist offices, and other amenities, Crocker found it confining.

Now that they'd missed the window to detain the HS *Star Helena* and capture Abu Omar, he was anxious to move on. Back to Kurdistan, he hoped, where they could join Colonel Rastan in the fight against the Islamic State.

It still bothered him that Black Cell's work had been interrupted and the town of Qabusiye had been overrun.

Just this morning, he'd communicated with Colonel Rastan via Skype. The battle to liberate western Mosul was under way, Rastan explained, and Black Cell's infiltration and leadership skills were badly needed. Crocker promised to return as soon as he got permission from his boss.

He'd also had a conversation with Jenny, who complained about her boyfriend. They had just moved in together, and already he was trying to control her.

"What do you mean by 'trying to control' you?" Crocker asked. She rarely discussed her personal relationships with him, certainly never one involving a boyfriend.

"You know…"

"No, I don't, sweetheart." His protective instincts rallied. Five years ago, when he caught some sixteen-year-old boy she was dating driving home with her drunk, he'd pulled the kid out of his car and kicked his ass.

"He yells a lot. He wants everything his way."

This time, he decided to take a more considered approach. "Have you explained to him that his behavior bothers you? That any positive relationship is based on mutual respect and compromise?"

"I have, Dad, yes. And he agrees. He's usually kind and reasonable, but sometimes, he gets…like… demanding. Mean…"

Red flags rose in Crocker's head. "Mean…in what way? Does he get physical?"

"No, but he threatens to."

Crocker wanted to say: Put that punk on the line. Instead, he tempered his response. "Don't let him intimidate you, or push you around. It's not easy living with someone from the opposite sex. If you love each other, you'll talk things over and work them out. But if he touches you in an aggressive way, do me a favor and get away from him."

"I will, Dad. I promise."

Despite his own problems with women, Crocker had never been abusive. Ex-wives might have complained that he lavished more attention on the teams than on them. But he'd never raised a hand to them in anger even when he suspected that his ex Holly was having an affair.

Akil appeared in the corridor of the communications center, signaling to Crocker that he was needed. "I've got to go, sweetheart. But I love you. Stay true to yourself. Be strong."

"I love you, too, Dad. Thanks for the advice."

CHAPTER NINETEEN

I have, indeed, no abhorrence of danger,
except in its absolute effect — in terror.
——Edgar Allan Poe

THE AL-HARZAT Children's Clinic occupied a former school auditorium with few windows and basketball hoops on both ends. The wooden floor was stained with blood and lined with cots. The smell of ammonia, sickness, and death filled Séverine's nostrils as they entered that warm, unventilated space.

She was trying to hold herself together. The clinic director, a white-haired man named Azmed Aman, explained that most of the children housed there were healing from severe injuries and amputations. He stopped at the bed of one young girl who was suffering from chronic dysentery and looked like a skeleton. Iodine used to clean mouth sores caused by a vitamin deficiency had dyed her lips purple. Her emaciated right hand was wrapped in gauze to hold an IV in place.

The girl's mother sat beside her, attempting to cool her with a straw fan.

Dayna whispered into Séverine's ear, "How could they let her illness get so bad?"

Séverine shook her head. "First thing…they need to let in some fresh air."

"I agree."

Clearly, the clinic was understaffed. She doubted if any of them had more than rudimentary medical training.

As Nabhas checked the girl's heart rate and other symptoms, Azmed Aman escorted Séverine and Dayna to a section of the room that had been separated by sheets tied to flagpoles. As soon as Séverine saw the four children on beds healing from wounds and showing signs of *cutaneous leishmaniasis,* the thought of asking the director to open the windows flew out of her head. One boy with a missing arm had sores over his nose and cheeks.

"Oh, my God…." Dayna gasped under her breath.

"Be professional," Séverine whispered back.

The two women donned plastic gloves and medical masks, and were preparing to clean the lesions when they heard shouting outside. A heavyset woman with a black scarf over her head hurried up to them and indicated that Séverine and Dayna should follow her.

"Why? What's going on?" Dayna asked.

Over her shoulder, Séverine saw Azmed Aman running toward the front door. Another man in a blue medical tunic had taken Nabhas by the hand and was hurrying in the other direction—to the rear of the clinic where she and Dayna stood.

"What's happening?" Séverine asked in English.

"Some militants…outside. They're hiding us in the basement as a precaution," Nabhas whispered back.

"Militants?"

She heard what she thought were muffled gunshots outside as two medical workers led them down a dark stairway in the far corner. Dayna, at Séverine's side, slipped on one of the cement steps and started to cry.

Nabhas said, "It's okay. We'll be fine. They'll leave us alone."

"I think I hurt my knee."

"Be brave."

Crocker felt anxiety tightening the muscles in his neck, thighs, and stomach as he sat in one of the *Roosevelt*'s secure communication rooms, facing Captain Sutter and Lt. Colonel Barbara Smithson on the large LCD screen. The coffee he sipped from the "Big Stick" mug was bitter.

He felt as though he was in some sort of prison—artificially confined when he was needed elsewhere.

"The good news is, we've got another op for you," Sutter started in his west-Kentucky drawl. "Current thinking says it'll launch tomorrow night."

"What's the bad news?" Crocker wanted to get back to Kurdistan as soon as possible to help Colonel Rastan and be closer to Séverine.

"The bad news? None really, unless you think enjoying the comforts of the *Roosevelt* until then is a negative."

"Why are we waiting until tomorrow night?"

"Because we're looking at another ship takeover," Sutter replied. "Similar-size vessel to the *Star Helena*. Similar cargo, also bound, we believe, to the IS in Syria."

"Fine, sir. But…"

"But…what?"

There was no point arguing that the fight against ISIS had entered a critical stage, and Crocker and his men were needed on the ground. Captain Sutter knew that. Clearly, one way to weaken the enemy was to cut off their supply of weapons.

Smithson cleared her throat. "The target this time is a general cargo ship registered in Antigua and Barbuda called the MCL *Tunis*. A hundred meters long; eighteen wide. Currently berthed at the Benghazi seaport and taking on cargo."

"Got it. Same entry procedure as last time?"

"You'll fast-rope onto the deck. Yes."

"We'll be looking for HVTs?"

"Not this time. Just take over the vessel and inspect the cargo."

"What about the Russian and Chinese naval vessels?"

"Don't be a wise-ass, Crocker. If they become a problem, we'll let you know."

The overhead light didn't work, which made it impossible to see in the small basement room. Screams echoed down the concrete stairs. Now she heard the sound of approaching footsteps.

Séverine's chest tightened and she stumbled across something in the tight space.

Nabhas whispered, "Quiet!"

Dayna sobbed and gasped by her side. She held on to Séverine's arm as Séverine felt along the walls in the dark. A row of metal lockers stood along the back wall. She opened one of them.

It seemed big enough to accommodate one person. She guided Dayna inside. "In here. Lower your head."

"Why?"

"Go on. I'll stand right here. I won't leave without you."

"What about…"

She covered Dayna's mouth with her hand. Closed the locker door. Turned and felt Nabhas's hot breath on her face.

"I'll talk to them.... You hide...."

"Where?"

The footsteps had reached the bottom of the stairs. Someone was turning the handle. She heard a man curse, then boots kicked in the door.

Nabhas said something in Arabic. Without warning a series of gunshots filled the little space like explosions, obliterating all humanity and reason. Blood splattered across Séverine's face, blinding her eyes. She stumbled backward, hit the backs of her legs on something, and flipped over.

One of the men shouted angrily, *"Allahu akbar!"* and fired his weapon. She saw sparks against the dark ceiling and lost consciousness.

Crocker and his men were in the Black Hawk again. This time the night sky was clear and the ocean still. He saw it passing by out the window.

"Fifteen minutes," the Night Stalker pilot said into his earbuds.

"Copy, Scarface."

Time passed like a dream. He saw Séverine's face. She was calling to him. He wanted to reach out and pick her up into his arms.

"You okay, boss?" CT asked beside him.

"Yeah. Why?"

"You seem somewhere else tonight."

"I'm going over the op in my head."

He tried to focus, but was having a hard time. Some other part of his brain was pulling him away. To what? ... Why?

"Ten minutes."

He'd tried reaching her by Skype before they left. She hadn't answered. Now he tried to imagine how their lives could fit together. It seemed easy in some ways; almost impossible in others. She wasn't like any other Frenchwoman he'd ever met. So grounded and practical. He wondered if she was a good cook.

His body moved automatically. He was on his feet, pulling his gloves on. The green light illuminated. He grabbed the rope last. Wrapped his ankles around it, came down smoothly, spotted a man on the bridge leveling an AK. Saw the sparks coming out of the barrel.

Hit the deck and fired.

"Go! Go!"

He was the first up the steps to the left. CT close behind him. Sporadic gunfire echoing off the deck.

He reached the bridge and was greeted by Akil's grinning face. He was holding a small bearded man by the front of his shirt. The man's feet were off the ground.

"Say hello to Orhan."

"Hi, Orhan."

"He's the captain of this piece of shit, and he's Tunisian. And he's admitted that the hold is packed with weapons. He's going to show us where they are, aren't you?"

Akil shook the captain like a puppy and the captain nodded eagerly. Crocker smiled.

What's next?

He felt as though he was needed somewhere. Mancini was already behind the wheel, bringing the vessel to a stop. And Danny Chavez was on comms, messaging the guided missile destroyers USS *Mahan* and USS *Ramage* in the vicinity. CT guarded six crew members who sat with their wrists zip-tied together along the back wall.

Crocker looked out from the bridge to the light chop of the sea. A bowl-shaped moon glowed in the distance. Everything had gone smoothly; but he had an ominous sense that something was wrong.

Séverine dreamt that she was on a wooden swing going back and forth, up and down. The wind tickled her ears. Tears streamed down her cheeks. Scenes from her childhood flashed before her—candles burning atop a birthday cake, a big smile on her grandfather's face, joy in her mother's eyes. She filled her cheeks with air and blew out the candles.

She didn't remember her mother ever being this happy before. She wanted to say something, but a strange guttural sound came out of her mouth instead.

She was in a boat on a silver lake. Her father held a fishing pole and puffed on a pipe. She watched the gray smoke disappear into the air.

The boat started rocking back and forth. She heard a voice calling "Miss…miss…" with a strange foreign accent.

An amorphous shape came into focus. A man's battered, swollen face.

She tried to sit up.

"No, miss.…No. Don't move.…We take you. We carry…Don't move.…"

She recognized Azmed Aman, the director of the clinic, by his white hair. She wanted to ask, *What happened to your face?* because his nose had been broken, and his left eye was swollen shut.

But it was so much easier to close her eyes instead.

Strong hands lifted her. Her face turned hot. Opening her eyes, she blinked into the harsh light. Saw blood splattered across a dirty wall. Glimpsed a body on the floor covered with a piece of canvas. Strands of longish black hair that reminded her of Nabhas's peeked out the top.

A horrible feeling came over her as she remembered—the dark basement room, the men shouting, guns firing, and the awful terror.

"Dayna! Where's Dayna? Where's Nabhas?" she asked frantically.

"Stay still," Azmed Aman warned her. "Don't move. Be calm...."

She was back on the swing, sailing up and down, back and forth, gulping the fresh air.

Something rubbed against her back. She opened her eyes and saw that she was outside the clinic and about to be loaded into an ambulance. One of the UN jeeps that had escorted her, Dayna, and Nabhas sat to her left, riddled with bullet holes. Blood dripped from the driver's seat. She gasped and covered her eyes.

Crocker lay in his bunk on the USS *Theodore Roosevelt,* staring at the ceiling half-asleep when Akil, on the bunk below him, whispered, "Boss....Hey, boss....You awake?"

"I'm trying to sleep. What's up?"

"You better see this."

"What?...If it's some stupid video with cats, I'm gonna kick your ass."

"It's not."

Akil handed up his laptop. On the screen, Crocker read the headline, "Doctors Without Borders Workers Attacked Near Aleppo."

"Oh, shit!" He sat up and read it again. The headline didn't change.

He opened the article from the Associated Press. It reported an attack by ISIS on a clinic in the outskirts of Aleppo. Several local doctors were severely beaten, one DWB worker had been kidnapped, and another killed.

Crocker immediately thought of Séverine. His blood pressure rose precipitously.

"Fuck me!"

He slipped off the bunk, handed the laptop to Akil, and quickly pulled on his pants and shoes.

"Where are you going, boss?" Akil asked.

"I gotta call Sutter."

The clock in the communication room read 0220 hours, and anger coursed through Crocker's head and body as he listened over the secure line.

"Yes, we just became aware of the attack. But we don't have many details."

"What have you heard?" Crocker demanded.

"A group of ISIS militants arrived to inspect a clinic west of Aleppo. Apparently they had heard that Assad's soldiers were being treated there."

"Were they?"

"It turned out to be a false rumor. But when they arrived they found some foreign doctors. They killed one and took a female doctor hostage."

"A female doctor?"

"Yes."

"You know the nationalities of the dead and captured doctors?"

"Nothing has been confirmed yet. But reports from Syria indicate the seized medical worker is an American."

"An American woman?" Crocker asked.

"That's correct."

The news, if true, brought relief and alarm.

"The woman was with Doctors Without Borders? You're sure of that?" Crocker asked.

"U.S. officials haven't been able to confirm that directly. But that's what we're hearing from news reports."

"Do you know if the doctor killed was a man or woman?"

"A man, apparently."

"What was his nationality?"

"We don't know."

"And the people who attacked the clinic were from ISIS?"

"Yes."

The rough garment scratched her skin. Her feet hurt. A bad-smelling person held her by the arm. She stumbled over her own feet.

"Where…am…I?" Her tongue was thick and heavy in her mouth, making it hard to form the words and get them out.

"Where?…Who?"

Half thoughts were all her brain could manage. She tried hard to concentrate; then a voice told her not to bother. "Let go, child. Let go…," it said calmly.

Let go of what?

Her head felt as though it had swollen to the size of a pumpkin. The boat she was in bounced and rocked from side to side. But it wasn't a boat, because they were traveling over something harder than water. And whatever she was riding in moved fast. Cool air reached her nose and lungs, but she still couldn't see.

She caught a whiff of lime-scented cologne. "Dad?"

She pictured his handsome, chiseled face. He waved at her as he pointed a camera. She started to smile, and the image dissolved.

She was being led up a set of stairs. Men around her mumbled in a foreign language. They spit the words "United States" and "American" with disgust. The sounds grew closer and closer until they felt like they were invading her skin.

She felt rough hands on her body. They poked, slapped, kneaded, and pinched her.

"Stop!"

She felt fingers between her legs. A man started laughing. Others joined in.

"No, no!" she protested. "You can't do that!"

Her body and mind were numb. She still couldn't see. *Why? Am I blind? Has someone done something to my eyes?*

It had always been a fear of hers since childhood. She'd had many nightmares of being lost in the woods and turning blind. Her mother told her the best way to chase them from her head was to think of something pleasant—like standing in the kitchen with her mother and grandmother and baking pies for Thanksgiving. Pecan was her favorite.

The pinching continued. Her body turned hot. She wanted to wake from this nightmare, but couldn't.

She hovered at the ceiling, looking down at her body, pale and half naked. Young men with black beards pawed at it and took pictures of it with their phones, like she was a prize pony or a rare animal in a zoo.

Why? she wondered.

She wasn't afraid, but felt a vague sense that something wasn't right, that she should be inhabiting her body, that both her mind and body were in a place they didn't belong, that maybe someone had roofied her drink.

Logan....Logan, I don't feel well....I want to go home.

She imagined she was at a party with her high school boyfriend. The two of them were fooling around on the sofa at a friend's house. She felt him pulling away her bra and ripping off her underwear. "No, Logan. Absolutely not! Not here!"

She was growing desperate. She wanted to push him off, to squirm out from under him, but no part of her responded.

"Logan, stop!"

The slaps came hard and swift from all sides, as though Logan had sprouted multiple arms. She tried to raise her hands to cover herself, but they wouldn't move.

"No....No, please. I'm a good person. I told you....I worship God. I love Jesus!"

She lost control of her bladder.

A man shouted something in a foreign language, and the slaps suddenly stopped. Fears, impressions, and memories flooded her brain. And all of a sudden she was able to focus. This wasn't a friend's house. It was a strange, dark room with strange slogans sprayed on the walls. She wasn't with Logan. She was surrounded by a group of wolflike men with wild, hungry expressions on their faces.

"No, God. Get me out of here!"

She felt their hot breath on her skin and passed out.

CHAPTER TWENTY

The cruelest thing of all is false hope.
—Sister Jude

CROCKER SPENT the rest of the night tossing and turning, unable to quiet his mind enough to sleep. All the time, plotting how he would return to Kurdistan, and from there make his way into Syria to rescue the American, or Séverine, or whoever it was who had been kidnapped.

All of them melded into one in his head. National identity wasn't important. All that mattered was humanitarian workers had been attacked by ISIS thugs. One of them—a female—was in their custody and needed to be freed! No ifs, ands, or buts. No concerns about risks, or how a rescue mission might affect the Russians, Chinese, or anyone else.

Waiting for more news from HQ was like torture. Crocker tried to alleviate his frustration by doing squats, lifts, and running on the treadmill at the gym to the point of exhaustion.

No one had come to alert him, nor had anyone called his cell phone. He hurried back to his room now, past framed photos of former *Roosevelt* commanders, hoping a "go" order from HQ awaited him.

The tiny room was still and empty.

He opened his laptop and logged into the secure server to check his e-mails. Mostly solicitations for vitamins and other crap. His father had sent a photo of him and his new girlfriend standing in front of Mt. Vernon, Crocker's favorite historic site. George Washington had been an inspiration since fourth grade.

The Viber icon pulsed at the bottom of the screen. He clicked on it immediately.

"Yes?"

"Tom?" He recognized the timbre of Séverine's voice.

He wanted to reach through the screen and embrace her. "Séverine, is that you?"

"Tom...."

"Séverine, can you hear me? Are you safe?"

"Yes, Tom. Yes! I'm in Erbil."

A tight knot of tension eased in his chest.

"I heard what happened. Were you there? Are you okay?"

"I wasn't hurt, Tom....But I was there. It was... horrible, horrible, so horrible. I've been busy. I haven't had time to think about it. To process everything, you know. It will take time...."

Years, probably. The psyche was fragile. He'd seen traumatic experiences alter lives forever.

He said, "I understand."

"ISIS shot one of my colleagues right before my eyes. They kidnapped another."

"I'm sorry."

"An American girl. A nurse from Georgia. A sweet girl...That's why I'm calling you."

"Séverine...."

"Her name is Dayna Hood. She's twenty-four years old and as American as can be. Daesh took her. They took her away, Tom. You know what those savages will do?"

"Séverine, listen.... This girl Dayna...she was still alive when they kidnapped her?"

"She was. Yes."

"Do you have any idea where…"

The line suddenly broke up, and the connection went dead. He pounded the little metal desk.

Fuck.

Then he gathered himself and dialed. His three attempts all met with failure. Instead of screaming or punching the wall, he took a deep breath and tried a fourth time.

The connection was made and he heard Séverine's voice. He asked her to remain in Erbil if she could, to gather as much information as possible without putting herself in any jeopardy, and communicate everything she learned to him. She agreed. He was going to do everything he could to meet her there and rescue the girl.

"Do you know when you'll arrive here, Tom?"

"No, but I'll get there. I promise."

"I believe in you, Tom. Believing in you gives me strength."

"We'll do this, Séverine. I know we will!"

Sheikh al-Sufi had spent the last four days in self-imposed confinement in the little room at the back of the Uwais al-Qarni Mosque, mourning the death of his wife Fatima. Tomorrow he would emerge to lead his men.

Tonight he faced another sleepless night of memories, regret, sadness, and anger, and warding off the gargoyle-like figures of the many-eyed man and Ibah, who waited in the corners like vultures.

They waited for him to renounce this life, calling like sirens: "Sheikh....Sheikh, come with us....Give up the struggle, Sheikh....Surrender...."

"Don't you know that I don't want to listen to you?" he asked from his knees.

"You are ready to come with us, Sheikh. You feel this in your heart."

Anguish gripped his soul. Tears spilled from his eyes onto the cold stone floor. "God has a plan for me! God has a plan!"

"There is no plan, Sheikh. There's only death. Your wife's death, your sons' deaths, your friends' deaths. You're next."

"God has a plan!"

"Look at yourself," Ibah snorted, wiping snot from her nose. "Look....Can't you see that you're disgusting, like us. Why would God care about you? God has rejected you. Come with us."

"No. No. No! Go away!"

The many-eyed demon issued a high-pitched laugh that grew louder and hurt his head.

The sheikh covered his ears. "Stop, demon. Stop!...Maybe God has taken everything—my family, my youth, my vanity. But I still have my body, my brain, my will, and my belief."

"All you really have, Sheikh, is bitterness and anger. They are worth nothing to God."

"You're wrong! He has brought me to this condition to reveal his plan. I see it now. It is time for me to surrender to him completely."

The demons laughed and sang together. "You're a fool. Old fool. Fool…."

Al-Sufi clasped his hands in front of him as their voices grew louder and echoed off the walls, repeating over and over, "God, I'm your obedient servant. I heed your words and direction. It has never been my intention to offend you in any way."

The laughing continued. He tried to summon an image of God. But nothing came. Instead he saw the face of Fatima.

She looked at him with sad, disapproving eyes. "Fatima," he said out loud. "My heart is numb. My soul is wounded and in pain."

The demons continued to circle and taunt him.

"Fatima," he prayed out loud. "Fatima, I trust that now you are in the garden of heaven, which is rich with wonders I cannot imagine. I trust that you are there beside the fountain of God with our children, friends, and other family members. I hope that one day I will join you there. First, it is my duty to fulfill the word of God. To lead his believers against the unbelievers and blasphemers. To bring God's will to his earth, whatever the price, whatever the sacrifices, whatever the pain, degradation, and loneliness. Goodbye, my love. I know you will understand."

The sheikh sank on the stone floor and beat his chest as he shouted: "I am ready, God. I am ready. I am ready. I am ready. I am yours…like I never was before!"

His jaw ached from the clenching he'd done all day, waiting for HQ to call. Inaction was driving him crazy.

Daesh had already released a photo of the kidnapped American girl, one of their black death flags in the background, sick fuckers dressed top-of-head-to-toe in black on either side of her holding swords, a terrified, confused look on the poor girl's face.

And ISIS had announced the terms of Dayna Hood's release—immediate removal of all U.S. troops from the Middle East and South Asia, and public withdrawal of U.S. support for Israel. If unmet within thirty-six hours, they promised to lop her head off and post the video on the Internet for all the world to see.

"She will pay the price of all infidels and unbelievers. This is God's will," proclaimed the official announcement.

Crocker had no doubt they would carry out their threat. He also knew that it was U.S. government policy to never give in to the demands of terrorists. That meant the clock was ticking, and down to less than a day and a half.

Now he paced the floor of the video comms room of the USS *Theodore Roosevelt* waiting for Anders and the others to appear on the screen and sketching out a search and rescue plan in his head. CT, Akil, and Mancini occupied chairs behind the central table and manned laptops and phones. All of them were querying friends in the field—military, local, national, or private military contractor—for any shred of information about Dayna Hood.

Tiny Chavez was on a plane back to Virginia Beach, where his wife was scheduled to have a baby any minute. Their second, and he hoped, their first daughter.

Crocker had spoken with Colonel Rastan in Erbil a short time ago. All he had to convey were rumors from his intel people, saying Dayna had been taken to an ISIS stronghold in either west Mosul or Raqqa.

Both cities were relatively close to Aleppo, where she'd been seized.

No one had direct confirmation. Some sources said there was a possibility that she'd been taken into Iraq.

"Get me a solid fix on her location. Work your sources. I'll reimburse you myself if I have to. This is that important," Crocker had said to Rastan.

Now, Anders, Sutter, Smithson, and Crocker's former teammate Davis appeared on the video feed— seated beside each other, glum expressions on their faces.

Crocker couldn't wait for a brief. He said, "If we don't act soon, we might as well pack in everything: the teams, the helos, the aircraft carriers, the one trillion our country spends on defense."

"Watch what you say, Crocker," Sutter warned.

"I agree with Crocker," opined Davis. "What good are we if we can't rescue our own people?"

Crocker wanted to reach out and high-five him through the screen.

"Fuck waiting, and careful," Crocker continued.

"You feel better now that you got that off your chest?" Sutter asked.

"Not really, sir. What's the plan?"

"I'm totally gung-ho about doing something," Smithson added. "But let's not forget that this young woman isn't a U.S. official, and she had to understand the risks she was taking when she went to Syria."

"Screw that."

"Crocker, I don't appreciate your—"

Anders cut her off. "There's no point debating what Ms. Hood did or didn't understand. She's been kidnapped. Since we're not conceding to any Daesh demands, there's a very strong likelihood she'll be executed in a brutal manner, if we don't mount a rescue."

"That's real talk," Crocker agreed.

"We're all professionals, and we know how this works. It's our job to analyze intel from multiple sources, and come up with a plan that we then present to the White House. I suggest we start by answering the fundamentals…who, where, what, and when?"

"The who and when, we know."

"Yes and no," Smithson interjected. "Daesh is a big, unruly organization. We're going to have to ID the particular brigade and brigade commander."

"Yes."

"So what do we know so far?" Sutter asked.

"Not a whole hell of a lot," Smithson answered. "Aleppo and the surrounding area is no longer under Daesh control. So whoever took Ms. Hood was most likely a roving band of some sort. Maybe looters and opportunists. According to the director of the clinic, they were looking for wounded Assad regime soldiers. They found some DWB doctors and nurses instead. They killed one and grabbed another. When they realized that they had an American, they probably sold her off…possibly to a Daesh commander."

"Which one?"

"That we don't know."

"What do we know about the doctor who was killed?" Sutter asked.

"He was a UK citizen whose parents emigrated from Bangladesh. He was unarmed and was apparently trying to defend his colleagues."

"Do we want to get the Brits involved in this?" Smithson asked.

"They've volunteered to help," Anders answered.

"But making any rescue international just makes it more complicated in terms of coordination and approvals, and we don't have much time."

Crocker glanced at his watch. "Thirty-three hours, twenty-five minutes. It's going to take us roughly three hours to fly to Kurdistan, and another several hours to get from Erbil to wherever we're going in Syria."

"We don't even know if the hostage is in Syria, do we?"

"It's 1715 Friday where we are," Crocker continued, "which translates to 1615 in Erbil, Aleppo, Mosul, or Raqqa."

"So?"

"If Daesh stays true to their deadline, the execution will take place at around 0230 Sunday. Any mission we launch we're going to want to do under the cover of night. So we've got a shitload to do before Saturday night."

A tall, handsome man in a khaki uniform ushered Séverine down the hall of Kurdistan's Ministry of the Interior, pointed to a door, and stood shoulders back to stand guard. She adjusted her long skirt and scarf, took a deep breath, and entered.

The size of the room surprised her—a large banquet hall with mirrors along one side, and lit by three enormous crystal chandeliers. At the far end, she made out a little man behind a huge wooden desk. Behind him stood a large red, white, and green flag with a gold sun in the middle, and two aides—a young man and a middle-aged woman with a white blouse and glasses.

The little man beckoned to her. As she crossed the

floor, an antique clock chimed seven times, indicating that it was 7 a.m. local Erbil time, Saturday April 22, less than twenty hours from the deadline.

In halting English, the man behind the desk introduced himself as Ibrahim Bashur, the head of Kurdistan's secret police, known as the Asayish.

Séverine sat in one of the formal chairs, fighting off nervous exhaustion, and passed along greetings from Colonel Nesrin Rastan, who had arranged the meeting. She'd been up all night on the phone with Crocker, Per, and her ex-husband, Alain. In between the calls, she'd squeezed in meetings with Colonel Rastan and other Peshmerga leaders in the lobby of the Rotana Hotel.

All of it was a muddle of warnings and frustration. Per had ordered her back to Istanbul. She and Alain had argued, as they usually did. Crocker had vowed to take matters into his own hands if his superiors didn't act promptly.

All she knew was that despite her efforts, she was no closer to locating Dayna than she had been the day before. Now, as Mr. Bashur cleared his throat, the photo of Dayna in Daesh captivity flashed in her head, causing desperation to spread from the pit of her stomach.

Mr. Bashur—long face, sad eyes, and a small mouth—seemed to have little to offer but sympathy. "At the present time we do not have reliable knowledge of where Ms. Hood is being held. We understand and appreciate your concern. Our resources have to be focused on securing the homeland of our Kurdish people. If we learn anything about Ms. Hood's location, we will pass it on to you and the Americans."

Séverine swallowed to lubricate her very dry

mouth. She chose her words carefully. "Thank you, Mr. Bashur, for taking the time to meet with me. Ms. Hood is a colleague and a friend. I was with her when she was kidnapped. Mr. Bashur, it could have been me."

"Ms. Tessier, I am here to offer my services in any way I can. Before we start, would you like some tea or coffee?"

For a universally feared man, he had a gentle manner.

"No thank you, Mr. Bashur. You are very kind. I want you to know that I'm willing to do anything to help my friend. I have friends in the U.S. military who want to rescue her. But first we have to find out where she is being held."

Mr. Bashur nodded, seeming to weigh each word she said. "I understand. Yes...I can tell you, Ms. Tessier, that Ms. Hood is not in Kurdistan."

"You know this?"

"With certainty, Ms. Tessier. Yes."

"Then where do you think she is?"

"Syria."

"Syria is a big country, Mr. Bashur."

"Yes, and extremely dangerous." He summoned the woman with the glasses and whispered something in her ear. She whispered something back.

"This is Mrs. Bozarsian," Mr. Bashur said, nodding to the woman. "She just reminded me that we have certain friends who operate with us in Syria. They know the militias there, and the different groups. They sell us information. Sixty percent of the time it is reliable. They could be of help, if you are able to come up with the funds."

Séverine sat up. This was the first moment in her

meetings with Colonel Rastan and Kurdish officials that she felt the slightest spark of hope. "Thank you, Mr. Bashur. If you would be so kind as to introduce me to these people, I will find the money to pay them."

"Very well." He turned and nodded to the woman to his right. "If you go with Mrs. Bozarsian, she will take you to meet someone."

"Thank you, Mr. Bashur. I'm extremely grateful."

He stood and offered his hand. "Good luck."

CHAPTER TWENTY-ONE

*Labor to keep alive in your breast that
little spark of celestial fire called conscience.*
— George Washington, *Rules of Civility
and Other Writings*

SEVEN O'CLOCK the morning of the fifth day since Fatima was killed, Sheikh al-Sufi rang the bell beside his desk to summon Yasir Selah.

The commander's chief aide didn't know what to expect when he opened the door to Sheikh al-Sufi's room. Frankincense and myrrh incense wafted out, indicating that the sheikh had cleansed the space of spirits. The room stood in order, and the sheikh seemed more energized and better groomed than he had been in months—his silver and black beard clipped to a sharp point, his long hair slicked back, his eyes clear and sharp.

"I have completed my *Isra,* Yasir," he said, meaning his *night journey.* "Now is the time for me to resume my duties and lead our forces to victory."

"Yes, Sheikh. God in his benevolence has willed it."

Sheikh al-Sufi grinned and puffed out his chest. Even his teeth weren't bothering him this morning. "Take me to see my lieutenants."

Yasir Selah bowed his head. "Yes, Sheikh. But first I bring good news. Commander Saddam Jamal has come to visit and is waiting in the command center."

Sheikh al-Sufi paused. A visit from his rival surprised him. Whether it augured a bullet in the head or something more pleasant, he was ready to accept his fate without fear. Everything had been predestined, and the will of God was the will of God.

Séverine had been waiting in the small, windowless room for more than an hour. She'd consumed two cups of green tea and a small plate of dates and crackers. Now she wondered how much longer she could sit there without falling asleep, and whether she should go look for Mrs. Bozarsian or give up on her altogether.

Time was her most precious commodity even as she stood on the precipice of nervous exhaustion. She'd wasted so much of it on meaningless pursuits and worries. Her concerns were real now.

Today, or one day soon, Nabhas would be buried by his parents somewhere in England. She had no additional information to share with Crocker. Nothing that brought her closer to finding Dayna and rescuing her. She prayed for stamina and luck, and her friends Dayna and Nabhas.

Séverine wasn't sure if she'd actually heard or had imagined the knock on the door. Then Mrs. Bozarsian stuck her head in.

"He's here," she announced.

"Who?"

"Asso Bekas.... You ready to see him?"

"Yes. Yes."

She stood and straightened her black skirt. A

smartly dressed, diminutive young man entered and offered his hand. "Ms. Tessier. It's a pleasure to meet you." He spoke perfect English. "My name is Asso Bekas."

As they sat, she couldn't help feeling disappointed. He seemed like a soft, slightly pudgy hotel clerk—not the rough, wily operator she had expected.

"I'm looking for information about my friend, Dayna Hood," said Séverine. "Mr. Bashur said you might be able to assist me."

Asso Bekas nodded. Above his upper lip she made out the hint of a mustache. "I am Syrian, Ms. Tessier. I live in Erbil now. But I have many friends who are in the fight."

"On which side?"

"Most of them are anti-Assad. We hate Assad. But, you see, there are many groups. They have different motives and goals. I can explain, if you want me to."

"That's not necessary now."

"Sometimes these groups fight against one another; sometimes they cooperate. It's a confusing situation. It's very hard for people on the outside to understand."

"Do any of your friends know where Ms. Hood is being held?" Séverine asked.

He furrowed his forehead with concern. "If I had this information of course I would tell you. I don't, but I think we can find out. In a situation like this, communication is difficult. The closer we get to the front, the more we can talk directly to the people who know what is going on."

He spoke with confidence.

"What would you suggest that I do?"

"If you really want to find Ms. Hood, we need to

enter Syria," Asso answered. "And we need to bring cash to pay for information."

"U.S. dollars?"

"Dollars are best."

She wondered if he was a con man, taking advantage of a desperate situation. "How much?"

"That depends on who we meet and what you want from them. If we're asking people to take risks, they'll want to be paid more. That's the way it works."

"I understand." She reminded herself that Mr. Bashur, the head of the Asayish, had vouched for this young man. "I need to find out where Ms. Hood is being held, the exact location—the neighborhood, the building, the address, the room, if possible. And I need to do this quickly."

Asso rubbed his round chin as he considered. "Maybe we're going to need as much as five or six thousand. Ten is better. Can you get the money in cash?"

"I think so." She had about three thousand in her checking account, but had an idea of where she could get the rest.

"You have it with you now?"

"No. I have to call someone and have him wire it to me. Ten thousand?"

"Yes. Two and a half thousand for my time and expenses. You can pay me one up front, and the rest when we return. In cash, please."

He seemed to have a plan. She wondered if Mr. Bashur had sanctioned it.

"We? You keep saying 'we,'" pointed out Séverine.

"Yes, Ms. Tessier. You have to come with me. We can say you are my wife or my girlfriend, and that we are traveling to the coast to see my family for my mother's birthday."

"When?"

"As soon as possible. I suggest you dye your hair black. The way you're dressed is fine. We should leave right away if the information we get is going to be of any use."

"Of course...." She considered everything she had to do—secure the money, call Crocker, let Colonel Rastan know where she was going. "Do I need to take anything?"

"A change of clothes, a toothbrush, and the cash. The money is the most important."

"I understand."

"I should remind you that it's Saturday, Ms. Tessier. If you're expecting to get the approvals and make a wire transfer, the banks close at noon. I have a cousin who works at the Kurdistan International Bank. He can facilitate everything."

Sheikh al-Sufi's special guards, dressed in black, escorted him from the mosque to the command center down the street. As he walked, he reminded himself that it was the tenth day of Rajab, according to the lunar calendar, and ten was a number of completion.

He planned to enter the conference room, where Commander Saddam Jamal waited, alone. This would let Jamal know that he wasn't afraid.

A saying he had learned in madrasa entered his head: *The command of Allah is a decree determined. He has appointed the night for resting and the sun and moon for reckoning.*

The sun burned in the sky. Whatever it was that Jamal wanted didn't matter. He would accept God's fate like a soldier. Let each individual moment unfold like he had as a child discovering the world for the first time, walking hand in hand with his mother. The sunlight, red dust, wind in his face, passing donkeys and cars.

Sheikh al-Sufi climbed the concrete steps and entered through the sandbagged door. Odors of charcoal and urine hit his nostrils.

Yasir Selah, a black prayer cap covering his shaved head, pointed to a room at the end of the hall. Exhausted-looking soldiers stood at attention.

"God be with you," the sheikh said.

"God be with you, Sheikh."

Two long fluorescent bulbs buzzed from the ceiling and lit the rectangular room. Commander Saddam Jamal rose to his full height of six-feet-two in the shadows at the far side of the table. When Jamal's face reached the light, Sheikh al-Sufi saw a wry smile playing on his full lips. His hennaed beard and shoulder-length hair glistened.

The two commanders embraced, and al-Sufi noted that Jamal reeked of orange cologne.

"Welcome, my brother. Peace be with you."

"Peace be with you, too, my brother."

Saddam Jamal clasped his hands in front of his heart and offered condolences to Sheikh al-Sufi for his wife's death. The two men prayed together.

Everything seemed to unfold the right way. Everything in its place except for the almost gleeful glint in Jamal's eye. He reminded the sheikh of a fox.

Why is he so pleased with himself? Does he know he's going to arrest me?

Also seated at the table were six of Commander Jamal's lieutenants, who had stood when al-Sufi had entered; they remained on their feet.

"Sit, please," al-Sufi said. "Let's talk about the state

of things. I haven't heard any news in five days, while I was in my *Isra*."

Jamal pointed to the chair at the head of the table.

"Please, Commander, take your rightful place. We are all grateful to Allah that you have returned."

"Inshallah."

"God has willed it," said Saddam Jamal. "He has also instructed us to take a life for a life, an eye for an eye, a nose for a nose, an ear for an ear, a tooth for a tooth, and wounds equal for equal."

"This is all true," al-Sufi responded, settling into the wooden chair. "God does not allow us to inflict greater injuries on the wrongdoer than he has caused."

"Sheikh, soon I will bring you news from the battlefield of Mosul, where our followers fight bravely to resist the infidels. First I have something special to show you."

Sheikh al-Sufi's heart missed a beat. He held his breath.

"It is a gift that has come to us from God...." Saddam Jamal clasped his hands in front of his heart and bowed his head. "I know that I am not as devout as you are, my brother, but I see this gift as a form of reparation for the death of your wife."

"A gift?"

"Reports from Kirkuk tell us that her body was destroyed by an American bomb. According to the *Hadith,* the instruments of retaliation for carrying out the will of Allah must be sharp and sterile." The *Hadith* were the reports of Mohammad's words and actions outside of the Quran.

Commander Jamal clapped his hands twice. The sheikh knew him as a man of dramatic gestures, but was now completely confused.

All heads at the table turned to the door. Two black-clad militants entered, escorting a short woman covered in a black *burqa*.

"What is this?" Sheikh al-Sufi asked. He imagined they had brought a relative, maybe a cousin, to look after him in his time of grief. But who? And what did this have to do with retribution?

Commander Jamal nodded to the two militants, who removed the *burqa*. Underneath stood a pale woman with light hair, wearing a sweatshirt and jeans. Her eyes were covered with a black blindfold, her wrists were tied behind her back, and tape covered her mouth.

Sheikh al-Sufi squinted at the strange vision. A light-haired woman? He suspected a joke, or some form of blasphemy.

"She's an American, Sheikh al-Sufi," said Saddam Jamal. "Our men captured her near Aleppo two days ago. She is fated to die by your hand tonight. It is God's will. It is God's will. It is God's will...."

Crocker looked at his watch. It was 0834 on the USS *Theodore Roosevelt,* 0734 in Kurdistan and Syria, and 1334 in DC. His nerves were raw from waiting and his quick, jagged mental rhythm was at odds with the gentle rocking of the ship.

He knew that if he didn't calm down he would explode. The people he wanted to hear from were either Séverine or Colonel Rastan. The grim triad of Sutter, Anders, and Smithson beckoned to him from the giant screen instead.

"Crocker?"

He swallowed the bile in his mouth. He was the sole occupant of the secure conference room this time.

Akil, Mancini, and CT were back in their cabins packing their gear, getting ready to deploy, even though they lacked orders.

The back of Crocker's head was inflamed from nervous scratching.

He swallowed hard, sat tall. "What's the latest? What have you got?"

Anders started.

Crocker wanted to dislike him, but couldn't. As always, the CIA officer was reasonable and as forthright as he could be. "Not a lot. Some chatter referring to Ms. Hood coming out of Raqqa, al-Bab, Mosul, and Kirkuk. We figure the Kirkuk chatter is linked to Daesh's propaganda arm, which is located there."

"Where's al-Bab?"

"It's an ISIS-occupied town about forty klicks north of Aleppo, not far from where Ms. Hood was taken."

"What's your best thinking on where she is now?" Crocker asked, his jaw tightening, the nerves in his forearm acting up.

"We believe she's somewhere between Aleppo and Raqqa. That's roughly 160 kilometers of territory. We base that on the little intel we've received and the work of our analysts, who figure that Daesh has no reason to move her far from where they seized her, given that much of the land around both cities is contested."

"Sounds about right." The bitter reality of the situation didn't sit well in his stomach.

"That's all we've got. The Asayish, Turkish, and Jordanian intelligence have nothing specific, either. We've even appealed to the Russians, who might be privy to information from the Iranians because some

Hezbollah militias are active in the area. But that's a long shot."

"I don't want to depend on them."

"No," Smithson echoed.

It sounded as though they were already preparing themselves for Ms. Hood's execution.

"Even if you deploy, it will be like looking for a needle in a very wide haystack," Anders continued. "We think they're keeping her in an underground bunker or some other highly secure location."

"Is there any possibility of a prisoner exchange of some sort?" asked Crocker.

"You know our policy is never, under any circumstances, to negotiate with terrorists."

A long pause followed.

Finally, Crocker groaned. "I'm not going to sit on my hands while the girl is killed. Me and my men are ready. We're going to deploy!"

"Not without orders," Captain Sutter responded, strongly.

"With orders or without orders, sir. We'll commandeer a plane from the flight deck if we have to," said Crocker. "We're going to Syria!"

"The fuck you are!"

Anders cut in. "Captain, Crocker…Let's all take a deep breath.…I don't see a problem with flying Crocker and his men to Erbil to be in theater…in case we uncover some specific intel at the last minute."

"Pride and stupidity," Sutter protested.

"Think about it."

"I see where this is going."

"I, personally, don't have a problem with that contingency," offered Anders.

"Neither do I," Smithson added.

"Captain?"

Sutter sighed. "All right. Crocker…let's get you and your men to Erbil, just in case."

Crocker felt slightly relieved. At least they'd be moving. "We're packed and ready, sir."

"All right. I'll talk to the ship's flight coordinator now."

"Tell him it's urgent."

"I know what to say. Thanks."

CHAPTER TWENTY-TWO

The superior man acts before he speaks,
and afterwards speaks according to his action.

—Confucius

SÉVERINE HAD spent thirty minutes haggling with her ex-husband, reminding him that she hadn't asked for a penny from him during their divorce. Now she needed help—at least $8,500 to add to the $3,000 and change she had in her bank account in France. That would give her around $11,500—$10,000 for bribes and information, and $1,000 to pay Asso up front. She wasn't thinking about the remaining $1,000 she would owe him, which in her current state of exhaustion was understandable.

She'd never had much interest in financial and banking matters, which Alain pointed out, explaining that the amount she had in her bank account in Paris was irrelevant because of the time and fees that would be required to transfer it to Kurdistan.

Séverine suspected that was true, but didn't care. She needed money, and threatened to call Alain's mother, Madame Delage, if he didn't get it to her immediately. That's when Alain offered to wire $11,500 to the account she had set up at the Kurdistan

International Bank, with the promise that she pay back the $3,000 she had in Paris when she returned.

"What I really think you need to do is come home and see a psychiatrist," he said before hanging up. "You need professional help."

Because of local bank policy, Séverine wasn't able to draw cash from a new account. So Asso got his cousin who worked at the bank to forward the cash in return for a $1,000 fee. He also arranged for the money to be converted into dollars, and provided a locked briefcase for Séverine to carry it in.

Everything seemed to be working out. Now her Canadian DWB friend Kat was applying a box of dark-brown Revlon ColorSilk to her hair. She stood naked on plastic garbage bags in the bathroom of the DWB dormitory in downtown Erbil, shivering.

"Why are you doing this?" Kat asked.

Séverine lied. "For my boyfriend. I'm going to meet his parents."

"Where?"

"They're Syrian. They're meeting us at a town on the border. It's complicated."

"You're going to Syria. It's not safe."

"My boyfriend says it is."

"I'm not sure I believe you. You sure this has nothing to do with Dayna Hood?"

Séverine covered her face with her hands. She didn't want to mislead her friend further, but she couldn't be dissuaded, either. And she still had a lot to do, including reaching out to residents of Raqqa through the "Raqqa Is Being Slaughtered Silently" Facebook page—something that had been suggested by Mrs. Bozarsian as a possible way to find out if her friend was being held there.

Kat kneaded her shoulders and whispered in her ear. "I'm sorry, Séverine. I don't mean to stress you out."

While she waited for the dye to set, she tried to reach Crocker via Skype and Viber. He didn't answer. Asso called from his car.

"It's almost noon. We have to get moving. It's a very long drive."

"Ten minutes."

"I'm downstairs in the blue Toyota Corolla. Make sure you wear your *shayla*."

The Gulfstream IV Crocker, Akil, Mancini, and CT rode in passed over the south coast of the island of Crete, which according to Greek mythology had been the birthplace of Zeus—god of the sky and thunder, ruler of the Olympian gods.

"Crete is where Athenian boys and girls were sent to be devoured by the half-man, half-bull monster Minotaur," Mancini said from the seat across the aisle.

Crocker had other concerns on his mind. "That's great, professor."

"Until the warrior-hero Theseus entered the labyrinth to rescue them and slay the beast with his sword. Kind of like what we're gonna do, right, boss?"

"I hope so. Some things don't change, right?"

"Zeus's mother, Rhea, hid baby Zeus in a cave on the island because his father had a thing about swallowing his children. When Zeus became a man, he forced his father to disgorge his brothers Poseidon and Hades. Generous guy, Zeus....He shared the world with them. Gave Poseidon dominion of the seas and Hades the underworld of the dead."

"Thanks for the lecture."

"Any time, any subject."

Crocker sat next to Akil, who opened a digital map of Syria on his laptop.

"I guess we should assume the girl's somewhere between Aleppo and Raqqa," Akil said.

"Her name's Dayna Hood."

"I know her name. I've seen her photos, too."

"Why the hell is the map taking so long to load?"

"You gotta chill, boss."

"Don't tell me what to do."

"All right....Here's Aleppo. Here's Raqqa," Akil said, pointing at the map on the screen. "If we infil by road, we're looking at around seven hours of travel time from Erbil."

"Seven hours! Why so long?"

"We have to cover 372 kilometers, or 231 miles, which doesn't take into account the shit conditions of some of the roads and various roadblocks. You know we're gonna run into militia checkpoints once we enter Syria."

"Right," Crocker said, remembering the close calls with various militia members two years ago as they drove from Aleppo to Turkey—experiences he'd rather avoid repeating, if possible. "The 372 kilometers—is that to Raqqa or Aleppo?"

"Raqqa," Akil answered. "Aleppo is another 160 klicks west."

The Gulfstream hit an air pocket and bounced. Didn't faze either one of them. "Looks like we're gonna need a helicopter or two," said Crocker.

"Raqqa is on the Euphrates River. Maybe we parachute someplace east or west of the city and infil the city by boat." Akil pointed to the patch of green and blue on the map that snaked northwest.

"You know which militia group controls the territory east and south?"

"Last I heard Daesh occupied most of it. Syrian armed forces and the Russians and Iranian militia groups are pressing them from the west. The SDF have control of a little piece of land near the Tabqa Dam...here."

Akil pointed to a spot along the Euphrates between Aleppo and Raqqa.

"The SDF?" asked Crocker.

"Syrian Democratic Forces," Akil answered. "A coalition of Kurdish militia groups—the YPG, YPJ, Kurdish antiterror units, and Baggara tribesmen."

He knew the YPG, and had heard of the YPJ, which were Kurdish female militia units, but the Baggara were new to him.

"They're a tribe of cattle herders that occupy villages throughout northern Syria and into Iraq," Akil explained. "They're Arabs who oppose ISIS."

"Why?"

"Hell if I know."

"I'll huddle with Rastan soon as we land."

"He's in Erbil?" asked Akil.

"I hope so."

The bigger issue on both of their minds was the exact location of Dayna Hood. Without that, there would be no mission to rescue her.

Crocker checked his watch. "We've got about twelve hours...."

"Plenty of time," Akil shot back.

"No fucking time to joke around."

"We're gonna find her, boss. Relax."

*　　*　　*

Séverine tucked the dark-blue *shayla* under the shoulder of her jacket to hide her wet hair, and then swallowed two Percodan with a gulp of water. Her lower back and neck had been killing her since the incident at the clinic two days ago. The Indian doctor who examined her in Erbil and prescribed the Percodan told her the pain was the result of severe compression of the muscles caused by trauma and tension, and advised that she have an MRI to see if there was any structural damage to the vertebrae.

That was the last thing on her mind now. All she could think about was who and what they would encounter on the road to Syria, and if Asso Bekas, seated beside her, would deliver on his promise, or betray her in some way.

It was a chance she had to take. She knew she wouldn't be able to live with herself if Dayna was executed and she hadn't done everything she could think of to prevent it.

Beyond that she worried that she hadn't heard from Crocker in hours. She prayed he was on his way to Kurdistan, and the CIA was either negotiating a secret deal for Dayna's release, or had a clear fix on her location.

She'd brought two laptops, her own and one borrowed from Kat, her cell phone, and a satellite phone lent by the DWB office in Erbil.

Via her own laptop she had posted a message on the "Raqqa Is Being Slaughtered Silently" Facebook page before they left, saying that she was a colleague of Dayna Hood's from Doctors Without Borders and pleading for help in finding her. So far she had received thirty-two messages of sympathy, and requests from two people to communicate with her via Facebook Messenger.

Asso warned her they could be ISIS trolls. Despite that she accepted their requests. One called himself Mohammad, the other went by BFOR. She lost cell phone and Internet coverage as they left the outskirts of Erbil heading west.

"Merde."

"What's wrong?" Asso asked.

"No coverage."

"This isn't France."

You can only control what you can control, she reminded herself. It was one of the things she'd learned during her study of Buddhism at the Sorbonne. Now she composed a list of things she could control in her head:

My levels of exertion and honesty
How well I prepare
How I act on my feelings
How I interpret situations
Whether to give people the benefit of the doubt
Whether to think negative or positive thoughts
The time I spend worrying

Asso, beside her, hummed to himself. She thought he looked like an engineering student, dressed in new jeans, a blue oxford shirt and sweater, a black leather jacket, and round, wire-rimmed glasses. He had impressed her with the way he'd coolly separated five hundred dollars, put it in the briefcase, and hid the rest of the money inside the spare tire in the trunk.

He turned to her and half-smiled. "You okay?"

"What do you do when you're not working with the Asayish?"

"I buy used cars in Germany and sell them for a profit in Erbil."

"How do you get them there?" she asked.

"I drive them through Greece and Turkey."

"You do that yourself?"

"Sometimes, yes."

"You're enterprising," she said.

"Many of us Kurds are. We have to be."

"I thought you said you were from Syria."

"Many Kurdish people live in Syria, you know. I'm from a city called Latakia on the Mediterranean Sea. The largest port in Syria. It was where some of the most violent protests against the Assad government took place in March 2011. The regime cracked down, arresting Sunnis, Christians, Armenians, and Kurds. Now it's a peaceful sea resort. When you're there you can't believe there's a war going on...."

The Percodan had taken effect and was making her sleepy. She closed her eyes.

Major Fendo Jahani, a Peshmerga officer and aide to Colonel Rastan, and a middle-aged CIA officer named Baldwin "Bones" Doyle greeted the SEALs on the tarmac of Erbil Airbase as U.S. and UK jets taxied in the background. Bones was a tall, balding man with a slight paunch. He looked like he'd slept in his pants, shirt, and sweater.

"Let's talk inside," he said.

Crocker and his team followed them into a room with green walls at the back of the newly constructed concrete terminal. Armed soldiers guarded the door.

"Colonel Rastan sends his regards," Major Jahani announced. He cut a sharp contrast to Doyle—new camouflage fatigues, a maroon ascot around his neck, and a matching beret worn at an angle. Good-looking with black hair and a strong jaw. "He's detained in Mosul. He told me to assist you in any way we can."

Crocker was disappointed that Rastan wasn't there when he needed him. Instead of dwelling on that he asked the question foremost on his mind. "What new intel have you developed on Ms. Hood?" He and his men looked like members of a rowdy motorcycle gang with tats, beards, and long hair.

"Well, sir—"

Doyle cut Major Jahani off. "Not much." He had a seen-it-all, no-BS manner. By no means the usual tight-lipped CIA case officer you encountered in the field. "Same worthless crap from the NSA. Rumors, but zero specifics. Fucking useless, if you ask me."

Crocker's stomach started churning. "We've got ten hours until the deadline. Ten hours!"

"We know that," Bones Doyle countered out of the side of his mouth. "Don't expect anything to change."

"What's that mean?"

"Chief Warrant, it means even if we get something from one of our sources, there's not gonna be time to confirm the information to the satisfaction of the suits in Washington, which means zero percent chance the White House approves a rescue mission in time."

"Call me Crocker."

"Crocker...I don't think I have to tell you why."

"No, you don't."

"They're gonna hope the Daesh savages don't cut Ms. Hood's head off because they're afraid that will piss off the big, bad United States and we'll bomb the whole place into oblivion. But Daesh will execute her exactly for that reason. And tomorrow the president and members of Congress will express their outrage, and approve more aid to the anti-ISIS rebels, and then they'll all return to Chevy Chase and Fairfax to drink their cocktails, and watch mindless shit on TV, and that'll be that."

Crocker considered Doyle's blunt assessment, and concluded it was spot-on.

"You see the plea from Ms. Hood's family?" Doyle asked.

"No."

"Brought tears to my eyes, and I don't cry."

An aide in civilian clothes hurried in and handed Crocker a phone. "Sir, your commander."

"Crocker?" It was Captain Sutter at ST-6 HQ.

"Yes, Captain. We just touched down in Erbil."

"I'm calling to tell you that we're working on some things intel-wise and to remind you that we can't make any moves without executive approval."

Crocker knew that already. "What are you working on?"

"We're looking at some links to Sheikh Abu Samir al-Sufi, a.k.a. the Viper. We're trying to confirm them now."

"What sort of links?"

"The possibility that he's the commander holding Ms. Hood. Nothing confirmed, but the NSA has picked up a couple interesting things."

"Makes sense. He's the chief Daesh commander in that area of Syria, isn't he? And didn't one of his wives die recently as a result of a U.S. air strike?"

"That's unconfirmed."

"Doesn't matter if it's confirmed or not, if you're looking at the situation from his point of view," countered Crocker. It was a skill he was still developing—seeing things from the other person's perspective—and one that he continued to put more stock in.

"Listen, Crocker…You're to stay in Erbil and be ready to deploy only on orders. Understood?"

"Understood." Another part of him was thinking, *fuck that*.

"You need anything, talk to Colonel Connelly." Connelly was the Air Force colonel in charge of the Erbil base.

"I will, sir. Thanks."

Crocker handed the phone back to the Peshmerga aide and returned to the confab in the middle of the room. Major Jahani and Doyle stood with the members of the Black Cell team—a scruffy lot all dressed in civilian clothes, duffels packed with gear at their feet.

He overheard Mancini say, "She's a young woman. No goddamn way we're sitting here with our fingers up our butts." It made him feel proud.

Doyle crushed a Camel with the heel of his boot and lit another. Frowned and looked up at Crocker. "This bother you?" he asked, pointing to the cigarette.

Crocker shook his head.

"Anything new?" Akil asked, scratching his grizzled chin.

"Nothing specific on the girl's location. She might be in Sheikh al-Sufi's custody. We're not to deploy until we get an okay from the White House."

Mancini groaned. "I got kids of my own, and a conscience to live with."

CT said, "I gotta wife I gotta answer to. I don't do something to help that girl, she'll kick my ass."

All eyes turned to Crocker. "No wife, but I'm going in no matter what DC says."

Akil gave a thumbs-up. "Make that four!"

CHAPTER TWENTY-THREE

Any fool can learn from his mistakes. The
wise man learns from the mistakes of others.
—Otto von Bismarck

SHEIKH AL-SUFI stood at the metal rail looking down at the young American girl praying by the window. The way the afternoon sunlight glanced across the pale skin of her face and her blond hair stood out against the black of the *hijab* made her look like an angel.

Her appearance reminded him of the pretty schoolgirls he'd seen during the months he'd spent training in North Carolina. Before they became women, they were innocent and friendly. In their teenage years they turned immodest, unchaste, and vain. They imagined their role was to make men weak.

The American girl confused him. Parts of him wanted to hate her, befriend her, and take her into his bed.

The Quran said, "Good women are obedient. They guard their unseen parts because God has guarded them." It instructed men: "As for those wives from whom you fear arrogance, admonish them first; and if they persist, forsake them in bed; and finally, strike them."

Though this girl was an unbeliever, she seemed to have a good soul. He'd heard she'd come to Syria to help heal the sick and wounded.

Al-Sufi wanted to approach her, but was wary. She could be a demon who would beguile him with her youth and beauty. Since her arrival yesterday, Ibah and the many-eyed monster hadn't appeared.

Seeing how her smooth skin glowed in the light, he wondered what it would be like to take her into his bed. If he truly wanted this, it would be okay. As the divine verses said, "Women are your fields, go, then, into your fields hence you please."

But did he? Maybe sleeping with her would please him too much, and lure him into an impure place, and, therefore, weaken him before the eyes of his men and Allah.

As he continued to stare at her, he wondered if there was another way. Maybe he could give her the opportunity to embrace the Faith, and after that decide to take her for his wife.

But even that would come with risks. And he'd been raised to distrust beauty. For all he knew, she was the most deceitful kind of demon—the kind that appeared as an angel, but was really born of fire and not from light, and refused to bow before Allah.

A local man in a white tunic brought tea and peanut butter sandwiches and set them in the center of the table. Through the window to his right, Crocker saw a big white praying mantis–like RAF MQ-9 Reaper drone being refueled and wondered where it was going next. Doyle fired up the black laptop he carried under his arm.

"This is the Viper's stronghold," he said, pointing at

a map on the screen. "This strip of land along the Euphrates River. Extends from the outskirts of Aleppo on the northwest, through Raqqa, and all the way southeast."

"How much land we talking about?" asked Mancini.

"Twenty thousand square miles, give or take. Other IS commanders rule territory north of Damascus, including the city of Palmyra, parts of Kurdistan, and northern Iraq."

"That's a whole hell of a lot." Crocker exchanged looks with the rest of his men.

"Even if we knew for sure that Ms. Hood is in the Viper's custody, we'd still be looking at a massive challenge to find her."

"I get it."

"What I'll do, which the suits in DC won't," Doyle continued, "is trust my powers of deduction. I'm no Sherlock Holmes, and I'll probably get canned for this, but here goes…"

Crocker leaned in closer.

"The Viper's stronghold is Raqqa. He's got complete control of the city and anywhere between fifteen thousand and thirty thousand militants protecting him. They're heavily armed and deeply dug in. So if I'm wearing his shoes, that's where I am now."

"Agree."

"Also, Raqqa is where Daesh has its propaganda people, TV cameras, satellite feeds, and all that technical shit. In other words, it's a perfect place to stage a public execution."

"Good point…."

"By the way, I looked it up, and ISIS has never publicly executed an American woman," Mancini added. "This would be the first time."

"True," Doyle countered, "but they've been taking it on the chin in Mosul and other places, and need some way to strike back at us and rally their troops."

"So you're betting they go ahead with the execution?"

"Hell, they've issued a public statement. They can't back down now."

"You agree, Major?" Crocker asked, turning to Major Jahani.

"I do."

The situation seemed dicey all around.

Crocker said, "We can't take a chance that they'll change their minds."

"No."

"But…what do we do? Where do we deploy?"

Doyle cleared his throat and pointed to a spot on the computer map. "A few days ago we gained a stronghold here…around the Tabqa Dam, which is about fifty kilometers southwest of Raqqa and along the Euphrates River. We did it as part of a strategic plan to cut off the city of Raqqa and take it before the Russians, Assad's forces, and the Iranians do."

"Who's we?" Crocker asked.

"U.S. Special Operations—a combination of Marine Recon and Special Forces—and various Kurd militias. It's now being held by the SDF. Their units are made up of militiamen equipped and trained by us, and led by a guy named Commander Kassim. Not my favorite person. Spends too much time flapping his lips on YouTube in my opinion. But he's there now and he's what we've got."

"Will he cooperate?" asked Mancini.

"If he doesn't, we'll push him aside."

Crocker slapped the table. "Then let's get shaking.

I'm gonna need a couple of Black Hawks, weapons, ammo…"

"When, sir?" Major Jahani asked.

"Now! We leave as soon as it turns dark."

Asso had taken Route 1, to Route 2, to the M4 highway in order to skirt the Turkish border and to stay within the Kurdish area of the region of Rojava and Northern Syria. Along the way, they'd encountered windstorms and SDF checkpoints, but found almost no cell phone and wifi service.

The ride had been long and uneventful so far—six hours over two-lane asphalt and dirt roads and mostly flat parched land. Séverine felt disoriented and sick to her stomach. She couldn't tell if it was a result of the tension, the continued pain from her back, neck, and shoulder, or the Percodan.

Now as they entered the town of Al-Hasakah, she saw that she had a couple bars of reception on her phone and sat up.

"Look," she said, pointing to her cell phone as they rolled into the city—a sunbaked mud grid, home to roughly two hundred thousand people—that boasted more than forty mosques, eight major Christian churches, and a large soccer stadium.

"Careful with that. Daesh monitors all cell and wifi activity in the area."

Asso explained that Al-Hasakah had been the scene of fierce fighting between Syrian Armed Forces, the al-Qaeda allied militia group Al-Nusra, and the Kurdish YPGs. During the summer of 2015, the town had been subsumed as part of the ISIS caliphate. A year later, Kurdish militias coordinated by the Asayish drove ISIS out.

Subsequently, Syrian armed forces had launched a brutal air attack against Kurds controlling the city. In August 2016, Syrian government forces withdrew and ceded control to the Kurdish Federation of Northern Syria—Rojava under a cease-fire brokered by Russia. The new governing council currently ruled under a Charter of the Social Contract that guaranteed all residents gender equality and freedom of religion.

As Asso slowed at a checkpoint flying a yellow and red Kurdish Federation flag, Séverine opened Facebook Messenger and saw that she had a message from the guy who called himself Mohammad, who had contacted her through the "Raqqa Is Being Slaughtered Silently" Facebook page.

She waited until Asso stepped out of the car to confer with the soldiers at the barricade to read it. The message said: "I am a student. My mother and sisters are trapped in Raqqa. I'm in a town nearby. What is going on there is a human rights nightmare. Maybe we can help each other. We are all human beings."

Despite Asso's warning, she typed back, "If you can help me find my friend, how can I help you?"

"Who is your friend?"

"Dayna Hood, the captured American. She is a good person. A nurse. We worked together in Doctors Without Borders."

"She is in Raqqa? You want me to try to find her?" Mohammad asked.

"YES! How can I help you in return?"

"My mother is very sick. Her kidneys do not work properly. She needs to get out of Raqqa for medical help."

"I will help you if you can locate my friend. Please… HURRY!!! It has to happen…now!!!"

Dusk started to fall and Asso was still chatting with the soldiers. Séverine got out to stretch her legs and use the bathroom.

Asso pointed to a restaurant across the street. He said, "If anyone stops you and speaks English, tell them that you're with me, your boyfriend. Stick to the story."

"I will."

"You can't trust anyone. There are spies everywhere."

She couldn't tell if he was just being overprotective. When she emerged from the little bathroom, Asso stood in the hallway talking with three serious-looking men, two of whom were in uniform.

He took her by the forearm and said, "Come with me."

Asso sat across from her at a wooden table in a private room filled with the scent of roasting lamb seasoned with rosemary, and said in a conspiratorial tone, "It's too dangerous to travel farther south or west without an escort."

"Who told you that?"

"They did....One is an officer in the YPG. The other two are Asayish."

She didn't want to be sidetracked into wondering what Asayish's interest in the case might be. They would either help or they wouldn't. "Do they have any information?" Séverine asked.

"Just confirmation that Ms. Hood is in Raqqa."

"Okay. That's important." One of the Asayish officials joined them. When he grinned, his mouth was filled with stained and broken teeth. "Raqqa is a large city, isn't it? Do they have sources there who can locate her?"

Asso spoke to the official and translated his answer for Séverine.

"The situation there is very dangerous right now. A siege is imminent. It's coming from Assad forces and the Russians from the north, and from Kurds east and west. So it's difficult to move around the area without being stopped by the religious police. But Asayish sources are active. They're transmitting information twenty-four seven."

"Thank you," she repeated, grasping her hands in front of her for emphasis. "Thank you very much. Please tell us anything you learn immediately."

"He will. He also wants to warn you about trusting anyone you meet on a Facebook page. They could be ISIS."

The short, pale Asayish official nodded and waved his finger. "Very bad. No trust."

The tone of his deep voice sent a chill up her spine. "Time is quickly running out for my friend. What does he suggest we do?"

He and Asso conferred, then Asso said, "He thinks we continue on to Ayn Issa. It's the last town under Kurdish control before Raqqa. Only fifty kilometers north of Raqqa."

"Why?"

"The few people who are getting out of Raqqa arrive there. Maybe one of them will have some information."

It was worth a try. But the road to Ayn Issa wasn't secure, so they needed to hire an armed escort. While Asso and the Asayish official hurried off to attend to that, Séverine ordered a bottle of water and checked her messages.

The first one was from Crocker. "Leaving Erbil now. Will land in Tabqa, west of Raqqa, in an hour. Will contact you when we land."

She texted back, "Great news! Thank u, thank u, thank u with all my heart. I'm leaving soon for a town called Ayn Issa. Hope to learn more there. Much luv."

She also had several messages from Mohammad, asking where she was and offering his services again. One of them read, "Please. My mother is dying. I will take whatever risks u need in exchange for medical help! I am taking risks now. I can be stoned to death for talking to you!"

She wrote back, "I understand. You're a brave man. I'm on my way to Ayn Issa and will contact you when I arrive there."

"I will meet u."

Armed men led her through a courtyard with a tree in the center. Since they were taking Dayna outside, the men had removed the hijab she had been wearing and replaced it with a *burqu* so her face was hidden. Through the mesh that covered her eyes, she spotted small tapestries with Arabic sayings woven into them hanging from the limbs of the tree. She wondered if they were prayers, and hoped that she was with people who believed in God.

Now they were leading her downstairs to a dank cement basement. Chills spread through her body into her hands. At the bottom, they arrived at another courtyard and gate. Two armed men opened it. They pushed her into a little room with no windows and thick cement walls, and left. A plate of food and a glass of hot tea sat on a table.

A single bulb hung from the ceiling. Dirty pillows leaned against one wall. Arabic calligraphy covered another. An old sweater hung from a nail by the door.

Listen to my prayer, O God. Do not ignore my cry for help....

She was trying to keep track of time in her head. Approximately forty Mississippis later, footsteps echoed from the passageway. She heard a key in the lock. The door swung open and six men crowded into the little room. There was hardly room enough for all of them to stand.

Please listen and answer me for I am overwhelmed by my troubles....

One, with a long, slender face, pushed the plate of food aside and placed a microphone and tape recorder on the table.

"Sit," he said.

She obeyed. "Good. You speak English. Where did you learn English?"

"I'm not here to talk about myself. Be quiet!"

He lifted the hood of her *burqa*. The other men were fierce-looking and bearded.

She recited some verses from Psalm 55 to herself. *My heart is in anguish. The terror of death overpowers me. Fear and trembling overwhelm me. I can't stop shaking. Oh, how I wish I had wings like a dove; then I would fly away, and be at rest!*

"We want you to answer some questions."

She thought she sensed a little drop of sympathy in his voice. "What's your name?"

"You can call me Rasul."

She wanted desperately to cling to it. "You are a good man, aren't you? You're my Angel Rasul."

"Just answer the questions."

He pushed the microphone under her chin. The questions came fast. "Why are you in Syria? Who are you working for? Where do you live in the United

States? Who hired you? What was the nature of your mission to Aleppo? What are the names of the people you were working with? When did you become a spy? What are the names of your contacts in Syria?"

She answered as best she could, but the questions kept coming like lashes. The men were practically shouting them at Rasul. She became confused and exhausted, and noticed that Rasul was gently encouraging her.

"Answer....Do the best you can....Don't hesitate.... Don't look at me, look at them....This will be over soon...."

When she said at one point that her beliefs came from the Bible, Rasul said, "I won't say that."

Under her breath, she recited two verses from Psalm 27 to resist the negative thoughts that invaded her head. *Though a host encamp against me, I will not show fear. Though war rise against me, in spite of this I shall be confident.*

She tried to hold on to God as her shield, her defense, but her will was starting to crumble.

Her answers to the men's inquiries no longer made sense. She swore that Rasul was answering them for her. She held on to the spark of empathy in his eyes.

"Are you married?"

The question surprised her. She wasn't sure if it was coming from Rasul or the others.

"They want to know if you're married."

"I'm not married. No."

"Were you ever married?"

"No!"

"Why not? Are you a nun?"

"No, I'm waiting for the right person."

When Rasul translated, the men looked puzzled

and whispered among themselves. Then one of the fiercest of them looked at her and nodded. It was the first time she sensed the least bit of humanity in any of them.

Rasul said, "He thinks you should become a Muslim. He thinks you will be happy if you become a Muslim and marry a Muslim man."

"Tell him thank you, but I love Jesus."

"I don't think I should tell him that."

"Tell him that Jesus changed my life, and I'm very happy, even here, even if I have to die."

Rasul didn't bother to translate this to the other men. Instead, he spoke to her directly. "How did he change your life?"

"I did lots of bad things before I invited Jesus into my life. He gave me a clean heart. He changed me."

Séverine rode in a covered jeep with three female fighters from Kurdish YPJ. The dark outlines of cotton fields passed on either side of them. A night breeze caressed her face, carrying the sweet scent of chamomile and almond blossoms.

Asso and two more YPJ fighters followed in the car behind them.

A round-faced girl in camouflage sang from the backseat, reaching for notes until her voice cracked. The other women laughed.

Séverine didn't have to remind herself that they weren't on their way to a party, but headed into the most dangerous territory on the planet, especially for a Western woman like herself.

"This is a beautiful area when there's peace," commented Roza at the wheel beside her. She had a bony face with sunken cheeks and eyes, and straight brown hair parted in the middle and pulled back. An M4 rifle rested on the console between them.

"How long have you been fighting?" Séverine asked, as she checked her phone for wifi or cell reception. Nothing.

"Two years," Roza answered. Séverine noticed a large bump at the top of her forehead and wondered what had caused it. "Before, I had no social or economic life. You know, my life was between four walls. Very traditional."

"You grew up in this area?"

"In Al-Hasakah, yes. My father repaired cars. My brother repaired cars and motorcycles. I was expected to get married and have children. This war has brought me freedom."

"I wouldn't have expected that."

"Expectations are for dummies." She smiled. "Maybe I should write a book."

She translated what she had said into Kurdish for the women in back. The bond between them seemed strong.

"For me, this war is not just about defending our land," Roza continued. "It has changed me. It has changed all of us."

They passed a burned-out tank alongside the road. Some clever artist had spray-painted it with cartoon-like graffiti.

Séverine hadn't had time to think about the ways the war had changed her, too.

"I never believed that a woman could be equal to a man before," said Roza.

"Have any of you been involved in combat?" Séverine asked.

"All of us, yes. We fought many battles. Many times

they put us on the front line to shoot at the ISIS, because the ISIS have great fear of us."

"Why?"

"They don't think they will be admitted to heaven and be welcomed by dancing virgins if they are killed by a woman."

CHAPTER TWENTY-FOUR

*He who wants pearls has to dive
into the ocean.*

—Kurdish proverb

CROCKER GLANCED at his watch as the Knighthawk passed over a modern hydroelectric dam. It read 2249 hours—a little more than four hours from the dead line.

He was thinking about the time he had driven cross-country with his red-haired girlfriend Leslie to start BUD/S (Basic Underwater Demolition/SEAL Training). He was twenty-two; she was twenty. The VW they drove in had broken down five times. By the time they reached Nevada, they were down to their last twenty dollars.

"That's Tabqa Dam," Doyle shouted into his ear. "Built in the '70s. The body of water behind it is called Lake Assad."

"It's still called that?" Crocker asked. Hydroelectric dams had always fascinated him. He and Leslie had stopped to tour the Hoover Dam during their cross-country trip.

The CIA case officer shrugged. "Daesh controlled all the land around it until a couple weeks ago. They left the guys who run the dam alone, and the men kept working and receiving their weekly paychecks from the Syrian government."

"That's wack."

While he'd been suffering through timed runs along Coronado Beach, ocean swimming, calisthenics, and timed obstacle course runs, Leslie had stayed in a trailer on the edge of the desert waiting for him to come home.

"Very wack."

She'd gotten bored and after a month or so returned home. He couldn't blame her.

The helo circled over rocky hills, past the three-quarters moon, and descended sharply into a valley to the south, near a town and temporary military camp.

Doyle said, "The pilot says he's going to touch down and take off quickly. So we have to move fast."

As they approached the ground he saw men waving pink and green glow sticks and shouting in the dark. "Run! Run! Run!"

They waved them into a bunker carved into the side of a hill and reinforced with sandbags. Inside Crocker and company were greeted by a self-important dude in camouflage. Looked like he spent a lot of time in the mirror grooming his mustache.

"This is Commander Kassim of the YPG," Doyle said.

Around him stood an assortment of heavily armed fighters, some in uniform, others in civilian clothes. One older guy with a big belly wore a plate vest over a dirty white University of Miami sweatshirt. They looked more like members of a gang than a military force.

"Crocker."

Kassim started talking excitedly to Doyle in Kurdish dialect.

Meanwhile, Akil fired up his Garmin GPSMAP 64st and said, "We're so close to Aleppo we should be able to smell it."

Crocker saw that a local highway—marked #4 on the map—followed the branches of the Euphrates that snaked west to the city. A big hand squeezed his shoulder from behind.

"Yo, Dez," Akil exclaimed.

"Akil, you ugly motherfucker."

Hugs and high-fives were exchanged between the former Delta operator Dez, now a private military contractor, his colleagues Oliver and Rollins, and Crocker and members of his team. The last time they had seen each other was at the nightclub in Erbil.

"What the fuck you doing here?" Dez asked in a west Texan drawl. He was a mix of African American, Mexican, and white, and had a massive chest and arms covered with tats.

"I was about to ask you the same question."

"We're bunking with a dozen smelly contractors in an abandoned house at the edge of town, waiting for shit to happen. You?"

"We're here to rescue the American girl."

Dez's eyes lit up. "Sweet, man.... Very cool."

"We're trying to figure out how to get into Raqqa and where we might find her. Any ideas?"

Dez had an almost childlike manner. "I don't know....Ollie and Rollins here did some recon on some antiaircraft installations west of the city two nights ago."

"How did that go?"

"Hairy as fuck," Rollins answered. He was a compact guy with an East London accent.

"It's a big town. Spread out along the river," added Oliver—a big bloke with the scarred face of a boxer. "Mosques, boulevards, traffic circles, archaeological sites. You know where you're bloody going?"

"Not yet."

"Unfortunate. If the jihadis find you they'll bugger you first then cut off your heads."

"Nice."

They were drowned out by shouts from Commander Kassim, who looked like he was about to have a stroke. "What's all the drama?" Crocker asked Doyle.

Doyle answered out of the side of his mouth. "He's freaking out because he thinks they're going to be bombed by Russians or Turks. Both nations' jets have been spotted in the area. He says he needs Stinger missiles and air defense immediately."

"The Turks?"

"Yeah, the Turks don't like the Kurds, either."

"Nobody fucking does, except us," Rollins commented.

By "us" Crocker hoped he meant the U.S. Coalition, but didn't have time to question him further. Instead he nodded toward Kassim and said, "Tell him we need his intel on Dayna Hood. Ask him to focus on that now."

Doyle answered, "He's sent some men to a nearby camp to fetch some recent deserters from Daesh."

"What for?"

"Hopefully, they'll know something."

"That's what he's using for intel?" Akil asked. "Deserters? Can they be trusted?"

"About as far as you can throw them," commented Rollins.

"We've got nothing else."

The YPJ and YPG had set up their Ayn Issa head-quarters in the lobby of a small hotel called the Ni-nava—a pale-blue three-story cement structure on the town's main square. Tonight it bustled with militants who came and went, and sat at tables resting, talking, and drinking beer, sodas, and tea. An electric current of expectation crackled through the air.

Past one of the wide arches, Séverine saw Roza sit-ting on the tile floor devouring a lamb kebab.

"We're waiting for orders," she said, wiping sauce off her mouth with the back of her hand. "The U.S. advisors are coordinating everything. We're going to liberate Raqqa. It will be a difficult battle, but we will win!"

"You're leaving tonight?" Séverine asked.

"Tonight? No.... Tonight we party and rest. What about you?"

Asso waved from a table in the back, under one of the lobby's ceiling fans.

"Excuse me," said Séverine as she went to join him. A soldier strummed a guitar in the corner. A heavyset man sang a sad lament that was swallowed up in the din of voices.

"What's he singing about?" Séverine asked.

"A beautiful girl named Helime who falls in love with a young farmer, but her parents don't consent. So she and the farmer elope and escape to another village, when war with the Turks breaks out, and many Kurds are killed. Helime's lover is wounded and sent into exile. He misses her so much that he sings this song."

"It's lovely. Tell him…"

"I will…. The song is old, but still speaks of our situation. Don't you think? We Kurds are a proud people with many beautiful traditions, and for centuries we have longed to have our own homeland and live in peace."

"Maybe you'll achieve that now."

"We haven't had good luck." Asso pushed a plate of food in front of her. "This is fried *kubbah,* a specialty from around here—bulgur wheat, onions, finely ground lean beef, cinnamon and other spices. Very delicious."

"No thanks." Her stomach was still unsettled. She ordered a bottle of water and a dish of plain yogurt.

Asso went to thank the singer and hand him some money. When he sat down again, he paused to listen to two men seated behind his left shoulder, talking at once and waving their arms dramatically. She suspected they were Asayish.

"What are they saying?" she asked.

"They're talking about your friend."

"What have they heard?"

He shook his head. "Just rumors, bits of information. Daesh has ordered everyone in the city inside their houses."

"What does that mean?"

He shrugged. "Don't give up hope."

Cold desperation spread from her stomach into her chest. Even the water tasted sour. She couldn't help looking at the time on her cell phone. 11:22 p.m. They had less than three hours. Exhaustion and defeat wanted to overwhelm her. She pushed them back.

I've come this far…. I have to be strong.

Her cell phone vibrated. Someone was trying to contact her via Skype.

"Excuse me," she said to Asso, standing and hurrying to a back patio.

The connection was lost. She waited, praying for the little screen to light up again.

"Séverine?"

"Crocker? Crocker, is that you? Oh, my God. It's so, so good to hear your voice."

A couple sat in the shadows of a leafy tree. She seemed to be intruding on an intimate moment.

"Where are you, Séverine?"

"I'm in Ayn Issa. I'm not far from Raqqa. North, I think."

"Okay," Crocker answered, his voice breaking up. "I'm…I'm near the dam called…Tabqa. We're on the other side of the city. We're not far from each other."

"What have you heard about Dayna?"

"Séverine….Séverine…."

"Crocker!"

The connection started to break up, then quickly was restored.

"I hear you now," said Crocker. "What were you saying?"

"The people I'm with…they're Asayish. They say Dayna's probably in Raqqa. Daesh is clearing the streets, ordering everyone inside. What do you think that means?"

"Don't know….Me and my men are ready to launch. We've got air surveillance moving in. Keep… faith."

"I'm trying."

"If you hear any specifics, let me know right away."

"Of course. Crocker—"

The line went dead. When she tried to reach him the call didn't go through. She squeezed the phone in frustration. The couple under the tree was making out furiously. It seemed like the perfect thing to do under the circumstances—lose yourself in the heart of another, and grab a few moments of pleasure.

A serious man wearing black-framed glasses was standing with Asso when she returned to the table.

"What?"

"He says someone is waiting for you outside. His name is Mohammad."

"Where?"

"On the street out front. Do you want me to come with you?" Asso asked.

"No. I'll be fine."

They stood in a small, windowless room at the back of the bunker—eight anxious men staring at computer screens linked to surveillance drones flying high over the city of Raqqa—Crocker, Akil, Mancini, CT, Doyle, Dez, Oliver, and Rollins. Sandbags lined the walls. A mixed assemblage of modern weapons stood propped up by the entrance.

"What are we looking at?" Crocker asked.

Doyle pointed to the four-color images on the screen. "That's the river...there. And that's downtown Raqqa...the equestrian center, the main avenue..."

"Looks fucking empty," Akil commented.

Despite the low cloud cover, the infrared imaging beamed from the two MQ-9 Reaper drones was impressive in its detail. Mancini explained that their highly advanced optical features included two-color DLTV cameras with variable zoom and 955mm Spotter, and allowed them to pick up small objects on the ground from an altitude of fifty thousand feet.

Technical shit that Crocker didn't understand. He wanted a target, a sighting of the woman.

"What happens when the storm blows in, which is supposed to happen soon?" CT asked.

"The drone operator can shift to the TESAR synthetic aperture radar, which provides all-weather surveillance capability, and has a resolution of one foot," explained Mancini. "The MQ-9 is also equipped with thermal imaging that can see through smoke, mist, fog, and even vegetation. But if it starts raining hard, we can expect it to stop being effective."

"In other words, we'll have no eyes overhead and no air cover."

"Air cover will be limited under the circumstances," Mancini answered. "The MQ-9 is armed with four Hellfire missiles and a pair of five-hundred-pound laser-guided bombs."

"Sufficient bang for a strike on a few selected targets, but not enough to keep the enemy pinned down," commented Crocker.

"Yeah."

Doyle said, "We fly these babies over the city constantly, and Daesh is aware of that. So they employ countermeasures, like hiding weapons systems or stationing them next to civilian targets. Apparently they've killed the lights tonight."

The city appeared abandoned, which made Crocker wonder if maybe Dayna was being held in another location.

"Is it always like this?" he asked.

"Quieter than usual," Doyle answered as the

Reaper cameras zoomed in on a series of larger buildings around a traffic circle, and a wide boulevard that cut north-south and ended at the banks of the river. "That is known as the Governate Building...there. And that's the museum."

"Why are they significant?"

"In the past, Daesh has staged big public rallies there," Doyle said, pointing to a courtyard adjacent to the Raqqa Museum. "Doesn't look like they'll be doing that tonight."

Crocker's heart started to sink. "If she's inside, she could be anywhere."

Doyle continued to point out major landmarks in the downtown area. "The Seray Building, the national hospital, the Fawaz Mosque, the Al-Firdous Mosque...."

"Aren't we better off looking for heat signatures?" asked Mancini. "If they're assembling somewhere, they're gonna need wheels to get there."

"Not necessarily," Doyle countered.

"What's that?" Akil pointed at what looked like two cars stopped at a roadblock farther up the road.

CT tapped Crocker on the shoulder. "Boss?" he whispered.

"Yeah."

"Captain Sutter's on the sat phone. What do you want to do?"

"I'll take it."

"He sounds ultra pissed."

The twelve members of the Ar Raqqa Sharia Court sat in a semicircle on folding chairs in a basement room of the Governate Building down the street from the Al-Firdous Mosque and catercorner with the

Raqqa Museum. Sheikh al-Sufi and his military advisors faced them from behind an old wooden table along the back wall.

The court was composed of a dozen serious-looking men with long beards, some of which hung to their chests. Many of them wore long black robes and prayer hats. Some fingered prayer beads that hung from their waists and muttered verses from the Quran under their breath.

In the dank room lit with electric torches and candles, rail-thin Imam Abu Anau Zabas of the Al-Firdous Mosque stood first and spoke passionately about the steady defection of foreign fighters that had started a year ago.

"With all respect, Imam, what does this have to do with the issue before us?" a younger, stouter member of the court asked.

"Because we are judged by our actions by believers all around the world," Imam Zabas explained. His thin face and sunken, burning eyes gave him the look of a prophet. "I warned you a year ago against the burning alive of Jordanian pilot Muath al-Kasasbeh and the slaying of the two Japanese hostages. These acts were violations of Sharia law and have led to defections and a loss of support."

"You speak nonsense!" another member of the court shouted.

"Kasasbeh wasn't an infidel," Imam Zabas exclaimed. "He was a devout Muslim who prayed before he took off on the mission that ended with his plane crashing, and his murder!"

"Traitor!" one of the emirs shouted. "You speak words of treachery!"

Sheikh al-Sufi, who as commander of Raqqa supervised the court and carried out its rulings, raised his arms and said, "Respect. Let the imam speak."

In a high voice quivering with emotion, Imam Zabas suggested that the execution of a woman, even an infidel from the West, would only bring more questioning of the Court's application of the law of God, and more defections.

"We have questioned her," Imam Zabas said. "We have observed her behavior and collected evidence from the Internet. This woman traveled to Aleppo as a doctor to help heal the sick. It is our duty as men of God to show forgiveness."

He quoted from the Quran, "'Instead of taking vengeance, turn to forgiveness and enjoin the good, and turn aside from the ignorant.'"

Then he proposed that instead of executing the American woman, a swap be arranged for Sunni militants held in jails in Iraq, Syria, and Turkey.

Imam Zabas's words were met with jeers and hisses. The hardline clerics shouted him down, calling him a fool and a heretic.

Their leader, Emir Ayub al-Kuwaiti, called on the head of the al-Hisba police—who had conducted the investigation of Ms. Hood—to testify.

The police chief said, "Our investigations of the subject are conclusive of several areas. Number one, this woman traveled to Syria under false pretenses. Number two, she is not a doctor. Number three, she is impure. Number four, it is our conclusion that she came to Aleppo to spy for the infidels."

Sheikh al-Sufi covered his mouth and tried to hold back a yawn. In the last year and a half, he had witnessed many court debates over the proper way to implement Sharia law. The hardliners always prevailed.

*   *   *

Séverine rode on the back of a motorbike that sped down a narrow asphalt road with her cell phone taped to the inside of her right thigh. A light mist coated her face; the vibration of the engine buzzed through her body. As she held on to Mohammad, she felt his heart beating under his ribs.

Between the Percodan, hunger, and exhaustion, her mind kept pulling her inward and back to her childhood, when she felt loved and protected, and the world demanded nothing of her but to be herself.

How did I get here? What brought me to this strange place?

For the answer, she had to reach way back to a sense of inherent honesty and fairness that she felt as a young child. She'd never been able to lie, even about the littlest of things, and had always been sensitive to the plight of others.

She wished Mohammad would focus on the slick road and leave her alone with her thoughts, but he kept turning back to her and talking over the engine. She caught only snatches of what he said.

"All I want…is to take care of my mother and my sisters.…You know…women under forty-five are banned from leaving the city.…You don't know how difficult our lives have become.…Music is forbidden.…Food is more and more scarce.…"

She'd always been trusting, too. Too trusting, her mother had often warned.

She drifted off and dreamt that she was flying over the rooftops of a city, steering around black smoke that rose from the chimneys. The smoke curled and formed into the heads of monsters.

It was too late to turn back. As long as her

intentions were pure, she believed good forces in the universe would take care of her.

"Séverine....Séverine...."

Someone was calling to her. She opened her eyes. Mohammad was slowing the bike. People up ahead were waving electric lamps.

"Séverine!"

"Who are they?"

"Séverine," he said urgently. "It's a Daesh checkpoint. Pull down the hood of your *burqa*.... Remember, you are my wife. You are not allowed to speak to men outside your family. Don't answer their questions....Get rid of your phone. Quick! Women are not allowed to carry phones!"

CHAPTER TWENTY-FIVE

It is impossible to convey the life-sensation of
any given epoch of one's existence—that
which makes its truth, its meaning—its
subtle and penetrating essence. It is
impossible. We live, as we dream—alone.
　　　　—Joseph Conrad, *Heart of Darkness*

CROCKER WAS still reeling from the severe dressing down and threats of court-martial he'd received from Captain Sutter. It's not that he had expected his CO's support, but he didn't need to hear his anger, either. Not now.

He sat with Doyle, Akil, Mancini, and Commander Kassim, who was questioning a nervous Libyan man who called himself Hamza Jibril and claimed to have spent the last eight months in Raqqa working for ISIS as a civil engineer.

He'd defected recently and swore that he had never played a military role of any kind.

Unlikely, thought Crocker, wondering how carefully this man had been vetted, and weighing the possibility that he was an ISIS informant.

Doyle and Akil were asking the questions and doing the translating. Their main interest was the best way to get to Raqqa undetected.

Hamza Jibril warned that the main road, Highway 4, was controlled by Daesh and contained many moving checkpoints—teams of two or three pickups traveling together that would stop and block the road at random locations. The Libyan also didn't recommend traveling to the city by boat down one of the estuaries of the Euphrates River, because many of them, he said, were mined, and others were heavily patrolled.

"Ask him how he would get to Raqqa, if he had to go there tonight," Crocker said.

Hamza chewed his bottom lip as he considered the options. When he spoke, Doyle translated. "He says he would go by foot and walk along the south bank of the river, away from the main road."

"What if he didn't have time for that and had to get there quickly?"

Crocker watched the Libyan carefully, looking for obvious signs of deception—hands near or covering the mouth, obsessive blinking.

"He said he would probably use a bike or a motorbike, but a motorbike would attract more attention."

"Would he follow the same route along the south bank?" Crocker asked.

"Yes. He says they are dirt paths. The safest ones follow the south bank. He says the closer you get to Raqqa, the more dangerous they become. These are the paths most people use to sneak out of the city."

Everything he said sounded reasonable. No other options came to Crocker's mind, so he turned to Commander Kassim and asked, "Can you get your hands on some motorbikes?"

"How many?"

"Seven, if possible." Crocker glanced at his watch. It was already 0117 Sunday. They had a little more than an hour.

"Eight," Doyle interjected. "I'm going with you."

"I'll see what I can do," Commander Kassim answered, his hands folded together.

"You'd better hurry."

Dayna sat in the corner of the dark room surrounded by dirty pillows. Flies buzzed around the untouched plate of hummus, yogurt, and cucumber on the table. A sliver of light entered through a crack near the ceiling and bisected the floor.

Her mind was on her friends and family back in Savannah, the tree-lined squares, the raw smell of the river, and the riverbank. She focused on one young man in particular, named Austin, who she'd met at church.

He taught English part-time at a local middle school and sculpted figures out of wax. She hadn't found him physically attractive at first. But his intelligence and sensitivity had slowly won her over.

Austin introduced her to art and classic literature—Shakespeare, Flaubert, Dickens, Tolstoy. Her favorite of the books she had read so far had been *Great Expectations*. She identified with Miss Havisham's adopted daughter Estella, who was given a great education and all the creature comforts, but lost the ability to return Pip's affection.

During the three months she spent with Austin, she'd learned that it was possible to be with a man you were attracted to and remain pure. The two of them laughed, prayed, dined, danced, and went on long walks and bike rides together, and parted friends. Only now did she realize how much she missed him, and even loved him. It pained her that she hadn't told him, and might never get the chance.

She didn't want to remain friends apart, like Estella

and Pip. Or end up entrapping and marrying someone she didn't love, if she ever got that chance. Or die in a foreign place and be forgotten.

On her knees with her hands clasped in front of her, she prayed out loud. "God, please come close to me and heal my heart. I would love to be with Austin again. If I get that chance, I will open my heart to him. I promise this, and I trust you. Whatever you want for me, I will do with gratitude. You are my Lord and savior."

She tensed up upon hearing steps in the hallway, and then remembered what she had just said—*Whatever you want for me, I will do with gratitude*. A key turned the lock. The door groaned open and Rasul's full face shone in the light from an electric lamp.

Concern creased his narrow forehead. The pounding of a hammer echoed in the distance.

"Is something wrong?" Dayna asked.

He pointed to the plate of food. "You did not eat."

"I lost my appetite and I don't think it will come back anytime soon."

He grinned. "Are you making a hunger strike?"

"No. I just don't feel like eating."

He draped an orange jumpsuit over the chair. "This is for you to wear. I'll come back for you in ten minutes. Put this on first."

"Rasul," she said. "Are you taking me somewhere?"

Halfway out the door, he stopped and shrugged. "I think so."

"Can you tell me where?"

"I don't know."

"Rasul, please. Can you stay just for a minute… and talk?"

He shook his head. "No."

"You're scaring me, Rasul. Do you mean to scare me?"

He looked at her hard, then shifted his gaze to the floor. "No."

Everything was happening so fast that it was hard for Séverine's brain to catch up. Guttural voices snarled at her in a foreign language; Mohammad pleaded with the IS soldiers, then turned and whispered assurances in her ear. Rain water dripped off his wide face.

"They have to check. It's their job. It's a precaution. I told them you're my wife and you lost your papers. There's no reason to be afraid."

Then why do I detect fear in his voice? Everything seemed dark and unfocused. There was no one to appeal to. She couldn't even speak. Then she felt rough hands exploring her body and feeling under her arms and breasts.

What are they looking for? What do they want?

She pushed them away. Someone slapped her and she hit the ground. The fabric grill over her eyes shifted so she couldn't see.

Mohammad's voice became more desperate, as he pleaded in Arabic. Hands reached into her pockets. She felt one squeezing between her legs.

She wanted to scream, *Stop! Stop! What are you doing?* But she didn't dare.

Men shouted at one another. They pulled her roughly to her feet. They started shaking her shoulders violently.

Mohammad whispered into her ear, urgently, in Kurdish, which she barely understood. "They found your phone. Give it to me! I told you to get rid of it."

She passed it to him.

Something hit the back of her head. Hands pulled her so her feet dragged across the pavement.

Mohammad whispered in Kurdish, "I will follow you. You are my wife, remember. They're going to punish you, or maybe keep you in jail overnight."

Why? she asked herself.

They pushed her violently toward the back of a truck. She lost her balance and hit her face. Warm blood dripped from her nose onto the front of the *burqa*. An engine growled and the vehicle lurched forward.

Her mind flashed to the story of Jonah being swallowed into the belly of a whale.

Crocker stood on the same field where the helicopter had landed hours earlier. He faced a woman with thick, dark eyebrows and a large nose. His men waited beyond with an odd collection of motorbikes and motorcycles. He wondered what she wanted.

"Why are we stopping?" he asked Doyle.

"Her name is Dr. Sahari. She used to run the museum."

In his head, he was running through a checklist of equipment—suppressors, C-4 charges, grenades, radios, cell phones, medical kits, GPS… "I'm sorry. But we don't have time for this now."

"Crocker…listen to what she has to say. It's important."

"This can't wait?"

The woman spoke English with a thick accent. "I know you have a deadline. If you show me a map of the city, I can show you the location of the tunnels."

"What tunnels?" Crocker asked. "We still don't have a target. Do you know where the American woman is being held?"

Dr. Sahari looked confused. "The tunnels under the city. They were dug by Daesh. I don't know anything about the American woman or where she's being held. I can tell you about the tunnels."

"There are tunnels under Raqqa?" Crocker asked, his attention suddenly riveted on the small, dark-eyed woman standing before him.

"Yes. They're linked to a three-thousand-year-old Assyrian temple made to honor the Babylonian god of wisdom—Nabu."

Crocker wiped the rain from his forehead. "I don't care about the temple or its history. Please tell me about the tunnels."

"The tunnels, yes...."

He called to Akil. "Bring a map of the city!"

Akil brought up a satellite feed of Raqqa on the Garmin device. Doyle, Dr. Sahari, and Crocker leaned into it.

"They use them to move around the city without being seen from the air," Dr. Sahari explained.

Akil said, "That's why we saw nothing on surveillance."

She pointed to a section at the south of the city, where Crocker remembered the main buildings were located. "Here and here," she said. "The tunnels start at the museum....The Raqqa Museum. It was built over the temple....Much of the collections have been looted. Incredible vases, art, and jewelry. The loss is inestimable, unimaginable..."

"We need to get from the river to the museum," Crocker instructed. "How?"

"There's a way. You can enter the tunnels. You enter here. I'll draw you a map."

Doyle handed her a pad he kept in his backpack. One of Kassim's men provided an umbrella. She drew a web of six vectors that originated from a central point.

"That's the museum," she said, indicating the central point.

"Where's the river?"

"It runs along here...to the south."

"We need a point of access," said Crocker.

"There's one here, near where the main avenue intersects with the river."

"Which side of the river?" Crocker asked.

"North. Yes, the north side."

"We'll be coming up a path on the southern bank."

She pointed to the Garmin screen again. "Okay. See...there's a footbridge, here.... The entrance to the tunnel is near these cypress trees...here. Last time I saw it, there was a sheet of corrugated metal that was used as a cover."

"Was the entrance guarded?"

"I don't think so."

"Should we expect soldiers nearby?"

"I would. Yes."

The first lash felt like a hot wire burning into her skin. Séverine bit down so hard her gums started to bleed. An image popped into her head of her father pouring red wine from a decanter into a glass.

Cold air tickled her back and she realized it was exposed and her feet were strapped to the floor. The fabric of the *burqa* covered her chest and hung around her ankles. Her hands were strapped down so tightly that the device she was tied to cut into her breasts.

In her brain she searched for a way to prepare for the abuse that she was sure would follow as black boots and shadows crisscrossed the concrete floor. Light spilled from a doorway ahead.

The second hit came like a bolt of lightning. The pain was so acute, it blinded her. Warm urine dripped down the inside of her thighs.

She felt anger and shame. A long pause followed, as her father stared at the glass of wine. She counted in her head. *One, two, three, four....*

It was the only way she could establish any kind of control of herself. At the count of eight, her vision cleared, but her back felt like it was on fire.

Ten, eleven, twelve...

BAM!!!!

The third lash cut even deeper. The violence behind it seemed immeasurable.

How can they hate so much?

Her father lifted the glass to his mouth, and the fourth blow followed right behind it. Something exploded in her head and she passed out.

Mancini had done everything he could to dampen the sounds of the motorbikes—wrapping pieces of blanket around the mufflers and pipes and securing them with gaffer's tape—but the noise was still too loud for Crocker's comfort as they bore down parallel paths that ran along the south side of the Euphrates River. The wet wind in their faces, they rode eight feet from one another, Crocker and Akil in front, CT and Mancini in the rear, Dez, Rollins, Oliver, and Doyle in the middle.

They were in ISIS-controlled territory with no location on Dayna Hood. No news had come from Tabqa or DC. He wasn't sure HQ was even talking to him anymore.

They're probably operating under the assumption that we're dead, or will be soon.

All eight of them had shed all signs of identification, even the plastic chits that identified their blood types. They'd agreed to take their own lives if injured or about to be taken prisoner. They were going in completely black—no backup, no plan, no sense of the level of resistance they would encounter, or how they would get out.

Still, Crocker had no doubt that they were doing the right thing. According to the deadline set by Daesh, there were only twenty-two minutes left.

He hadn't heard from Séverine in a while, and pictured her in his head—dark, searching eyes against pale skin. The Honda dirt bike hit a furrow in the path, jutted right, and came off the ground. Crocker managed to hold on and keep the bike upright. Landed hard on his nuts and winced. *Fuck!*

"Boss?"

Stars danced in his head. He hurt too much to answer.

I deserved that for not maintaining focus. His eyes lasered on the muddy path in front of him.

"Boss?"

"Quiet!"

Fields passed on his right; the rain hissed against the leaves; his boots were covered with mud and water.

Akil veered closer and waved from his Kawasaki to get Crocker's attention and pointed to the left.

Through the slanting rain, the Black Cell leader made out a guard shack near the river flying a black flag.

Here we go...

He looked for a way to avoid it; thought for a second that it might be unoccupied. Then a light lit up the doorway and two men stepped out. They seemed to have been attracted by the noise from the bikes. One pointed a weak flashlight in their direction and shouted.

"Waqf! Waqf—!"

Akil said, "They're telling us to stop."

"Not happening."

"I can feed them some BS story, then we can grab 'em and find out what they know."

"No time."

A Daesh guard stepped away from the little wooden guardhouse and waved his arms. The second man stood behind him, smoking a cigarette, his rifle slung over his shoulder.

Crocker growled, "I got the one on the right."

When they were within seventy feet, the militants readied their rifles.

One hand guiding the bikes, one hand grasping their weapons, Crocker and Akil took them down with suppressed bursts from their MP7A1s. Done, and done.

All in a blink of an eye. They zipped past the bodies bleeding out on the ground, cordite burning their nostrils. Crocker knew men who enjoyed killing, but he wasn't one of them and didn't want them on his team.

Taking a life, even in combat, wasn't supposed to be easy. It wasn't for Crocker. Each enemy he killed took a piece of his soul.

*   *   *

"'Where are you taking' me?" Dayna asked the two big guards on either side of her as they followed Rasul down a narrow corridor. She hadn't realized how weak she'd become as a result of fear, hunger, and exhaustion. The orange jumpsuit bagged around her ankles and dragged across the wet concrete floor.

"Will you please ask these men where they're taking me?" Her voice had become higher pitched and more desperate. She hadn't remembered putting on the black plastic sandals, which worried her. She was losing track.

Rasul stopped, turned, and barked something to the guards in Arabic. They held her as Rasul removed a black bandana from his pocket and tied it over her mouth. The cloth cut into the corners of her lips. He secured another over her eyes.

Why is he doing this? she asked. Negative answers buffeted her from all corners of her brain.

She noted that her head was uncovered, and her wrists were tied behind her, and Rasul, who had been sympathetic, hadn't bothered to tell her what had changed, or what lay ahead.

God, I know you love me....

Does he?

The negative voice appeared again—the one she had started calling The Shadow, and that had told her to give in to her old boyfriend Raymond and take drugs with him, because if she didn't he'd leave her for someone else. The voice that told her now that she had to denounce her country, and even demean herself to mollify her captors.

As though she had no choice. But she did. Jesus Christ had taught her that. Even though her body was shaking and she couldn't think straight; even though fear threatened to devour her, she had a choice.

Though I walk through the valley of the shadow of death, I will fear no evil, for you are with me; your rod and your staff, they will comfort me.

Cold sweat sprung all over her body and started to ooze down her legs and arms.

She pictured Austin's face, his sweet, loving smile; her father holding out his hand; Jesus being nailed to the cross. She clung to them, warding off fear, pain, and exhaustion.

I am the resurrection and the life. He who believes in me will live, even though he dies....

CHAPTER TWENTY-SIX

How can you rise if you have not burned?
—Hiba Fatima Ahmad

SÉVERINE DREAMT that she was trapped in an underground room and the walls were closing in on her. She felt the bones in her chest breaking, and tasted blood.

The taste was bitter, and caused her to choke. Strong hands held her arms and someone was dragging a wet rag across her mouth.

"Arrête!" she mumbled.

A man responded with a question in what sounded like Arabic. She reminded herself that Mohammad had told her not to talk.

Past sour-smelling men, she saw black walls and Arabic slogans painted in white. Men with black masks were holding her head and washing her face roughly through the mesh grill of the *burqa*. They had freed her hands from the table. She tried to straighten her back, but the pain stopped her.

She wanted to protest, but bit her tongue instead.

I'm in Raqqa. I'm being punished for having a phone. They haven't found out where I'm from . . . yet.

The men took her by the arms and pulled her forward. She stumbled and started to fall because her legs were numb. They caught her. Their nails cut into the skin of her forearms.

She wanted to ask a question, but stopped herself.

I'm supposed to be Mohammad's lightskinned Kurdish wife. I can't say anything.

The men urged her forward. All she could manage was little steps across the rough concrete floor. Her arms and legs barely functioned, and her back was a swirling mass of pain. At least she could see, breathe, and hear.

Where are they taking me?

They passed through a doorway into a larger room. Stopped at a table and one of her captors spoke to a man with a red beard. The bearded man recorded something into a ledger. The men pulled her arms again. They continued walking slowly, past two other women in black hijabs being held by more masked men.

I'm alive. I'm not the only woman. Maybe they're about to be punished, too.

She paused to collect her strength. The men urged her forward. Their voices weren't as harsh as before. She wanted to obey, not to please them, but to remove herself from this dreadful place. They slowly entered another, wider hallway.

What's this?

She was growing impatient with herself. She wanted to sit and rest. When she looked up she saw a group of men dressed in black walking toward them on the other side of the hall. All she could make out of their expressions was their cold, stern eyes.

As they passed, she noticed a small person in an

orange jumpsuit in the middle of the men. She wore a black blindfold and had tousled reddish-blond hair.

Dayna?

She had to stop herself from calling out Dayna's name. When she turned to look back to see where they were taking her, she was sure it was Dayna by the way she walked.

Yes…It's her! Yes, it's her! Oh, my God!

Excitement surged through Séverine's body. She and the men escorting her entered a large room divided by a metal fence. On the other side of the fence a crowd of people was waiting. She recognized Mohammad. His eyes lit up when he saw her, but he didn't move.

Does this mean they're letting me go?

One of the men who had been escorting her scolded her in Arabic. She lowered her head to the floor.

She imagined she was walking down along the Seine with Notre Dame Cathedral on her right. Cherry trees bloomed on both sides of the river— vivid pink against the clear blue sky.

A door in the fence buzzed open and she was pushed through. Mohammad caught her. She still couldn't straighten her back.

"Mohammad…" she whispered, not daring to embrace him or even look in his eyes.

He turned without saying anything, and led her out of the building. She stumbled out into the sweet, cleansing rain.

As soon as they reached the corner, words burst out of her. "Mohammad, I need my phone. Please hand me my phone…Which building is that? Where are we exactly?"

*   *   *

Crocker looked across the river at the dark city shrouded in mist. Behind him his men were hiding the bikes in the shrubs and drainage ditch behind him.

This is gonna be a bitch.

He tried to separate the best way to proceed from the dozens of warnings flying through his head. Once they reached the museum, they'd find someone to lead them to Dayna. Maybe grab a militant and beat the information out of him. Somebody had to know where she was.

"The bridge is there, boss," Akil said, pointing to the right. "Time to cross."

"Yeah."

Time was running out. Their mission seemed preposterous—eight men with no specific target against an army of dug-in fighters. None of them had been in the center of the city before.

His boots slid across the wet wood. Akil pointed past two cypress trees to the entrance of the tunnel.

He hurried in a crouch, the MP7A1 clutched beside him, when something vibrated on his combat belt. Simultaneously, Akil signaled for everyone to hit the ground. He went to his knees, retrieved his cell phone, then lowered himself to his stomach and readied his weapon.

Through the NVGs, he saw two militants standing on the other side of the bridge with their backs to them. He waited for CT and Dez to come up behind them and slit their throats before he answered.

"Yes."

"Tom? Crocker?"

The connection broke up.

"Hello."

"Tom, it's Séverine. Tom, is that you?"

"Yes, Séverine. I have to whisper…Can you hear me? Where are you?" he asked, shielding his mouth around the phone.

"Tom?"

"Séverine, are you okay?"

"Tom, I'm in Raqqa. I saw Dayna! I just saw her!"

"Where?"

The connection broke up again. Akil was waving him forward. He held up his hand to indicate "wait."

"Séverine?" he asked into the phone. "Séverine? Can you hear me?"

Her voice fragmented with static. "Dayna….She's in the building…center of the city. It's called…the…Gover…nant Building."

"Governant Building?"

"Yes…yes, Tom. The Governant…Building. It's across the street…across the street…from the…"

"Séverine. Séverine. I didn't get that last part."

"Dayna…I saw her at…across the street…the…museum."

"The Raqqa Museum?"

"Yes. She's in the Gover…nant…now. Ground floor."

"Where are you? Where are you, Séverine?"

The line went dead. The rest of the team crouched, waiting at the entrance to the tunnel. The rain fell more heavily than before.

He wanted to call her back to see if she was okay, wanted to reach through the phone and hug her. But didn't have time for either. When he had glanced at his watch a minute ago they had thirteen minutes left.

Now he sprung forward and saw Akil crouched near a sheet of rusting corrugated metal holding up four fingers and pointing to the entrance. He was indicating that four guys had already entered.

"We have a target."

"Where?"

"Across from the museum!"

"Sweet!"

He wiped the rain off the lenses of his NVGs and entered behind Akil. Oliver and Mancini went in after him to guard the rear.

Slid down at a sharp angle for about eight feet, reached the muddy earthen bottom, knees bent, went down on his hands and knees and started crawling. Through his NVGs he saw the shapes of CT, Doyle, Dez, and Rollins in front. His shoulders grazed the sides.

The air inside the tunnel was thick and still. With a renewed sense of hope, he entered a wider space, which stunk of rotting garbage and human feces. In the corner, he spotted discarded clothing and a foam mattress. The ceiling was still too low to stand. A rat ran over Crocker's left hand and started to run up his arm. He flung it off.

Mancini grunted. "Animal cruelty."

Akil whispered, "One big fucking toilet."

"Who's in front?"

"Dez and Rollins."

For some reason his radio wasn't working. "Pass along the news. She's in the Governant Building across the street from the museum."

"Ten-four."

Akil whispered, "It's on the corner. I know it from the maps."

"Hurry! We're running out of time."

*　　*　　*

Events unfolded like a dark dream. The men in black with black masks over their faces standing at attention, the bright lights in her eyes, other men holding video cameras. One wore Converse sneakers.

Dayna wished that they hadn't removed the blindfold, but they had. What she saw conjured impressions of the apocalypse. A man with a thick black beard stood behind a microphone haranguing her in a foreign language. Her wrists and ankles were still bound together.

Hate poured out of him. Barely strong enough to stand, she looked up at the high, arched ceiling. Seeing cobwebs gathered in the corners, she remembered how the Book of Revelation had scared her, even though she couldn't help reading it a handful of times.

Darkness swirled everywhere. It came out of the mouths and ears of the men. It entered her nostrils and turned her cold. So cold.... She tried to resist it, to find the light inside of her, to feel the love of God.

A passage from Peter flashed in her head: *The day of the Lord will come like a thief, and the heavens will roar and the heavenly bodies will be burned up and dissolved....*

She trembled. One of the men in black spread a black sheet on the ground. Another forced her to kneel on it. The voice of the man speaking into the microphone reached a fever pitch.

And Satan who had deceived them will be thrown into a lake of fire with the beasts and false prophets, and they will be tormented day and night forever.

She bowed her head and waited. Two men stepped beside her and put their hands on her shoulders. She recalled the faces of Austin, her parents, grandparents, friends, and everyone she had ever loved.

"Thank you, thank you, thank you...." she muttered.

Crocker heard something crash ahead and pushed forward through the echo until he ran into CT.

"What the fuck happened?"

"Something fell. All good."

"We've got to move faster!"

He saw Akil standing in the entrance to a large chamber looking down at the map drawn by Dr. Sahari.

"What's this?" he asked, seeing plaster filigree on the ceiling.

"It's the entrance to the Assyrian palace. The museum should be over there."

Akil pointed left, near where Dez, Doyle, and Rollins were standing.

CT stepped out of the background, waving his hands and mouthing the words "A stairway! I found a stairway!"

Crocker raised his left arm and pointed.

Akil whispered, "Let me go first. I've got the map."

The men surged toward the arched opening, their weapons locked and loaded. There were too many things wrong with this mission operationally for Crocker to count. But they had come this far, and they weren't turning back.

He scanned ahead for targets, made sure the suppressor was on tight and the MP7A1 ready to fire, then followed Akil up the stairs. The first six or seven were made of stone, and the remainder were cut from uneven pieces of wood and made a clattering sound that couldn't be avoided even when he tried climbing on his toes.

One of the pieces of wood dislodged, causing Akil to tumble into him. CT was already at the top, crashing through a wooden door. He heard an explosion; saw a flash of light.

Fuck! Here we go!

It flung him back down several stairs and into Mancini. The three men helped one another up. Readied their weapons. Rushed through the door. Someone had discharged a grenade.

He heard the spitting of rounds from suppressed weapons and looked for targets through the billowing smoke and dust.

Someone crashed into his back. Turned and saw CT. He was a split second from ripping him apart. Took a deep breath, turned, and made out Akil's silhouette in a doorway, beckoning. It was fucking chaos already.

"This way," Akil whispered, stepping over a black-robed body.

Crocker's head was still messed up from the fall. They were outside now, running alongside the museum, past a burned-out car and other wreckage. Akil stopped in front of a big puddle and pointed at the five-story building on the corner. In the distance he saw the dark minaret of a mosque.

Crocker quickly scanned for targets, then turned and signaled to the men behind him. Counted six. Doyle appeared to be limping.

He waited for them to catch up. CT indicated that Doyle had been shot in the foot.

They ran together. He spotted Akil ahead turning to signal, and two militants emerging from an alley, aiming their weapons at Akil's back. Crocker motioned to Akil to get down, went into a crouch, lined up both targets, and fired in a contained line from left to right. Both militants buckled at the knees.

Akil, all balls that he was, didn't hesitate, jumped to his feet and barreled toward the corner of the building with CT on his heels. They both disappeared into the tall entrance and a split second later another charge went off. Pushed Crocker back on his heels and was followed by ferocious firing that lit up the window to his left.

Crocker hit the ground and scooted right around the corner through mud and water, into the marble entrance. It was hell inside—men screaming, rounds flying everywhere, smoke.

Someone pushed his head down, then another grenade went off, stinging his ears and sending waves of pressure against his face and chest.

"This way!" CT shouted in his ear.

Dayna, on her knees praying, waited for the moment the sword met her neck and hoped that the blade was sharp and she wouldn't feel much pain. Every part of her was shaking, flying apart.

The terror she felt…unimaginable.

What are they waiting for? Please, God…

A moment of silence and her heart skipped a beat, followed by a dull thud and the popping of what sounded like firecrackers.

The men beside her shuffled their feet as though they were dancing. A strange current of fear passed through them and entered her skin.

CT went first, crossing the slick floor and firing, bursting through a door into a back room and peeling right. Crocker bolted in behind him, going to his knees, sliding and taking cover behind a column. It was a banquet-sized room with a high ceiling, filled with rows of desks, laptops, boxes of papers, bicycles, and other miscellaneous junk. A group of armed men fired at them from behind desks at the far end.

"This isn't it," Akil said, his eyes blazing with intensity.

"What do you mean?"

Rounds zinged past Crocker's head, and glanced off the column in front of him.

"She's not here!"

"Séverine said she's on the ground floor."

"This is the ground floor!"

A grenade slid toward them. Crocker pointed right. He, Akil, and CT dove toward a low marble wall and fired. Jumped behind it as the grenade exploded and the whole room shook.

Motherfucker!

As soon as shrapnel stopped falling, they came up together and obliterated the men at the end of the room.

A breathless Mancini joined them as Crocker turned to Akil. "We're in the Governant Building, right?"

"This is it!"

"Then she's supposed to be here."

Dez, at his shoulder, shouted, "Duck!"

Rounds flew at them from a doorway to their right. Crocker slammed a fresh mag into his MP7A1. He and the men responded with suppressed fire of their own.

"Where does that lead?" Crocker asked. Before Akil had a chance to answer, Crocker answered his own question. "Maybe there's a downstairs. Let's go!"

* * *

Sheikh al-Sufi had experienced profound unease throughout the proceeding. Something didn't feel right. Were they inviting God's displeasure by executing an innocent woman?

He wanted to stop the proceeding, but didn't know how without inviting scorn. When he heard the firing above, he felt relieved of a terrible burden, which seemed wrong, too. The danger didn't alarm him at first. He stood in his own calm bubble as some men hurried to retrieve their weapons from the table by the door and others took cover.

"Sheikh! Sheikh!"

Someone was holding his arm. Men were shouting back and forth. He stared at the girl kneeling in the center of the room and wondered if he should take her away or signal the man standing by her side to cut off her head.

Crocker pushed through the twin metal doors and confronted a scene of utter mayhem. Struggled to make sense of it at first. Men in long black robes hurried toward him. Some were armed, some weren't. Some were running, others hiding behind benches.

He understood enough to go to the ground and open fire. Men fell; ones behind them shifted and turned like a herd of stampeding cattle and ran toward another exit. Breathless, he caught glimpses of what was going on in the rest of the room—photographer's lights on tripods, a makeshift grandstand along the opposite wall with black-clad men hiding behind it, a man running with a video camera clutched under his arm.

No girl. No Dayna Hood.

Someone screamed. Akil leaned into him and thrust his left arm forward.

"There! She's there!"

"Where?"

He followed Akil's finger to the center of the room, as a wild spray of automatic weapon rounds slammed into the wall and doors behind them. Still couldn't see the girl.

In the split second between picking out targets with his MP7A1, Crocker spotted two militants standing over an orange-clad figure kneeling in the middle of the room. One of them was holding a sword.

In the midst of the chaos, he had no time to calculate the risk of firing and missing. The person in the orange jumpsuit lifted their head. Seeing that it was a woman with a pleading look in her eyes, he unleashed a salvo at the man with the sword. The man's chest released a spray of blood, and a split second later something huge slammed into the ceiling and exploded.

Fucking hell!

CHAPTER TWENTY-SEVEN

*Everything will be okay in the end, and if it's
not okay, it's not the end.*
—John Lennon

SÉVERINE STOOD in an alley behind the Governant
Building when the first Hellfire exploded. She expected to be filled with terror, but felt an almost
overwhelming happiness instead.

Something had been accomplished. She turned to
thank Mohammad, but the look of terror on his face
as he looked up stopped her. She raised her eyes, too,
and saw part of the roof falling toward them, and past
tiles and chunks of mortar, the pitch-black sky.

Freedom... she said to herself as something hard
slammed between her head and shoulder and everything went dark.

Crocker couldn't remember covering his head, or going to the floor, but did experience the impact of
three more rockets hitting the building and exploding. Then something hard hit his back and he passed
out.

He dreamt he was swimming underwater.
Through very murky water saw the silhouettes of two

big sharks emerging from a cave. As they started toward him he heard the muffled sounds of men
screaming behind him.

They grew closer.

"Boss? Boss?"

He coughed, spitting out a tooth and pieces of plaster. Tasted blood.

Akil knelt beside him. His head and beard had
turned white. Three rivulets of blood ran from a cut
above his eyes.

"You're bleeding," Crocker said.

"Like I give a fuck," Akil shouted back. Sporadic
gunfire in the background; men crying out in pain.

"You're shouting, man. Your ears are shot."

"What?"

"What happened? Where are my NVGs?"

"Forget your NVGs. We gotta get out of here and
find the girl."

"The girl?"

Suddenly, it came back to him, and when he tried
to stand up, his left knee protested. So did his forehead and back. Still he managed to get to his feet
with Akil's help, recover his weapon, and brush off
the debris, all the time trying to peer through the
thick dust.

His field of focus extended barely three feet.

"Where is she? What the fuck happened?"

"Air strikes. We gotta get out of here before they hit
this place again."

"Recover the girl first!"

Dayna experienced the flames, heat, chaos, and shouting and thought for a moment that she had entered
purgatory. Someone was pulling her by the arm, and

she looked up into the face of the man with the silver-tipped beard.

He wiped tears from his eyes with the backs of his hands. Looked at her as though he wanted to apologize.

For what? What happened?

Then another big object slammed into the roof and exploded, throwing her off her feet and face forward to the floor.

Crocker and Akil were on their hands and knees, injured men around them groaning, Crocker wondering what had happened to the rest of the guys on their team. Six feet ahead he stumbled into a tangle of bodies under a pile of debris. Some were moving.

As he started to dig, his hearing sharpened and he heard moaning to his left—it sounded like a cat.

He crawled toward it, running into a militant with half a face. Pushed him away, and coughing from an intake of dust, saw a flash of orange.

Heard another low moan. Sounded like a woman. Something like, "No...don't..."

Sheikh al-Sufi saw a large golden gate ahead through the mist and imagined he was arriving at the garden of paradise. As he approached, two men in white robes appeared and started to wave him back.

"Go away!" one of them shouted.

"No, you're making a mistake. My wives and sons are in there..."

He blinked and someone was clearing rubble from the collapsed ceiling off his chest and helping him up.

"No...."

His mouth filled with dust, and his nostrils were

raw from the foul smell of something burning. He tried to get his bearings as Yasir Selah watched him with a stunned look in his eyes.

"Yasir….."

Yasir didn't respond. Chaos and smoke wanted to overwhelm him. The girl in the orange jumpsuit lay to his right with her back toward him. A foreign soldier crouched beside her. Seeing the infidel, he reached under his robe for his knife.

"Dayna?" Crocker whispered. "Dayna, can you hear me?"

He started to lift her up when something cut into his right forearm. The pain was so sudden and so sharp that he let go of the MP7A1 and rolled left.

Next thing he knew, he was grappling with at least two men, using the palm thrusts he had learned in CQD. Left, right, left, right, acutely aware of every movement from the enemy, anticipating the next punch.

As he reached into his vest for his SOG knife, a big man bit into his shoulder.

"You fuck!"

Grabbed the man by the beard, pulled him off, and met the man's eyes for a moment through the milling smoke. Middle-aged, intense, a silver-tipped beard, a gold star sewn into the black tunic.

"Savage motherfucker!"

Sheikh al-Sufi thought he was staring at Ibah. Her angry eyes burned into his, and the fierceness in them started to overwhelm him. Raising the knife, he shouted, *"Ebelizuh!"* ("Devil!"). But before he could drive the blade into her, she butted her head into his chin and he saw stars. Next thing he knew she was on top of him and suffocating him with her weight, pulling his soul out of his body. He tried to fight back, but couldn't find the strength....

Crocker saw the dread and confusion in the militant's eyes. Drove the butt of his left hand under the bridge of the nose of the man with the silver-tipped beard. Heard blood gurgle in the bastard's throat. Grabbed the knife away and finished him off with a slash across the throat.

Took a quick breath, when a younger man wearing a black prayer cap screamed *"Allahu akbar!"* and slammed into him, stunning him for a second and causing him to spin face-down to the rubble.

Dirt in his mouth, smoke filling his lungs, all the time the militant kicking and shouting like an injured dog. Words Crocker couldn't understand, maybe to Allah, maybe to his brothers. Retrieved the SIG Sauer from his combat belt and put three quick rounds in the militant's head.

On the verge of losing consciousness again, he still couldn't see for shit.

"Akil?"

Someone nearby whispered, "Help," or so he thought. Reaching toward the voice, he felt something delicate. An arm. Pulled the woman closer, wiped the grit from his eyes, and saw her face. She was having trouble breathing, so he cleared her mouth and windpipe with his fingers, then slung her over his shoulder, struggled to his feet, and staggered toward the stairway.

"Hold on."

*　　　*　　　*

Dayna imagined she was little and her father was carrying her on his shoulder. When she looked at the back of the man's head, he wasn't bald like her dad.

"Who are you?" she whispered, smoke burning her eyes. "Where are you taking me?"

The man moved like an animal, powerful shoulders and back. She heard another man's voice call in front of them. "This way, boss. This way...." Then passed out.

One step at a time, around debris, bodies, and twisted metal, somehow they found their way outside. Crocker crouched behind a pile of broken concrete near the side door. Took a deep breath to clear his lungs with Dayna in his lap. Felt for her pulse. Akil beside him slammed another mag into his automatic weapon.

"She okay?" he asked.

"Alive, but semiconscious. Probably the result of smoke inhalation. Where's Mancini?"

"I got no comms. Don't know."

"Where're the others?"

"Boss, we gotta get the fuck outta here!"

"Which way?"

"Follow me!"

He summoned all the energy he had left to stay upright and keep moving forward, stumbling, catching himself, only semi-aware of chaos around them—people running and shouting, flames shooting out of windows, bullets ricocheting off the street.

Akil stopped and was arguing with a thin man with a beard.

"Why are you stopping? Who is this guy? What's going on?"

"Name is Mohammad. Wants us to go back and dig out some woman."

"No time. We've got the woman we came for!"

"He says she's a Western woman. French."

Crocker's blood froze. "Séverine…shit!"

"Who's that?"

"Wait here. Hold the Hood girl. I'm going back."

Akil stood in his way holding his hands out to block him. "No, boss. Nix that. We can't now!"

"Out of my fucking way!" Crocker still held Dayna over his shoulder. He was trying to hand her to Akil and push him out of the way at the same time.

"Sorry, boss. No can do!"

Crocker couldn't remember what happened next. His next moment of consciousness was when he became aware of hot tears streaming down his cheeks. He was sobbing and walking with a half-conscious Dayna across his shoulder.

Couldn't figure out why he was so emotional, when he realized and stopped.

"Wait!"

The girl moaned. "Austin…Austin, is that you?"

He saw blood on his left forearm and thought it was hers at first.

"Wait for me, Austin…I'm coming…"

"Boss!" Akil tugged him by the shoulder.

"We forgot someone." He couldn't remember who.

Akil said, "Boss, keep moving, fast as you can. You need help?"

He saw the river ahead, and reached down deep through the pain, weakness, and exhaustion. Pushed forward blindly, intermittently aware of hands and voices guiding him.

"Where're the other men?"

He saw blood dripping from a slash across his forearm to the legs of his pants and stopped. He set Dayna down gently in the grass, and started to reach for his medical kit. Couldn't find it.

"Boss, what do you need? I'll take care of that…."

He looked up at CT, who had a bandage wrapped around his head.

"You get hit?"

"Nicked, man. I'm cool. You?"

"Where the fuck's everyone?"

He heard a gurgle of water, and realized they were sitting behind high scrubs on the south side of the river, near where they had hidden their bikes.

"Boss—"

Another explosion hit the city and lit up the sky. It was far enough away this time that he didn't even blink.

Felt a stab of anguish as he remembered Séverine.

It's a fucking shame…

"Boss, we got Mancini and Dez. Manny's fucked up. You got a radio that works?"

"Negative."

"It's okay.…Dez says he's got one."

"What's wrong with Manny?"

He was trying to think of what he needed to do, who he needed to call, what he needed to say to his men, but his brain wouldn't work.

CT said, "Boss, Dez's got water. You need some?"

He nodded. The liquid cleared his mouth and throat, and revived him for a minute. He fed some sips to Dayna. She opened her eyes enough to squint up at him and closed them again.

"Hey, boss. Sorry about your friend," CT said.

He turned to him, but wasn't sure what he was talking about at first.

"Yeah?"

"The woman.... The French one."

Then he remembered, winced hard, and covered his eyes.

The wind dried the tears and turned the dust and wetness into a crust that Crocker now brushed away from his eyes. He sat near the open door of the helicopter, watching moonlight reflect off the river, and turning it into a long silver snake.

Commander Kassim sat beside him talking excitedly into a radio, a silver Rolex on his wrist. All he cared about was that Dayna Hood was alive. Somehow they had managed to rescue her. Somehow.

But the price they had paid was steep. Rollins was dead, his body wrapped in a Kevlar blanket. Doyle was clinging to life after receiving multiple bullet wounds and fractures. And Mancini suffered from a broken clavicle, an AK round to his shoulder, a concussion, and cracked ribs.

He was almost positive they had left Séverine behind in Raqqa, presumably buried under rubble. Sweet, special, wonderful woman. He felt awful about that.

All he wanted now was to go home and rest, see his daughter, and heal his body. After that he'd try to get his head together, weigh the good against the bad, figure out the whys and what-fors, and face whatever disciplinary action HQ wanted to hit him with.

It was too soon to worry about that now. His mind was too clouded with pain and exhaustion.

Crocker had spent three days recuperating at the Landstuhl Regional Medical Center in Ramstein,

Germany, from the cut to his forearm, and other assorted injuries and bruises. Yesterday afternoon, he and Akil had bid goodbye to Mancini, who faced another surgery to repair his shoulder, and boarded a military jet back to the U.S. Last night was the first time in a long time Crocker had slept in his own bed, which felt like paradise.

Now he woke to the sounds of birds chirping outside his window and warm, sweet smells from the kitchen. A glass of orange juice waited on the night stand.

They felt like the first moments of a new life, a fresh start. As he sat up, the aches and pains returned and reminded him of the recent past.

He had an urge to free himself from all of it. To escape on his motorcycle and leave his old life and SEAL teams behind.

But he couldn't do that. He had teammates to help heal and support, responsibilities to fill, and at least one memorial service to attend.

He'd learned in Germany that Rollins's body had been cremated. At the end of the month Rollins's mother and girlfriend were holding a service for him in London. Crocker planned to be there. He also wanted to visit Doyle, who was recuperating at Johns Hopkins Medical Center in Baltimore. First he had to call Séverine's mother in Paris and express his deep condolences.

Séverine's face and voice haunted him.

In the shower, he thought he heard her calling him. "Crocker? Crocker?"

He answered, "Séverine, is that you? Are you okay?"

No answer. Now dressed, he shuffled toward the

welcome smells coming from the kitchen and was greeted by smiling Jenny and Bogart.

"Welcome back, Dad!"

They hugged him. Freshly baked muffins waited on the kitchen counter.

"You're a hero," BD said.

"I'm no hero," answered Crocker, "but it's good to be back."

"The newspaper says you are," Jenny offered.

The headline on the front page of the *Washington Post* read: "President Hails Heroes of Syrian Hostage Rescue." It didn't refer to Black Cell or mention any names, but it did quote the president, who said, "The men who completed this mission are the bravest men and best warriors in the world today. They're national heroes and make us all proud to be Americans."

Crocker was moved.

Three days later, dressed in his customary black, he sat in the departure lounge at Dulles Airport waiting for his American Airlines flight to Paris to board when his cell phone rang.

It was Captain Sutter. They hadn't spoken since before the mission.

"Crocker?"

"Yeah, Captain."

"You want to ride up to DC with me this morning for the ceremony? I figure we've got a lot to talk about on the way." His tone was friendly.

"I'm already there," replied Crocker.

"DC?"

"Yes, sir."

"Okay, then," said Captain Sutter, "I'll see you at the White House. Maybe we can meet up after. I know things were said between us, and other things happened. We need to sort through all that like professionals and resolve it."

"One way or another," added Crocker.

"One way or another. Yes."

He didn't know where he stood with HQ now. Didn't care, either. He'd been threatened with a court-martial for disobeying orders. Knew from his friend Davis that the NSA had intercepted Séverine's call informing him of Dayna Hood's location, and that information had been communicated to the White House, which authorized the drone rocket attack on the Governant Building in Raqqa.

In addition to killing Sheikh al-Sufi "The Viper" and other ISIS militants, the rockets had taken the lives of Rollins and Séverine, and injured Crocker and other members of the rescue team.

So he had reason to be angry, sad, and more than a little conflicted.

"Happy to do that at some point, sir," Crocker replied, struggling to maintain an even tone of voice. "But I won't be attending the White House ceremony this afternoon."

"Why not, Crocker? You're expected. Dayna Hood and her family will be there. They want to thank you in person. The president does, too."

"I've already spoken to Dayna and her family and plan to visit them in Georgia when I return. Right now I'm on my way to Paris to attend the funeral of the real hero of the operation."

"Who's that?" Sutter asked.

"She was the colleague of Ms. Hood's in Doctors Without Borders who went into Raqqa and found where Dayna was being held. This woman died in the rocket strike, and her body was recovered and recently turned over to Doctors Without Borders and returned to her family."

"I heard her mentioned, but didn't realize what she had done."

"Her name was Séverine Tessier. She was a brave and remarkable young woman, sir. You might ask the president to mention her name and the important role she played during the ceremony this afternoon."

"Text it to me, Crocker, and I will."

"Like I said before, she was the real hero of the rescue mission. She went into Raqqa unarmed and on her own. The tragic irony is that we launched the drone strike that probably killed her. It killed Rollins, too."

"Who's Rollins?"

"Rollins is the British private contractor who volunteered to join us. The president should probably mention his name, too."

"I'll tell him. What's his first name?"

"Don't know, sir. He went by Rollins. And another thing, sir. I assume you knew about the drone strike and didn't warn us. All I have to say about that now is a big…fuck you!"

ACKNOWLEDGMENTS

There are a number of hardworking and very talented individuals we would like to thank, starting with our brilliant editor, Emily Giglierano, and the rest of the excellent team at Mulholland/Little, Brown—including Pamela Brown, Ben Allen, Scott Wilson, Kapo Ng, Neil Heacox, Gabriella Mongelli, Elora Weil, and others. In terms of day-to-day support, we're supremely grateful to our families. Don wants to thank his father, who quit high school on December 7, the day Pearl Harbor was attacked, enlisted in the U.S. Navy, and served throughout the war. After he retired he devoted his time toward helping veterans through the DAV and the VFW. And Ralph wants to acknowledge his lovely wife, Jessica, and children John, Michael, Francesca, and Alessandra. As for inspiration, we get that from the men and women in SEAL teams and other agencies of government who do the kind of work we describe in these books. Thank you for your service!

ABOUT THE AUTHORS

Don Mann (CWO3, USN) has for the past thirty years been associated with the U.S. Navy SEALs as a platoon member, assault team member, boat crew leader, and advanced training officer, and more recently as program director preparing civilians to go to BUD/S (SEAL training). Until 1998 he was on active duty with SEAL Team Six. Since then, he has deployed to the Middle East on numerous occasions in support of the war against terrorism. Many of today's active-duty SEALs on Team Six are the same men he taught how to shoot, conduct ship and aircraft takedowns, and operate in urban, arctic, desert, river, and jungle warfare, as well as close-quarters battle and military operations in urban terrain. He has suffered two cases of high-altitude pulmonary edema, frostbite, a broken back, and multiple other broken bones in training or service. He has been captured twice during operations and lived to tell about it. He lives in Virginia.

Ralph Pezzullo is a *New York Times* bestselling author and award-winning playwright, screenwriter, and journalist. His books include *Zero Footprint: The True*

Story of a Private Military Contractor's Covert Assignments in Syria, Libya, and the World's Most Dangerous Places (with former British Special Forces commando Simon Chase), *Jawbreaker* and *The Walk-In* (with former CIA operative Gary Berntsen), *At the Fall of Somoza, Plunging into Haiti* (winner of the Douglas Dillon Award for Distinguished Writing on American Diplomacy), *Most Evil* (with Steve Hodel), *Eve Missing, Blood of My Blood, Left of Boom* (with CIA case officer Douglas Laux), and *Full Battle Rattle*.

MULHOLLAND BOOKS

You won't be able to put down these Mulholland books.